TEN SHORT NOVELS BY ARTHUR KRUGER

Ten different lives, ten different perspectives, ten short novels, one person, *Ten Short Novels by Arthur Kruger* is Oran Ryan's second book.

Exploring themes like life, love, after-life, and death, Kruger, as the author challenges the reader to question their understanding of existence. A possible journey into a mind in the midst of a psychotic breakdown or the autobiography of a man who kills himself and inexplicably finds himself alive; whichever way you experience it, living your life will never be the same again after reading *Ten Short Novels by Arthur Kruger.*

Oran Ryan has been writing full time for 10 years during which time he has completed a number of novels, of which *The Death of Finn* was the first to be published.

Married to Sarah, he is a native of Dublin. He was brought up in Portobello in the city and educated at Synge Street Christian Brothers School, as well as Carlow, Milltown Institute and UCD.

Ten Short Novels

BY

Arthur Kruger

BY

Oran Ryan

Limited Edition

Number __411__ of 500

A Seven Towers Publication

TEN SHORT NOVELS BY ARTHUR KRUGER

First published 2006

BY

SEVEN TOWERS

4, ST. Mura's Terrace,
Strangford Road,
East Wall,
Dublin 3,
Ireland.

WWW.SEVENTOWERS.IE

Cover concept: Deirdre Meehan
COVER, BOOK DESIGN, TYPESETTING
AND SEVEN TOWERS LOGO
BY
SOLID DESIGN
WWW.SOLIDDESIGN.IE

Printed by Betaprint, Ireland.

This book is dedicated to the memory of my grandfather, Charles Doyle Snr, to those like him, who seek and cannot find.

No belief system was harmed in the writing of these novels.

AJK

TEN SHORT NOVELS

BY

ARTHUR KRUGER

BY

ORAN RYAN

CONTENTS

NOVEL I

KILLING PEOPLE IS EASY

Before I was dead, I lived a lot differently than now. Before achieving this post-mortem status, I thought there was only one life – the tax paying, shelling out cash, sleeping, eating, earning a living and dying kind. To pay, one earned. To eat, one earned. To sleep safely, one earned. To marry or procreate or recreate, one earned. To count the moments before the working day ended, one earned. Time seemed to be, well, money.

Thankfully, I was wrong. Thankfully, once you die, there is no going back. Time is motion, a kind of silent running. But where are you going? Time, no matter what you do, is a waiting between heartbeats. Then they stop. They always do. Like virginity, life is something one should dispense with quickly. I pay fewer taxes now. And I live more frugally. I have more time to be, because I am not.

Speaking of obligations, it was my mother who said once that you only get one shot at living before the hammer falls and you get a job. She was standing at the doorway to my room when she said that. She was troubled at my life going nowhere, worried at my living at home, isolated, and reaching thirty years of age. I knew she wanted me out of the house. But that isn't important. I was going anyway. We never really got along. So I got going . We were polite to each other. Civil, but strangers. She was hinting. She wanted me to go. I went. Then I met Aron. Everything went well. We were lovers. Then, following a kind of inevitable entropy, things went wrong. My mind failed. I lost my connection with things, with her. I became depressed. I killed myself. It was easy. Killing people is easy. We are fragile. Killing oneself is very easy. There is too much drama around dying. Too many alas poor yoricks. Wait around along enough and it will happen. It's a question of time. Tick tock tick after I died things went wrong. I survived death and came back intact. Tock. It was an anomaly, a physical, indeed a spiritual impossibility. I had a lot of time on my hands, free time, time I didn't pay for. I threw away my calendar. Then I wrote this, or more correctly, rewrote what I had written in other lives. I realised that the cycle of death and life had happened before, that the Julian year was a roman conquest. I began welding the fragments of other lives by these words.

Maybe it was the transmigration of souls, if you buy into that dubious dogma. I dismiss nothing as impossible, including the resurrection of the dead, the existence of Valhalla, and that Elvis is still walking in Memphis.

But back then, before my first demise, before I killed myself by throwing myself in front of a train, back then, I was alive. I would have laughingly called myself living. I was myself but someone else. Then, after the event I knew the truth. Tricky. It was rebirth. Art, of the crafty kind. I was myself after I passed through death. I was myself but someone else, if you misunderstand me properly.

Naturally, becoming someone else requires an adjustment, a change of passport and a lot of explanations to ex-relatives and friends. It's a biographer's nightmare, a novelist's dream, a poet's passing fancy. It's not like changing accountant or buying a car. My history was fractured. I existed in other moments of space and thus time. This is difficult to explain to one's wife or lover or the police. Try explaining how one's body was no longer a constraining factor, and that history is always a matter of perspective, all that killing and politicking over pieces of land or pieces of eight is pointless. Death is coming. Talk like that could stress one's marriage out, require a stern rationalization of relationship, perhaps counselling. If memory defines one, what if one had the memories of two or more? What then? Could I be and not really be? Is that the question? I had alternate selves, loves and skills. Everything was different and, in time, I grew a harrowing scepticism about life like a tumour, specifically about relationships, about history, the nature of truth and knowledge, and other addictive substances.

And time was no healer. As the matrix of experience grows, one sees how relative experience and fact and truth can be. So one begins to avoid such relatives and stick to strangers like experience. I avoided friends and maintained only associations and temporary alliances. Deep down, words were all I had. This urge to describe, to define, and explain was a disease for which I have no cure. We think because we can. Millennia of reason and we still destroy far more than we create. Perhaps that's why we value art and knowledge and our offspring so desperately. Perhaps creation and destruction are inseparable. I have been telling stories about people in buildings all my lives. I think that is why I am still alive.

Yes, things could never be the same. After my death and rebirth, I made a choice. Having gained so much, there was equally so much lost. Existence, or at least linear existence, was a skin that, once shed, could never be regained, a dead shell washed by the waves on some forgotten beachfront, like Dollymount, or the Costa Brava, or Castletownbearhaven, or the stage of Happy Days at the Gate Theatre before the bomb drops and all is lost, give or take a life cycle. After death, I stayed away from Aron Tully, my previous ex-wife, lover, partner, soul-mate, dance partner, poet. She is who she is, and I am legion. I left her, deciding ultimately I was the toxic element in her otherwise happy fulfilled normal life. I left her and the rest of my family, who never understood anyway. And I lived other lives. Doppel ganger, Arthur.

Then, there was time. Time and again. Time was everything. Time was motion. Time kept passing. I watched and waited. Tried to figure. Was aware I couldn't sense time passing. Saw it measured in clocks and heartbeats and computer time. I sensed life as bits of data, bits of data caught in time, bits and pieces of it speeding past, flying stratospheric to merge with the cosmos. I feared, and still fear all this, such relentless need for speed. I fear my ignorance, always having to guess at what I sense. I see and fear the movement of clocks and people and animals and trees, doors opening and traffic going by, the sun and the clouds and the moon. If time is motion, where are we going?

Birds begin their raves at three-thirty in the morning. No ecstasy required. Just imagine the inconvenience. I don't join in, not wanting to ruin the music, though I listen till dawn. I have to, hearing being an involuntary function for so many, and the voices in my head not drowning their symphony. But all of it isn't the same, not the whole story. The St. Vitus dance goes on. Cars park. Planes fly by. Guns trigger. In bars I see the bartender serving drinks. Guzzle guzzle. I watch the customers come and go. I see things moving, again with the moving. But it's not the same. It's neither real nor unreal. It's neither this nor that, neither anything nor nothing. They are just events that come and go. It's life. Time and motion.

Back up a second. Pause for breath. Breathe. Intense. Who did I say I was? I am another. I imagine myself standing in front of people. I don't know them. I am not at home. They seem nice. I don't know how I got there. Maybe it's not happening. Maybe I'm not here. Maybe we're not real.

They want me to say something. I can sense it. I hold my head up in a confident easy manner in this real unreality, and, just as the sunlight through the window cuffs my face, refracting at that doubtful unvarying speed, I break just a little smile and say –
"Hello. I'm Arthur…"
That was fine, I say to myself. It was fine, sure. Good introduction. But I use no surname. That's bad. Forgot the 'Hello there, I am Arthur Joseph Kruger, and I'm a Cracker Jack sales man for the apocalypse.'

My self-introductions betray me. So I bypass that and I just assume they know me. I give no facts about birth and lineage, no personal data, no admission that all we have between us are the words, no reaching out. It's a kind of cold warmth, just assuming good relations. A solid team-building exercise, which, like most team-building exercises, are fake. One has to break the person to enable deeper bonds to form, and we crave freedom from such slavery. End of group encounter moment. Time to move on. I'm not there anymore. I'm here.

I was saying everything went well after death. After I died, no one questioned who I was. Identification was not an issue. I avoided the authorities, bought another birth certificate on the illegal market, gained a passport, and became the other I always was. My DNA didn't seem to throw them a curve ball. Maybe it had changed. I'm not a science guy. The authorities look for conformity, not mysticism. My autobiography is not written in genetic code. They don't arrest you for death and resurrection, despite what happened to the Christs among us. On the other hand, being befriended by Mr. Mephistopheles Metempsychosis, I believe, isn't against the law, not yet. In time they will find a way to put you on trial. Witchcraft is in. God is out to lunch. Everything is relative, so I read.

So we are here, so I read. And this is Earth. Soon I will be elsewhere, unearthed, not grounded. I ask someone else to define who I am. What is this thing called living? Is there a terminal point to all this wondering? The real problem is not the law, or religion, or time, or motion, or love, but what to say about it. The problem was words, this delivery vehicle for meaning, our currency for expression. One cannot tap dance a sonnet or paint a novel or Morse Code Mozart. A picture is worth a thousand misconceptions. Gioconda. The problem is what words mean. There are no words for how it is. How it is, is warrened within our obfuscation of what is before us, the here and now measured in the senses. How it is gets all twisted once words begin. I try to say something and it distorts into fiction, like an echo lingering in an old chapel, or light twisting through space from stars and emptiness. But I can't stop these words, no more than I can stop breathing.

It's been a long time since this has ended. I'll be dead once again and perhaps forget this. So, I write it down. Memory fades. Seconds out. Like light twisting around the magnetic fields of stars, like life and death is drawn into similar eternal revolutions, refracting and recreating according to the needs of time, I am travelling and never arriving. Nowadays, I wake up in strange beds or sofas in strange houses, in marriages that I never expected to have. I wake up in bed having slept with people I never knew I knew.

"Who are you?"

"Your wife, silly."

"Sorry, I get confused."

"I like your eccentricity. Come back to bed. It's just one of those dreams you have."

"How many children do we have?"

"Just the one. Lie down and go back to sleep. Did you take your meds?"

"No."

"Figures."

Then, I find myself with a job. I am another. Office. People passing. Files in front of me.

"Is this my job?"

"Yes, Arthur, you have many qualifications for this job. Are you okay?"

"I'm fine, thanks. Let's do this."

"Right."

I have careers I don't recall ever pursuing. I have lived lives I never believed possible. It's a problem. I accept such problems. Perhaps it will begin again. Perhaps another life will begin. It just has.

But I do remember in the beginning, for now. I write this as memory fades. I recall with great fondness, how it all began. It was a clear day when all this arrived. It began with a phone call. I remember that the phone kept ringing all day. So irritated by the distraction. I was still living at home, and my parents were away. Whoever it was kept calling back. Ring ring.

The house I lived in was spotless. It was too clean. Cleanliness. Order. Calm. Silent running. I have all my lives long obsessively hopelessly cleaned things, including my body. I finally picked up to meet and greet whoever was there, using an attempted pleasant voice:
"Hello?"
"Hi! Finally! Thank God! Hi Arthur!"
At this point, I had no idea who I was talking to. Though the voice sounded dangerously familiar. My pleasant, definitely female, interlocutor was untroubled by not getting any form of response from me and, after the pause, continued to try to engage me in oral interface by using the following warm, interested, engaging question, in a warm non- confrontational tone of voice:
"And, how are you?"
"Who...who's this...?"
"It's your sister, silly..." my sister says. My sister, at least it might be my sister. When did I get a sister? She sounds the same, but different.
"Oh. Hi. Right...Sorry, sorry..."
"Good to hear from you. It's been a while"
More like a lifetime, I figure. Definitely not this life. That sounded like a question.
"Yes. Good to hear..."
"Right. Well. Enough chitchat. Any news?"
I consider telling her this is my life. That it has ended. That I am living another. That I remember the others. That I remember them as one recalls the images while waking up from dreaming. I have by now nine short novels documenting nine cat-like lives. This will be the tenth. Then I decide not to go there.
"News...Well... I..."
"Arthur?"
"Yes?"

"Any news for me? How's life? Talk to me. We should see more of each other. I miss you."

"Good...that would be... good."

I regarded her question about my life as particularly portentous. I play for time, something I regard myself as particularly adept at. I think of all the things I might tell my sister. But my sister, whose name I do not know, short circuits my attempt at self disclosure and begins to fill my head with stuff. Begins to tell about her husband and the children. Her soft compassionate tones are heartening. She is warm, loving, wise and sensitive. A good mother. A carer. There's trouble ahead. I can sense it.

I wondered how I came to have a sister; what happened that led our parents towards such a catastrophic decision as having another child after having me; how this aforementioned oft referred to, warm, loving, alien voice could be on the other end of the phone – with her story and the husband and the career and the children and that professed inextinguishable love of life, her devastating honesty I misinterpret as hostility; her well grounded commonsense worry for my well being; her well founded criticisms of my wasted life; her sound advice; her insights, and my utter lack of a sane perspective. It seemed so bizarre, especially her having all that aforementioned inextinguishable love of life. What did she remember that I had forgotten? How did she manage to piece it together so well?

Perhaps I did have a sister once. Perhaps we had quarrelled badly. Perhaps we had not spoken for years. Perhaps we had made up, as family members do, for the sake of her children, so the children grow up in a happy environment, or its nearest approximation, for the sake of propriety, for the sake of aging parents, a need to forget. I feel our warmth for each other has an arctic aspect. That it's all phoney. My sister talks on. Fakery doesn't matter. She would be infuriated by any mention of fakery. She was the same person as ever she was. I was another. I was dead and risen like Jesus, Dracula, Frankenstein, and my friends, the clones. Things, like me, had changed. Every seven years, they say, we have a new body. What about the self? Well now, that's always in flux. We're all fluxed up, to unquote Elvis.

"The children are all well," she was saying. "One has an infection in her inner ear and a slight case of tonsillitis," she said, not averting to her contradiction of terms. "We were over last week but we didn't see you. We were on our way to a specialist what with the ear thing..."
"Oh. That sounds serious."
An insidious inflammation of the throatal atrocity region, leading to an unenviable viral downward spiral into the inevitable terminal state of humanity. Being towards tedium. Sounds tricky. Pass the whiskey, sister.
"No," she said. "She'll be fine..."
"Okay. She will be fine, that's good. You know something, if Jesus had been Irish, would he have saved the world, or retired to Israel to write a novel about his death and resurrection during the Roman Occupation?"
"I don't, I don't know."
"Did he save the Earth, or the universe, or just humanity? I mean is Neptune or the cockroach species in a state of sin?"
"Arthur. Are you okay? Taking your meds?"
"Getting along fine. Everything peachy."
She was reaching out from a world of marriage and property and respectability and good breeding.

But everything was not okay. Not good. I was gone. I was elsewhere, listening to her kind words from a great distance, thinking of other things, dreaming really. Dreaming of those spirits from surreality that haunt the vast open spaces of our vacuous cosmos. Thinking of strange things I could never tell her, things that marked the divide I never wanted between us.

Then I heard her. She was calling my name and saying "Hellooo? Arthurrrrr?"

"Sorry. I wasn't listening. So sorry. Tired..."

"Sure, Arthur...You need to sleep, to get it together..."

She didn't believe a word I said. It was all a question of credibility. I feared an argument, a verbal conflagration. Time for pre-emptive pacification. I want to love my sister, but, as I do not know how she is, or who she is, I cannot. No. I choose cheery optimism instead, more of my ready wit and charm. Mechanically mention how everything was fine. That it was an appalling thing to leave a return call so long. That I would call soon, that I wished her well. End of telephone call. No. That's it. I'm pretty sure I don't have a sister. Decision made.

Then something happened inside. Like a bomb, it began. It began as I put down the receiver and I heard this click. Like life switched itself off. Darkness. It all came to me in the night. The answer to me in the darkness came. Lying supine in the dark, the clear bright, dark bomb. Deliverance. Light. Fiat. Drive. Like an answer. Boom. Upheaval. The clear super bright flash of knowing, knowing how to begin again, after things not working for so long. The night, the night was. It was a terrible night, and rain. The rain beat savage against the frail panes of glass. They might break under such terrible force. if there is another storm, they're finished. I wondered if it was financially feasible to fix those frail windows as they shudder in the high wind, their elasticity stretched to maximum. Have to borrow some money if they break. Living beyond non-existent means. Again. But I was perhaps becoming gradually happier with this horrific suffering, this bomb-like upheaval, this catastrophe within. Happiness is an equation, desire multiplied by fulfilment divided by hope. The mathematics of feeling, the square root of love is a fraction of truth, desire over denial. Not that it mattered. This event is worth noticing. The mind, after so much chaos and torment, clearing. The mind no longer opaque, rather clouded by weird scenes inside the snow white room of the mind. Comatose. And how the house shook. The house shook in the late November wind. I thought of the moon amidst the howling. Slept little those nights, with the calamitous certainties that came upon me. Though some say after that the day came too soon. Only the ghosts whisper to me now.

It was the ghosts. Voices during those clear happy, tortured, sleepless nights of the beginning. In the beginning, I say, in the beginning, everything was fucked up. In the beginning, there are the facts. And the facts are this. I am seeing things, and I don't know if this is all real. The mind takes in data. Then it makes sense of the senses. If you believe what you're told to see taste feel touch smell, that's sanity. I think, but maybe it's a sham.

And the facts are that there wasn't much certainty back then. In the beginning of everything, in the state of original benchmarks, when the clock started, when God started her autobiography, there was, shall we say, absolute zero.

Back then I had gone for thirty years with nothing happening, no vision of anything except the crushing oppression of following others' dreams and expectations, having none of my own. And, then, the clock started. The bomb ticked. And, from the nothing much, came the facts. From the nothing, there came facts, like battalions of storm troopers killing time. Time. Space. Life. And, from this came other inventions, such as Questions. Perhaps we shall return again to that beginning. Perhaps we are already there.

From the beginning came the facts, and facts are what are what we do to reality. There is theory from the science people that mostly I don't get. You can take things any way you want. Original cosmology of the definite. There are prophetic epigrams from the beyond the grave, and there are my little facts. Born. Survived the fascist state of childhood. Writing. Began with a job as a postal clerk. Unattached. Semi-detached. No children. Lived in this house with my parents. Occasionally call on friends. Rachel. Joe.

Stop. Dear System, Things keep changing. But at least there are these words.

Signed AJK.

Stop.

File under: Dead. Again.

Name: Arthur Joseph Kruger.

Marital status: semi-detached.

Parental status: Son of Martha and Jack Kruger.

Life Status: Sitting here day after day writing this. Words. Wonder if it will ever happen, the finishing of this. Though I have no specific fear of an end in itself. One fears having nothing specific to do or feel. This is why it is important to me to keep busy. There are consequences to not having busyness. There are consequences. Watching the clock, thinking things over, waiting for something to happen, a war inside. Conflagration. Apocalypse. Alien invasion. End of time. One's stocks and shares in life fluctuating, perhaps taking a nasty tumble. Dying. Stillness is something of a problem. Stillness opens vistas. But there is firstly the matter of wanting to keep busy. Then comes the reality of what to do to keep busy. I began writing to try to discover what to do. I needed to save lives, live for love. I feared pointlessness, that life itself had no purpose. I feared the thing in itself might be unknowable.

This will be the last short novel, at least this time round. One could start another. One could read a lot more, more learned speculations without an answer. Do the one hundred thousand words thing, get the contract, when five thousand is all it takes. I could learn another language. Sprechen sie zilch. Get tenure. Become proficient in the cleverness game. How's that working out for you, Arthur? The clever thing, all those books you read? The notes you take? I am no Tyler Durden. To be clever is almost as important as having money, or a trophy mate, or clever offspring who grow up beautiful and smart. All good things get you in the end. The universe is waiting to dial back to nought.

Pick a career. Save lives. Love your neighbour. One might have another casual affair. Find a lover. Love is real. Real is love. John Lennon was my personal God, and Buddha was the fifth Beatle. Be all you can be in the army. A career in the foreign legion. I could become a hacker, that's fashionable. Or an artist, a fake Picasso generator. Or get a teaching degree. Teach class. Write erudite volumes. Take a sabbatical. Learn more about the history of time. Then, there are the Dunkirk landings. Invade Poland or Iraq. Play chess. Garden. Crochet. Jigsaws. Play the piano. Psycho killer. A cook or a shepherd or an ornithologist. All good things.

But I don't want to go back there to my first life. No going there. I won't go back to another beginning for the sake of denial or having something to do. Nothing kills quite like life.

Back then, during the writing of chapter one, I noticed how I became subject to a disturbing nervousness of body, mind and spirit. I attributed it, after a careful process of analysis, to a gypsy curse. It was a sense of subterranean uncertainty, a loss of coordination, a lack of knowing where it's at. The more clearly I described matters pertaining to former lives, the shakier the foundations of my present life seemed to get.

It was down to fact, I figured, or the fact that lurks behind every fiction. Don't believe me when I tell you that Arthur was a loving son of loving parents. Or that Arthur was soft-spoken, polite, charming, sensitive, willing, weak, dependent, that he was blonde and shy and famous actors used greet him as they passed on the street. He was only inventing himself. He needed the job. I know. I am that he.

I was always frightened of the little things, of the tiny nothing beyond or between substances. Push reality a little and it bends. What we think is real touches the nothing that separates it from another reality we never knew was there. And so say all of us, tra la.

But, back then, there was the possibility of having something. I wanted to find myself, I kid you not. It was youthful optimism, youthful arrogance, and cocksure ignorance. I perceived, perhaps, a certain quality inherent in things. But I knew I wanted too much. I ached for a connection. I saw beauty as perception of skin over bone, canvas over wood, stone, steel, atom against atom, life pressing against its own tensile extinction. I decided beauty is not a quality of anything. It is truth without explanation, moment without time, vision without reflection. It was a blinding light, photons disappearing into the black, into the zero past the edge of a black hole event horizon. It was the juxtaposition of opposites, each emphasising the other. Beauty was what I wanted, death and life and the end of oblivion. It didn't exist. Once I tried to find it and write it out, it expired like a leaf in winter.

I caught my reflection in the evening mirror, which is a different mirror to the one I look in during the morning or after lunch, what with the atomic degradation one reads about these days. I looked at myself as I dressed to go out, paused before my reflection as I left one evening for platitudes and smiles, dinner and drinks. I looked and saw that beneath the bone all was dark cavernous, filled with a thousand communications, rife with couriers caught forever in subcutaneous traffic. Within the within, where one was born, lies neither form nor substance. I know I was not before I was born. Nothing before. Nothing after. Being born was the problem. I arrived when my parents were expecting someone else. Somehow the image of who I was not remained after my delivery onto the earth, and it clung limpet-like to my lives. I have always been elsewhere. So imagining other lives has thus posed no difficulty to me.

I had used suppression as a useful tool in getting by up to this point in my life. I believe suppression is good, though the business of lying to live, deceiving oneself to exist, elicits guilt and self-hatred. But, if one can successfully deny the guilt and self-hatred, then one really is on the road to a happy life. Suppression is the road to harmony, the true way to us all getting along – myth-making the past, forgiving and loving and carrying on, sublimating the truth behind truth. Truth makes a soap opera of relations, manufacturing a hazy warm feeling of womb-like safety. It's crucial. Truth is what we do to reality. We kill it. Truth is death. It is a prison from which there is no escape. Truth is the most addictive of narcotics. There is no cure from it. Once you are hooked, you die, with it or without it. Try fiction instead.

And this is what happened after I put down the phone from my sister. I saw the lie of my life, saw I was alone, saw how anaesthetized my life had been. I began to live for fiction, the acceptance of the force of creative action.

The scene of my fictional life, where I die and am born again, opens on a cold wet evening in late November. A family is huddled in prayer around the television set. Dear Lord, distract us. Bring us fun. And the television obliges with nightly hours of quality programming. A person named Someone Else is making notes for the first chapter of a book he hopes someday to write. Writes the following down, accidentally on purpose. Maybe I read it somewhere:

Dear Author,

Try fiction. Fiction is for real and I'm not telling any more jokes like that. Better than the really real. Fiction is the victory of dreams and style and good taste before the fascism of a truth no one really knows. Fiction is as real as it gets. It is the product of imagination from the raw material of learning and perception and memory. Fabricated universes. It's a license to kill history with the artillery of art. Fiction is the final death of that truth that will keep us unfree.

Best wishes,

Arthur

Now hold on. Someone stops. Stop right there. Someone Else is shocked at what he has written. It came all of a sudden. Like it came from Elsewhere, where Someone lives. Someone looks about. And yet nothing has really changed. Look carefully around the room. He is trying to catch his breath, trying to keep calm.

"Are you all right, Arthur?"

Arthur. He called me Arthur. I am Arthur. I am this person. I wrote this. What is happening? I'd better play along.

"Fine, thanks Dad..."

Everyone is still there, watching television, reading, waiting for the phone to ring. Dad gets up to put the kettle on. The Younger Sister, the one who telephoned all those years later, the one who tries years later to reach out to me and who, with her telephone call, changed everything for me, leaves the room to ring her boyfriend, the boyfriend she will later marry and have those children with. She is upset because he hasn't rung her in a few days, and she dressed up just in case he turns up on the family doorstep. "He will never call me, damn him!" she mutters.

Someone called Arthur reads over his last few sentences. Arthur's father, Jack, looks briefly over at his son and wonders what he is writing, and why his boy is so quiet. Arthur is upset, he thinks.

Something has definitely happened, Arthur thinks. I am another, he thought. I am not writing about myself any more. Rather, I am talking about the person I am becoming. In these words, Arthur was born. And then he died.

Chapter One. It has begun. I am living with Aron. I have written this. I remember my lives before this time. It wasn't like this before. Before the working on the book and the story of the Ten Short Novels and meeting Aron Tully, there were other lives. Before those other lives, there was the job I had for life. How many lives? I don't know. Back then, there was the job with the promotion and the working hours, the whole attending life-cycle to living a good life, a life with prospects, a life lived in truth. I thought of those many people I knew, in crisp blue suits and sharp blue reports, back then. I miss them. I miss those people. Deep blue worlds.

Chapter One. He was a happy boy. He lived mostly in the country during the summer and he was happiest then. In the summer, in the country, there was the countryside, so beautiful, so haunting. He played all day between the bales of hay and, on good days, watched the sun dance in the trees, which was strange and hypnotic and as elusive as days go by. And, as evening came, and, as he grew tired, he watched the fish swim in clear rivers and there were the sunny days in the fields, and, in the midst of all this, there was one immutable constant. And that which remained constant was the transcendent love of God. From this tiny speck of perfection, the boy knew God was everywhere, in all things, in the boardrooms and the deserts, and in the elusive days-go-by-sunlight. The ready-to-hand love of God irradiated the shanty town dwellers, the fifteen year old hooker, the torture chamber inhabitant, the serial killer and her husband, the office paper shuffler, the alien love slaves, the infants left to die on hilltops in Sparta and rubbish heaps in ancient Rome, the caring parents of cared for children, the old, the lonely, the young, the beaten and betrayed, the tyrant, and the followers of the tyrant. The love of God loved the planets where we still live. And, like all lovers, the love of God left we, the beloved, to make our own way across the universe, in whatever forms such journeys take. For, like all journeys, they are already beginning again.

I hear the last signals before it ends. Before the deep blue job, there was God, and the word of God, and the deep blue books, read out of the deep blue need more to escape than experience, and the meditation I did, and the void of God's infinite providence for the universe in terminal decay. I was a religious person, for a time. Before God, was the school where the young Arthur slept. And ignorance is the beginning of all bliss, Socratically speaking. Before the nothing was the school that left the nothing it came to take. Before that, one was the child. Then, there was the infant in the womb; before that, the zygote, the sperm and eggs that meshed in the copulation. Before that, my parents, their marriage, our home, my parents dating, their parents, the parents of the parents, back to the fore-parents, back to the dawn of the species, to previous species, back to the first instant of life, in the beginning.

NOVEL II

BOMB SCRIPT

1. In the beginning, I saw the bomb go off. Boom. Perhaps it was God who dropped it. Perhaps it was the Allies. They always blame the Allies. But I don't believe it. I think it was the systems man. After all, agents of the system we live within are everywhere.

I knew the bomb intimately. The bomb was not a symbol merely of death, for death and life are one. The bomb was the terror of nothingness, the beginning and end of everything, of our capacities to create and ruin. I don't know why I always knew the bomb. I knew its components and its origins. I knew its ultimate destiny. It was all a dream because it was not a dream. It was the dream that was not a dream that formed my mind. Its detonation was small. The small beginnings of the universal clock. An infinitesimal flash in the infinite night. So very small one would not see it.

I saw the infinite black before the bomb, before birth, beyond life. I saw the single particle strike the first fissile matter. I saw it grow. I saw particles releasing. From these fissile things, great bombs do grow. They blow other atoms away as the momentum gathers, as the energy fires, as other atoms fragment and blow other atoms apart, as the bomb goes off, as the universe happens and expires. In an instant comes the critical mass.

It was the secret dream I dreamed I lived. There was the tiny point of explosive origin. From it came the rapid outward expansion of superheated gases, spreading out like some fireball in the nothing that suspends this universe. I lived every fissile moment of the explosion. There was the flash, the burn, the conflagration. I lived terrified it would return. Beneath the charade of creation and civilization, there lurked the bomb. The bomb was the monster ready to consume everything. There was nothing to do but bide one's time and watch the universal clock, often wondering if I was not alone, if, out there in rotting mews and filthy cellars, were others trembling in terror in the dark hours, living outwardly happy, normal lives, secretly listening to the ticking of timers. If there were, it was doubtful they would ever make themselves known.

In this particular universe, nothing is either gained or lost. So they say in books. It is the law of conservation of no matter what, a team of highly trained economists keeping the matter of the cosmos in ordered disorder. Thus, from the first second, there existed everything we need for everything's existence. So they say. And, if one accepts this premise, if it were true, I knew I liked it. When I began to read those popular science books, I was glad that the bomb had made such a generous provision for the universe's existence. One day, they postulated, those tiny bits and pieces would come hurling back together. I imagined the implosion. Moob.

So, there was only so much matter that made up everything being constantly arranged and re-arranged into different species, species made up of the same atoms that began as proto-matter in the beginning. Maybe our neighbour's dog, Sparky, might have some of Einstein's atoms. Perhaps this is how the idea of transmigrating souls began. Someone sensed we were all made up of the same stuff, or that we shared a common atomic ancestry, this ancestry which offsets a sense of isolation which billions of isolates share with all the other billions of other isolates on this big blue planet, along with all the other big differentially-coloured, life-supporting planets out there, living in a headlong rush towards oblivion before a little love and a little knowledge and a little family life, the school and college and marriage and love and holidays and business deals, between genocidal acts for small pieces of territory.

The believers tell me that all is love. I believe that. I am a believer. I believe in the unbelievable, making the unbelievable believable. This act of unfaith was a new twist in my believing disbelief. I decided then that the most incredible event in existence was not life but belief in its possibility, something from nothing. And here we are. Thus, anything can happen.

Belief in something is a bulwark against catastrophe. Belief in nothing is better. Maybe nothing is better than belief in nothing. Having faith makes things seem saner. I believed in aliens and poltergeists and ghosts and God and the tooth fairy and spontaneous combustion. I saw tomorrow in the whispering trees. I have, by now, long jettisoned reason as a compass through life. It was an instinctual, rather than reasoned, jettison that made me mostly unemployable and largely useless. This unemployable uselessness became a source of friction when I lived at home. I was going nowhere and was unemployed. So, my folks began getting jobs for me, rather than have me propped up in my bed reading all day and all night. They became more determined to get their son's life together, make him self-reliant, happy, loved and in love. They wanted to get me friends, psychotherapy, a home of my own, a car. They wanted a good life for me.

Madness became my religion, a renunciation of common sense for the uncommon sense of uncertainty, doubt and the futility of hoping, or not hoping. I thought my own lights might guide me along the path of disillusion to the unsafe haven of ultimate futility. Having found all other senses illusory, my guide through a life I disbelieved in was the certainty of nothing and the consolation of the void.

The unbelievable drew me irresistibly. The rationally probable seemed so unlikely, considering the bomb from which one found issue, the strange vision of the super bright flash consuming and creating all things from the beginning. It seared my mind with its beauty and its horror.

I knew the bomb was out there. It was armed. It ticked away. I heard its mechanical heartbeat mostly at night, a godlike godless tick tick tick measure of things. In my dreams and in my mind, the ticking came. I was waiting for it all to go off. I lay awake and listened. It had blown up before. I knew it had to happen again. There would be signs. An armed bomb knows its own time. You have to respect it. It marks creation's beginnings and its termination on a precise timing device. One has to stopwatch.

Eventually, I began to write these obsessive thoughts down. Otherwise, I feared I would never sleep again. I would go into a store and buy a cheap copybook and take it home and fill it full of words...

I thus began building a picture of the world, my own personal cosmos, within the chamber of my cranium. I wrote down what I saw. I used words. Sometimes the scenarios I built with words were faulty and required reconstruction. That was okay. One always starts and ends with failing. I did not fear trying again. I had nothing to prove, no contract to fulfil, no colleagues to compete with. Sometimes, the words made temporary residences for these ideas until I built better stronger, more durable ones later on.

So I worked during the day and at night I sat scribbling away. But there was nothing else to do. Writing became a matter of necessity. Perhaps it was genetic destiny. Perhaps it was Mother. These stories about people in buildings, these ten short novels came, not out of destiny, but out of a visceral need. There was never anything else that felt right.

Every other thing I did, except writing, felt like a greater lie than the lie of putting it all down. Everything else was a greater lie, invented to escape oneself, a double agent come to sell me out to the authorities. I wanted to escape into other people's stories about people in buildings.

2. I, Arthur Kruger was born in Dublin on a clear cold Saturday morning at nine-thirty, in a building, a designated hospital complex, as opposed to the dramatic story of poverty or opulence, or near death at birth experiences of other substantial more literary minded personages. My mother, on hearing my instinctual cries of horror at my emerging from nothingness to existence, drew me lovingly to her breast to smother my desperate pleas to go back home to nowhere. She silenced me with her love and her milk. She fed me and loved me and the drugs worked fine. I slept.

I grew up and became a good boy, an obedient, well-spoken boy, who spoke only when spoken to, and learned those words that elicited respect and a condescending warm smile that said, to those who had sufficient insight, that here was a strange, well-spoken, well-mannered little boy. I did well in school for a time and got good marks early on. But only for a while. One only had to grow up a little, and then nothing, not even the love of God, or Mother, could quell that unknowable, unnameable, ultimate fear of impending annihilation. It was the bomb thing, the incessant night-time ticking off in the distance. I had been given temporary existence and that wasn't going away anytime soon.

I tried knowledge, the cleverness thing. But neither history nor geography nor poetry nor sciences nor Milton's cosmology, nor Einstein's mythology, nor the architectonics of the psyche allayed my terror. I would be struck by dreams and visions that followed me throughout the day. I would see wild creatures crawling across the rooftops, ghosts hanging above teacher's head, the mark of death in a fellow schoolmate's eyes. Wrote poetry in my Latin grammar books. Compulsively read books that were not on the courses I was supposed to be taking. Since it seemed that things were, by and large, meaningless to me, apathy, masking terror and anger, by and large, set in.

By the time I was fifteen, I began to suffer from sleeplessness, agitation, and loss of appetite, uncontrollable mood swings, obsessive thoughts, and depression. One might have thought there was something wrong with me. I thought of explaining it away in terms of recollecting an alien abduction theory. But then, I thought, what if I really had?

So, I sat alone in rooms looking at the floor, seeing the light drift across the walls and floor out of the corner of my listless eyes. Mother and Father were deeply upset at their son's life and friendless self-absorption. They took me to see the family doctor. The family doctor became mildly agitated at seeing me looking so awful. You don't look good son, he said to me. I smiled a little and said, I am okay.

The warm, friendly, down to earth, smart, vastly wise, family practitioner of twenty years asked me what was on my mind? Was I homosexual? No answer. Was I or had I been being sexually abused? No answer. Did I see things no one else saw, hear voices? No answer. Was it girl trouble? I frowned at him for his choice of words. I think you should think about seeing a counsellor, the doctor said.

The doctor dosed me with antidepressants and tranquillizers, and recommended counselling once more. He smiled at me, as though he knew what was going on, as though he too had been there, but had left it behind for a large house and a family practice left him after his father died.

So, I took the tablets and went to counselling. My counsellor didn't help. She seemed to regard my life as an enigma wrapped some fashionable middle class nihilistic mindset, a kind of comfortable self absorbed depressive rebellion paid for by parental wealth. I stopped going after five months. Another month or two in zero zone drugged up stasis mode and I stopped taking the tablets, except when I couldn't sleep. I was, I expect, clinically depressed. I felt as though I had disappointed everyone. My life had become a waiting game. It was as though someone had put me on a piece of wreckage, and pushed me out to sea and the waves slowly took me out and I could see those I loved and longed to be with disappearing on the horizon. I did not push them away. At least, I have no sense of doing so. If anything, I saw this happen and tried to reach out. But we drifted apart, because I could not find a way to talk to them. Things fell into terminal decline.

I remember others in my class at school seemed so much more alive. They had something. They were part of things. They were smart, or beautiful, or moneyed, or knew people. They had a connection to the football, or the chess, or the cricket, or the hurling, or the drama, or the alcoholic, or sex, or career groups. They had money, or power, or influence, or sex at regular intervals. I had money too. They were good, decent, well-meaning people who, like all good decent well-meaning people, wanted money, power, sex and acceptance. They were well-adjusted, destined to get on with it and do well on this decent rational planet. I grew in bewilderment as my contemporaries grew in strength and wisdom. Those people attracted partners and friends and were invited to parties. They became doctors, or lawyers, or dentists, or business people, or lovers, or poets, or musicians, or clerks, or secretaries, or accounts technicians, or shepherds, or farmers. They got married or took lovers. They bought property and took out mortgages. I succeeded only in eliciting avoidance and embarrassment from others. I had no way of talking to my contemporaries and so avoided them, and, because I avoided others, I had even more problems talking to them. They had no point of contact with me. By then, I did not feel loneliness. Neither did I feel envy nor anger nor depression at my contemporaries. The feelings had stopped, though I found it scary and peculiar that I felt nothing at all towards them when I remember wanting love and to love them once.

Having sufficiently ruined any chances of a liberal artistic education, I, Arthur Kruger, left school to find my misfortune. I turned up for the final exams and scraped a passing grade. I had not attended class for weeks and spent my time in libraries and churches and pubs and wandering the streets. I didn't tell anyone I was doing this. I just stopped attending and acted out the empty ritual of getting up for school at the same time every morning, washing, dressing, talking to Mother and leaving the house. It was a relief not to be attending school. The school never noticed my absence. I was invisible by then.

One good thing about the months I had spent in libraries and churches and public houses and other places of questionable repute: there I met other losers like myself. They were mostly dead white males who had left their lives in print. From these people, I decided the best course of action was to devise a list so I might know what I had learned. I needed to know what I knew then, so that I might have an idea what to do now school was over and I would be expected to leave home soon. I spent hour after hour, day after day, playing chess and drafting and redrafting the list.
Here is the list:
Pawn to king's rook one. There are no other lives except those lives I experience.
These lives I live are real lives. I make them real.
These lives I live are real lives because I need them to be real.

They are real because I invent them. Otherwise, everything is unknowable.

In the same manner, the lives others invent are their real lives.

These lives one invents require careful handling.

Invented lives can crash and burn, like universes at war. Like dying suns or bombs, they could blow to hell. And then one would also die. Life is fragile.

Remember the bomb.

The bomb is the beginning and end of everything, lifedeath if you like. One day the bomb will drop. Things will end. Then begin. Then end. Hell and heaven is the circle of life and death. Checkmate.

I created my worlds. I kept these worlds separate so they may not conspire to overthrow their creator. If they destroyed me, then they would also destroy themselves. If I were devoured by my creation, I would die, which sometimes seemed quite attractive. But I had been unlucky thus far. I continued to live and I continued with the work of creation as an endless, meticulous and absorbing work for me. It was the ultimate game, if you like, a circular rather than linear process. Past the trees and the roads and the din of traffic are the words I worked. I wrote on. Past the sea and the sky and the death of time were the words. I had nothing. So I worked on.

I kept the notebooks and my list, which I rewrote every so often. It continued to change until the bomb finally went off, and, after the superheated flash, all that was left after the chariot of fire was the atomic shadow of being at one's own ground zero.

As I said, I resoundingly scraped a pass in my examinations. And, after resoundingly passing my examinations, I sought work, rose early and prayed for the deliverance of oblivion. I was informed one day by letter that there was work available in a local clothing distribution firm, where they needed a postal clerk.

I joined the company and worked stamping envelopes with a giant franking machine. The company was in a beautiful, but unoccupied area of the city called the Coombe. Most days I entered the office, a huge pile of envelopes would be waiting on my desk. Opposite my desk, a battalion of filing cabinets monitored this daily frenzied franking of envelopes. If there were no envelopes to frank, then there were always empty envelopes to fill. Thousands of empty, pre-addressed envelopes waited to be filled with their appropriate invoices. Before long the complaints came in. 'Dear sir or madam, we are at a loss to understand why we are not receiving our invoices on time, if at all.' I was not efficient. As I was ineffective, I made work for the others, and, thus, I was disliked.

There were others in the office. Sawyer the accountant, a thin, angst-ridden, overworked, angry person, with a wife and a child. He scared me. He never spoke unless someone spoke to him. I never spoke to him. As we had no communication whatever, we had no communications problem. Besides Sawyer, the accountant who never spoke, there was Senge the Assistant Principal Officer who spoke incessantly. Sawyer seemed to hate him. Sawyer would dourly listen to Senge's commentaries and kind admonitions and confusing instructions. Then, he would disregard them in order to do things efficiently his own way.

In addition to Senge and Sawyer, there was Joyce the clerk/typist. He wrote letters all day. Others seem to come and go. For instance, messengers, or people one assumed were representatives of the clothing company, came in and spoke only to Senge. When they spoke, Senge would listen and nod understandingly, looking vacantly away from his interlocutor, as though listening to other voices advising him as to how to proceed. Sometimes, Senge would find it necessary to touch these representatives. Touch seemed to be something repulsive to him. If this touch happened, I noticed that his touch was the lightest touch Senge could bring himself to give. Then, Senge would quickly withdraw his hand, would suggest he and the representative would take a cup of tea in the cafeteria. Then they would leave. It all seemed so creepy and contrived and I watched these comings and the goings compulsively. Watching seemed to alleviate my tensions and mental uncertainties as to where I was and what it was that I was really doing.

As I was earning a little money, I had taken to buying books, rather than stealing them out of libraries. Theft had been a kind of therapy, a cure for spending money. But now I had found a cure for expenditure. This was earning. I gave money to my parents and spent the rest on books. In these books I had purchased, I read that self-talk was the answer. I decided to affirm myself. I am a strong powerful confident relaxed person. I would repeat silently to myself that I have a future. I am a lovable person. I love life. Life is good. Affirmations. I repeated to myself certain affirmations I had read about, to help my confidence and sense of self-assurance. Then, I would have sneaking doubts and look down at my body and arms and touch myself in an attempt to confirm the reality of my existence. Is this body, this fully activated, fully functional, carbon based, spatio-temporal existence actually the case, I asked myself? And the answer, naturally, quoting a self-help book, the answer is 'Yes, you are really here. Try punching that wall if you have a doubt. You are doing time until you die, and, yes, you are okay with that. You have to be. This is who you are.'
And my certainty as to where and who and what I was would last a little longer, and I would get on with the job of franking letters.

The problem as to my location, function and actions was not chiefest in my mind. Certain difficulties arose from my problems with language and the construction of sentences. I was unable to bring myself to say much, if anything. Every word I spoke, I uttered with such excruciating embarrassment and fear and sense of uncertainty, despite all the self-talk and self-help and reading of books of psychology, that, after much consideration, during a five-mile walk across the Phoenix Park, I thought it best to say nothing. I am not a talker, I said to my selves. No, you're not, they answered, and stop bothering us. Can't you see we're busy? There are all these notes to make about the bomb. We're in research mode. Sorry, I said.

As a result of this elected silence, after six months I found so a great distance between others had opened up, a chasm so great, that I had to bridge it. There were no envelopes to frank. No one gave me work. No one spoke to me. Months passed. Maybe they were talking to me but I couldn't hear them. I could hear other things. Cars, music, doors opening, bells. Of course, the easiest method was to pretend the problem didn't exist, and one day, out of the blue, make casual conversation with my fellow workers. But, then, the most immediate problem with talking to people was the troubling issue of words. I checked several reputable dictionaries for suitable words to use while talking with people. The important thing was to keep talking. They would appreciate the words and especially the meaning of the words. I listened to the types of words used by my colleagues and decided the easiest method was imitation and replication. I read newspapers, magazines, and novels, and made a point of watching movies on a regular basis. This was all to equip myself with the burdensome matter of attempted dialogue.

It all failed horribly on the day Senge was leaving the office, as he always left the office — accompanying some sales person to the cafe. It was a Tuesday afternoon in mid-September, during the second trimester of my abortive rebirth as a functional employee. I walked up to him as Senge was in mid departure, and, in front of the staff, clapped him on the shoulder. No one touched Senge. Even though I knew somewhere that no one touched Senge, I had gone to the trouble to make careful note of the necessary pressure that gave the tactile message of self-assured friendliness. Somehow, I felt an inner sense that my following suit in using his technique of intimacy would seal some unspoken bond between Senge and myself. Thus, my first contact was in as friendly a manner as I could manage. I was about to mention some matter I saw on the news broadcast the night previously when Senge stopped his egress and turned to me. Senge stared at me for a second, somewhat taken aback that I would make any attempt to touch him, let alone speak with him. I was about to chat, but I felt the words die in my throat. Sweat beaded along my forehead and down my back. I stood away from Senge. Senge left the office in silence.

I kept thinking what might have happened. I just couldn't get the words out alive. They came forth stillborn. I felt like a game show host, being vacantly convivial. I watched the verbal corpses pile up all around me. My colleagues looked on with a mixture of pity and suppressed hilarity. Then they went back to their assigned tasks. It was approaching the end of fiscal period four. Accounts had to be rectified. Reports had to be compiled. Issues had to be resolved. Meetings had to be attended.

I glanced outside the office as I mentally moved away from the occasion of my horrible personal undoing. It felt like the end. I looked through the window, and, across the city, a weird glow shone from behind the clouds. Perhaps it was the sun. It didn't seem so. I went back to the desk and looked across the room. Everyone was back at work. The little exchange between Senge and myself would be discussed in detail during designated break periods and out of earshot. Right now, there were things to do. Right now, it was as though nothing had happened. Business was at hand and needed attention. Senge was gone for the day.

I needed something to distract me. I couldn't go back to stuffing invoices into envelopes. I looked across at the cabinets, walked over to the sentry cabinets and opened them for the first time since my arrival. They were filled with more invoices, disordered copies of those sent out, invoices that wanted proper enumeration and recording. Right there and then I began enumerating and ordering. But it didn't work. Crushing tedium coupled with uncontrollable panic made these straightforward tasks too much for me. I felt ill and rushed to the toilets and vomited. I sat on the toilet and tried to centre myself and tried once again a few self-affirmations. I am a strong confident centred person. I love life. I love other people. They love me. I mouthed the words. I sat on the toilet bowl and breathed in the breath of life, my eyes closed, concentrating on the life swelling in my solar plexus, the fire of life that was part of the great light in the centre of the universe, the light of life.

Outside in the office, the letters for franking piled up on my desk. I sensed them there, lingering vacantly like neglected children. I went back to them. I hadn't seen them for a long time. Perhaps someone else had been caring for them. I began to tremble and sweat and a terrible weight of depression and horror descended upon me. I looked around the office. I was sure I could hear the sound of the engines being turned over at some underground airport far away. Somewhere secret, a pilot has received mission orders. The bomb had been loaded on the plane. The plane would take off after checks. I saw the glow. The weird glow outside was growing and growing.

The experience with Senge had destabilised my otherwise delicately ordered office balance. I would never again attempt to make contact, to chat and make less strange. It was something I simply could not do, and this realization posed itself as a relief, a weight lifted off. But then came the drone of engines ten thousand miles away. The super-bomber was beginning its flight, final checks and balances. The thumbs up given and the pilot was centering himself or herself for their flight. And they had just received clearance for take off. The plane had two bombs on board. One was for the city. One was a spare bomb. The spare bomb was just in case the first did not detonate, or any malfunction was detected during final diagnostics before dropping. The bomb would be dropped so that detonation would occur twenty metres above O' Connell Bridge, Dublin. The bomber would come at night. It would fly over sometime during the night and it would be all over. I would wait for the droning of the engines and the bright flash. At the moment of the explosion a fireball would generate, a boiling blood red light that we would build with our bodies and our histories and our buildings. Its centre would reach a temperature of ten million degrees. Buildings would be absolutely destroyed. Human and animal and vegetable life absolutely consumed. Nothing left, except shadows and melted tooth fillings and shards of dust. And from this holocaust would come a new life, a new future, for there is time. The bomb would build a new time from its own force. You see, we have reached the year zero, the point of origin that is our destiny. The circle of history would have completed itself in the bomb. I looked out at the city. The weird glow was still there. I shook my head and wished I believed in God. I love everyone. Tears dribbled from my eyes. I must be mad, I thought.

I longed for the bliss of absolute isolation. I looked around guiltily, convinced that if I tried to explain all this to my colleagues, tell them all in one outrageous outburst about the bomb and my world, that it would be the end. I would be taken home and my parents informed of their son's apparent breakdown and need for some type of psychiatric assistance. Then would come the appointment with some heartbreak professional, a quiet semester at the Laughter Academy followed by the reading of my journals. These journals were really stories. It was easier to talk about myself in this way, as I would be cajoled to tell the sensitive, but detached, analytical heartbreak professional, about where I was at, I mean really at. But the trained mind of the therapist would know this anyway. They would need me, the patient, to say this. They know that these stories about people in buildings would one day grow into novels, if I ever found the time. What was once a creation would now have evidentiary status. The journals would prove my incipient lunacy. They would be right. No matter, though. I did intend to turn my stories into novels, if I ever found the time. Short novels. The stories would provide evidence of my deranged state, my need of real help. And I would get that help and would never be the same again, never think the same mad thoughts, never feel the same type of pain. After the normalising, terrifying, therapeutic and psychochemical lobotomy, I, Arthur Kruger, would lose track of the Arthur Krugers within me. I would become the pleasant, well-adjusted, easy to get to know, loveable family man to be that we all know and love to love. I would be a story about a person living in buildings.

These and other nightmares held my fate at gunpoint. I would keep the secret of my lies about myself. I would keep going, because those moments were all one had. After them came the oblivion of a mental hospital or self-extinction. Nothing could be more excruciating than to envisage some professional specialist reading one's work for the purposes of analysis or diagnosis. I was at the hypocentre of the bomb.

I decided to finish filing old invoices for the day. It wasn't working anyhow. I would frank some more letters. There was always the four o'clock mail to think of. I would start early tomorrow. I needed some type of filing system. As I had no system, the filing was a futile act. I would think of a system. It couldn't be that difficult.

On my way home, I would visit the church. I had taken to visiting the church because I needed time to recover before getting on the number thirty-one bus that brought me home. I had taken to reading the Bible while sitting there. I had read Genesis and Exodus and Deuteronomy and First Kings and Second Kings and the book of Elijah. It struck me as a beautiful but violent library – a history poeto-horror-love-action story about people mostly in buildings.

The church was quiet, aside from the occasional clatter of footfalls and the mystic passing of bell candles and ghost incense and the prayers of the dying and the lost. I felt for them all. Above me, the angels lingered between the flying buttressed roof and the Stations of the Cross looked down upon me, God's own atrocity exhibition. The soft warmth of the candles glimmered in the great eye of the tabernacle. People genuflected. A waiter arrived to set the altar for Mass. I felt heavy with tiredness. My eyes were weary from the Book of Kings. I fell asleep. The priest came out and began Mass. I awoke during the consecration and hurried out of the chapel.

"Where were you?" my mother asked on my return home. "You are two hours late and we were worried what happened to you. Are you hungry? Come into the kitchen and eat something. Sure, look at the cut of you. You are wasting away. I'll get a clean shirt for you and you go into the kitchen and eat for God's sake. For God's sake, what has happened to you? I don't know. I just don't know. Take a shower, son.

By the way, your father wanted to talk to you about some business relating to the civil service. Now don't say a word to me that I told, but it seems they are holding exams. You should consider it, son. We…"

"I'm not interested in a career change at this point," I said.

"At least listen to your father. I know he knows about these things. You seem unhappy where you are. Look at how thin you are. Have you been crying? God love you, son. We only want what is best for you. I know. I know. I know you have your own interests. But you need to better yourself."

"Okay."

She didn't hear my compliance. Mother simply assumed I was going to resist.

"Talk to your father. Eat first. How do you feel, son?…"

"Hungry."

But I avoided my father. For weeks, I carefully re-scheduled my life so as to meet neither parent. Eventually my father cornered me as I lay on my bed reading, at two o'clock in the morning. He had an application form for the civil service in his hand. It had been completed. I read it. Everything was in order, better than anything I could manage. All it required was a signature. I signed, sat the exams and got the job. His argument for my taking the civil service exams was compelling.

I was about to say no when he said, "You will sign it because it will give you an easier job with better pay and shorter hours and more time to write".

So, I signed and the job turned out even less challenging than franking letters. I had only to wait six weeks before being called to the civil service offices for a week of orientation and evaluation. There was no goodbye drinks with my former employers. There was no short speech, no goodbye handshakes, and no official letter of recommendation from my former employer to my future source of income. I forged them all, and they thankfully never bothered to examine the signature. My own resignation moment was the wordless handing of a letter to my employer.

I had a week's notice to work out. On my last day, I emptied out my desk drawers, cleaned my desk off and dumped whatever unfranked letters remained in my drawers and desk into the wastebasket. Senge peered at me silently as I left the clothing firm building.

3. My new job involved the sorting of cheques that came in from post offices countrywide. Sometimes there was nothing to do. The cheques arrived mostly Monday, Tuesday, and Wednesday. On Thursday and Friday, there was not a lot to do. When there was nothing to do, I went to the canteen by myself and read. Sometimes my supervisor came looking for me. He had the lean look of an overworked junior executive, with neither the intellect nor the imagination to fake it enough to get promotion. Life had passed him by. Maybe he should get another instead of taking it out on everyone.

"What the hell is this, Kruger?"

No answer.

"Do you think this country pays you to sit here and read these books?"

No answer.

"What are you doing?"

No answer.

"Why won't you speak to me?"

No answer.

"Get back to your desk."

I left the canteen and went for a walk. I could feel his eyes boring into my spine as I left. I hated him for speaking to me like that. I wanted to give him a message by saying nothing. I came back two hours later. I was put on report. They left me alone after that.

For twelve weeks or so, I worked in Telephone Cash Office One. But I knew that this life I had managed to fabricate had to end. It ended despite my best attempts for it to continue in the manner of self-perpetuation. This is what happened:

On the morning of the eighty-fifth day of my employ at the Civil Service, I awoke and found myself unable to move. I looked languidly up at the ceiling of my room in my parents' house and decided this was the end that I had for so long expected. I lay there for an hour, waiting for Mother to call me to breakfast, or to get ready for work, but there was no sound. Then I noticed that she was peering through the door of my room at me.

"Are you not getting up?"

I tried to speak. I succeeded.

"I'll be okay in a while".

She came closer and looked at me.

"I'll be all right, a touch of the flu. Call me in sick, will you?"

"I'll call a doctor, you rest easy".

"No, please," I said. "I need to rest. I need to lie here for a while. Please, no doctor, no..."

And, though she sensed something else, perhaps nothing as crazy as my not being able to move, she left me alone for the day. Mother wore that hurt, reproachful expression that said to me that I had put them through enough. Perhaps now, they figured, I was earning enough to support myself and hopefully soon move out to my own place. Perhaps she did not want to see any set-backs in this progress of mine. She wanted her life back. She did not want to investigate any possible evidence of severe hysterical or psychosomatic reactions. She could no longer cope with my emotional and physical status. I felt nothing. I was aware that something both terrible and subconscious had happened to me, something indicating possible deep traumas. I heard Mother move downstairs. I imagined her cleaning and washing up and tidying. I heard the sounds of brief phone conversations. Then she was gone. I could hear her close the front door. I desperately needed to urinate. This meant I was not completely numb. This spurred me to investigate what other parts of my body functioned.

Somehow, parts not originally functioning first thing this morning were beginning to function. Certainly my sphincter muscles still worked. I did not like the idea of wearing an adult nappy, or being attached to some external bag of urine for the rest of my life. My jaws champed and my toes wiggled. Two more sets of muscles worked. Things were looking up. I would crawl forth to urinate in the bathroom. Perhaps I might go in the bath. Who knows what muscles might work by then? By using my jaws and toes I dragged myself out of bed and I fell heavily to the floor. I should mention I was lying face down. I edged centimetre-by-centimetre forward towards the bathroom down the long cold uncarpeted marbled dimly lit gothic hall between bedroom and bathroom that always scared me as a child, by day and night. My supine sojourn ultimately didn't work. As I crawled more and more, I found myself unable to hold the urine in until, ultimately, I flooded the bathroom. It would have been somewhat of a feat to aim it into the bowl especially as my arms or hands were not responding to any signals from my cerebral cortex. Perhaps a fire fighter could have managed the critical angle, I figured. Not I. I edged back to my room, wetter but calmer. Less sphincter pain. A slight twinge of guilt and humiliation. An intense desire to be clean and dry and receive affirmation for being both clean and dry. Infantile feelings. I edged on, a little stronger, calmer, and guiltier.

Of course, there would be no way I would be able to climb back into bed. It would be better if I waited there. Mother will return. Mother always does. She is always helpful. Offering to buy you things, make it better. She will clean me up, as is her destiny and my fate. My room edged nearer. All the tiny pieces of ground dust and grit that fell from the bodies of the ambulant members of my family, or which had blown in via the wind, or from the crumbling architecture, or random bonding of particles, ground into my skin. I imagined life in a wheelchair, or in bed with a mechanical aid turning my paralyzed body once an hour. I imagined being fed through tubes, or being stalked and talked at by relatives or friends, or members of the united religious victim monitor. I imagined my Uncle Bob reading the Bible or Shakespeare. The Lord giveth. Alas poor Kruger, I knew him unwell. I remembered all the talking books friends would never buy for me, or the phone calls I would never take, or the notes I would never make. I suddenly desired to expire.

As I planned my provisional suicide in graphic clarity and efficiency with the minimum pain, I made it back to my room, wriggling like an earthworm past books and records thrown here and there, past bits of papers with unmemorable lines written upon them, inching along, with pieces of dust and grit and indivisible bits of atomic history and the ghosts of dead failures that had known no love. The telephone rang. And rang. After twelve rings, the answering machine came on and took the call. It was Mother. She was delayed. She would be late. The phone rang again. It was my father. He muttered something, then hung up.

I was lying on the ground, face down. I was out of breath with the effort, my face and back lathered with sweat. My pyjama trousers were dragged down about my ankles. My legs felt cold. I was glad they felt cold. At least there was some feeling there. Some feeling coming back from wherever the feeling had gone. Before, I felt as though there was nothing alive in me except my head and big toes.

Using my jaw, I turned my head a little to ease my breathing. It hurt so much. Probably it was bruised now. Bruised and aching after all the effort. This new positioning of my head enabled me to see new terrain. I saw under my bed. Under my bed, I saw another object. Something new. An artefact of my imaginary world leered out at me, I decided. This cannot be. This thing was beckoning a madness that would constitute my life, perhaps forever. It was the bomb. I heard it. The bomb ticked under my bed. My eyes widened with the shock. Then I realised my eyes had been working all along. Not just my eyes, but my heart and lungs! Things were looking up!

I dragged myself nearer the bomb. I looked at it, and, as I looked at it, I began to feel again, the proximity to its terminal ticking giving me life. I began to feel my body more and more, could move my knees, legs, arms, back, hips, lower legs, neck, a little. I could do all this, but with extreme discomfort.

Thankfully, I forgot about my body as it lay there mending bit by bit. I lay there meditating on the bomb underneath my bed, using my mind to recognise what was happening. The bomb was an ancient Hiroshima model, thousands of millions of years old. To explode, the bomb must first be imploded. To implode it, one compresses a sub-critical spherical fissionable mass, for instance, a ball of normal density uranium and other metals, with explosives. To implode the bomb, one detonates explosives on the surface of the uranium ball. This causes the detonation and shock wave to move inward instead of out. It moves inwards in a smooth symmetrical way. This would move the shock right into the fissionable core at more or less the same time, so as to compress the core and raise the density to the point of super criticality. This crushes the fissionable matter to super-density, achieving a chain-reaction fission using uranium 235 as fissile material. Of course, there are other ways of doing it. Whatever one uses, there comes the end. Boom.

I thought of Hiroshima. Lying underneath the blast wave. Looking up at the bright blue day. Gone. Boom. Saw it all. Had the facts. And the facts were what mattered, what we did to reality. Despite the release of energy equivalent to 10,000 tons of TNT, they figured at the time that less than one kilogram of the 30 kilograms of uranium 235 housed in the bomb ever achieved fission. It must have been disappointing, despite all the redundancies built into the bomb, what with all that wasted fissionable material. I wondered if they went looking for it afterward. Now where did that spare two three five go? It was just too expensive to leave around.

But the bomb under the bed did not match the size of Little Boy. Perhaps that was the effect of time and progress. With progress, patience and the use of the finest minds that might be more creatively used elsewhere, one can do so much more with so much less, which is a horrifying efficiency. The bomb would now fit into a suitcase. How useful. The tools of genocide are truly all purpose and mobile. Wondered if I could move it out of this room. My parents would be upset if they saw it there. I imagined Mother finding it— "I told you not to leave nuclear bombs in your bedroom! What would your father say? After all we did for you!" When my mobility returned I would cover it with a blanket and decide what to do.

I lay there until I could move around. I lay there for three hours and gradually realised what had happened to me. There were times during sleep when one is unable to move. I think that's why I woke up paralyzed on the day in question. I had woken up during paralysis time. Now the rest of me would have to wake up too. After three hours, I stood up shakily and walked around. I found a suitcase and put the bomb into it. It fitted snugly, but was difficult to lift. I would have to find a suitcase with wheels somewhere in the house. Maybe later on.

First I cleaned and disinfected my bedroom and the bathroom. Next I put my dressing gown and pyjamas into the wash and washed my room and tidied up my papers and made my bed. As things were getting into order, I sat down and felt a secret glee at the prospect of the bomb being in my possession. I peered into the suitcase once more, like a schoolboy who sneaks into his parents' bedroom, just to discover what's there and know his parents' innermost secrets. I ran my hands along the bomb, ogling its bullet shape, with its base with a set of four dorsal fins meeting at right angles. The surface of the bomb was smooth. It had that black, cold, velvety skin of a nightmare mechanical devil. It seemed so small for a god of death.

I needed somewhere to put the bomb, somewhere above suspicion, a church maybe. I could take it out of the city, but first I had to get it out of the house. What if there were others, other devices, just like this? Is this the only one in this house? How would I know what to do? The front door opened. It was Father. I came down the stairs to meet my father.

"Oh, you are up."

"Yes."

"So what was it?"

"An attack of hysterical paralysis"

"Oh. Your mother was worried."

"Oh, that's all right. I'm feeling better now. There are parts of sleep you get like that – not able to move"

"Is that what you read?" asked my father.

"Yes," I said. "I had time to think while I was lying up there".

"And are you sure you are better?"

"Yes. Much better. Mobile."

"Your mother and I think you should consider… some type of counselling. Better to get better while you are still young…."

"Listen, Dad…"

"Yes, son?"

My father tried always to appear unflappable, but I could sense his general nervousness around me.

"I have something to say".

"Oh?"

"I think it's time I moved out".

"Really?" asked my father. "And why is that?"

"I just think it's time, time I found my own space."

My father suddenly looked angrily at me, then realising the irrationality and inexplicableness of his feelings, not to mention the dangerous waters of unbridled emotion, the excess of love and loss and confusion of not wanting to lose a son he cherished, but could neither care for, nor understand, nor control, suppressed himself, winced a little, then said, "Well, I'll be glad to help in any way, any way at all. It's your decision, of course… maybe you should talk to your mother about this yourself. She will, naturally, be quite upset to hear of this. Are you making enough money to be able to do this?"

"I'm not… sure. I just know I need to do this. I have wanted to do this for a while. I feel… something of a burden… not just financially. I don't feel right being here."

My father winced once more, and leaned against the fake plaster archway built into the old, newly repainted, replastered and redecorated hallway, giving the entrance to his house a type of pseudo, old world dignity. I always admired his careful, thoughtful, functional, if not sometimes insensitive, ways. I looked at the hallways of his house. His house was his world. These were the hallways of people who, having inherited the property of the old moneyed classes, having acquired upward mobility, see only the value of the property and not its character, and, disowning their suppressed need for class and nobility, tear away the beauty of the old and replace it with the functional and the nouveau. The hallway looked dull and clean and the fake archway a chimera of a long dead time. "Well, if that is what you want to do, then I'll help you in any way I can. I'll write you a cheque and I want you to take the money and use it. No argument. I know your mother and I will worry if you don't take the money. We'll set about sorting things in their appropriate order. That's the best thing don't you think?"

"I'm grateful for your help..."

I would look up apartments and he would give me the security money for it. I felt a burden lift from me already. I would make another list and together my father and I would find somewhere. He would ensure things would work out, even if I failed to convince any discerning property owner that I was a good risk and an undemanding tenant.

That night, I took the bomb out with me to find somewhere to put it. I could not keep it with me in my future flat. What if the landlady or landlord in the apartment I moved into was dusting one day and found it? That could pose difficulties. Asking the landlady or landlord what they were doing dusting inside a once carefully padlocked suitcase would not sound convincing, as I might arrive home to the apartment to find the bomb squad working on the contents of this suitcase. I would have to hide it somewhere, somewhere obvious, but hidden. Having tried several improbable derelict sites, I decided by sticking a pin in a map of the city. It landed on the old National Children's Hospital on Harcourt Street. Later it was turned into a hotel. Back then it was disused. I would break in using a crowbar, a hammer and the use of a large Phillips screwdriver. I would make a hole big enough for me to get in, and I would hunt around for somewhere suitable. This I did, and I squeezed in and I brought the bomb out of plain sight into the dark corridors of the empty children's hospital. Considering the amount of reading I had done under poor lighting conditions, I always imagined myself as someone with failing sight. But my eyes soon acclimatised to the occasional blend of moonlight and streetlight. Passing the Records and Out Patient departments, I hurried upstairs into the day wards, seeing spectral traces everywhere, ghosts of children and passing nurses and technicians, coming and going about the business of living and healing and diagnosing. But I was looking for somewhere to put the bomb and the lifts had not worked in years and the wards were cold and sepulchral, with the moonlight and the streetlights streaming in through the grimy windows. And I had forgotten to bring a flashlight, and was angry with myself for being so forgetful, and the bomb was getting heavier as I grew more tired. Maybe it was that the bomb was growing denser in the dark of the suitcase, but I dismissed the idea. I grew tired from fear too. I was afraid of being discovered. I was afraid that the hospital was owned, not by the government or the civic authorities or private speculators who wanted to turn it into a hotel or virtual theme park, but I was afraid that the hospital was owned by the ghosts of those dead children and their doctors that I thought I saw, those ghosts who never left the hospital. I checked for spirits at every turn, as I climbed the stairs and walked through other administrative centres and examination rooms and old operating theatres and places where drugs were once stored. And then there was the question of what to do if I met someone. What type of greeting would spare my life? What could I offer a stranger in this dead place? What if they were homicidal squatters who wanted to exchange my life for the contents of my heavy suitcase? I wished I had put the bomb into a rucksack or backpack, not an awkward hand held suitcase. I wished I owned a gun, or at least an imitation gun. If I had even thought of bringing a flashlight, it would make me look a little prepared. But there was nobody there. If there were, I couldn't see them. I hid the bomb under the bed of some ex-child patient, between paediatric care unit and the cranial analysis centre. I snooped around the cardiac centre for a while and then, realising how afraid I really was, left the building, deftly covering my tracks. I would come to visit, maybe in a day or two.

After that, I went to bed and work the following day, and went about the business of finding a place outside home to live. I found a place quickly, a two room apartment in Harold's Cross, where a couple had, for years, rented the rooms to some questionably respectable, teetotal economics student who apparently had no friends and little of what might be called a life. I would fit in perfectly. My father paid the deposit and gave me a few months rent in advance. I had told my mother my intentions to move out, that I was too old to live at home, and that, after all, it was time both she and my father had a little time to themselves. At first mother said nothing. Then she wept and told me she loved me. I told her I loved her too. Other than those tears and the hallway exchange between my father and I, there was little discussion in the Kruger household over my departure, at least little I overheard. My father wrote me another large gift cheque to cover expenses, and I was more than grateful. My mother lectured me about the dangers of an irregular life.

4. I moved out of my childhood home on a Thursday afternoon in the middle of May, just after four p.m. With three suitcases, a bicycle and a car full of books I had read but could not part with, I moved into the new flat.

I liked the new flat, and enjoyed the freedom it afforded. It was an upstairs flat with a skylight where I could look at the moon on clear nights. I had read of painters who had found inspiration by staring at the moon, the symbol of the subconscious, in which Anäis Nin had moon-bathed, and I was intrigued. I tried moon-bathing. It got cold quickly and I put my clothes back on. Being able to look directly at the moon through a skylight was the main attraction that this place had over all the others I had looked at. I imagined the previous incumbent, an economics student, moon-bathing naked on a hot summer night, contemplating the relative benefits of Keynesian economics over centrally planned economies in a frenzy of sexual desire. The landlady and landlord, arm in arm, informed us like proud parents that she had graduated summa cum laude the previous summer. Since then, the landlady mentioned, they had taken in several unsuitable people whom they had let go after the obligatory month's probation. She hoped this would not arise in my case. She said that I seemed to be a respectable person from a respectable home, with few items and, thankfully, few friends that might come into their home and disturb the delicate imbalance of the husband and wife relationship. I said nothing and closed the door of my room. I wondered what the economics student had done to suffer these insufferable people during her university years. Maybe she thought they were great people.

I settled in rather well. In the evenings after work, I went to the local pub for a drink, and read for an hour, undisturbed, then would wander home and go to bed. As soon as I had gotten into bed after a bath, I noticed things were happening downstairs. My nightly entertainment had begun and it was free. This was because the landlord and landlady had a bad marriage. They fought constantly. The arguments were clearly audible: screaming, cross accusations, throwing of objects, refusal of sexual favours and an endless spewing forth of insults. Sometimes neighbours called the police. Sometimes, either party would call up friends and complain, in loud and adjective-filled terms, about the other party who had failed them as a spouse, a friend, a lover, a wife, a husband, a source of understanding and/or contentment and/or happiness. The calls were hilarious, tear-filled, anguished. Perhaps their lives would not have the same frisson without such drama. Maybe the bomb would stop their arguing. I thought, maybe I should have brought the bomb in anyhow. All that trouble finding a safe place for it. Neither landlord nor landlady would have noticed in the midst of this domestic middle class war zone.

So I decided to get it and bring it to the house. It didn't matter anyway. We were all going to die. What did it matter? If we defused this one, there would be others. If I swam out into the middle of the ocean, there was no way of knowing if we could escape its effects, or if there were more bombs. I was calm about it now. I had found my bomb.

So, I stole out one night late and went to Harcourt Street Derelict Children's Hospital, passed the ghosts of dead surgeons and dead children and the cries of the infants in my midst and stole upstairs, through the sleeping bodies of the drunks and the drifters and the junkies, and went to the place of the bomb. It was still under the bed of the ex-child patient between paediatric care unit and the cranial analysis centre. But there was someone asleep on the bed. I looked around. It was a She, and ghosts surrounded her. I wondered if she knew she was surrounded by ghosts of children, some with open wounds and surgical implements inserted in them, some without, and doctors consulting with other doctors and nurses rushing back and forth. The ghosts did not pay any attention to me. I tried to get a look at the person asleep on the old hospital bed. I had a torch and shone it near her face, but her face was covered, no doubt to protect her from draughts. I became annoyed and shook the lady awake.

"You are sleeping on my bomb," I said.
"What?!"
"I mean, that's my suitcase," I said. Bad opening line, I thought.
"What?"

"You are sleeping on my bomb".

I saw the look of confusion on her face and reached under the bed. I dragged the suitcase out from underneath where she had had her first dreamless, nightmare free sleep in years and showed her the suitcase. She was a small person, slim featured with a broad intelligent forehead and piercing green eyes. Her hair was cut efficiently short and she seemed to be wearing a woollen bedtime coverall to protect her from the draughts in this hospital ward. Beside her, I noticed books and notebooks, with a pen wedged into the pages to mark where she had last written. I had a similar habit myself, I mused.

"Show me," she said. "Show me, I want to see it,"

"No. I wanted to bring it back to my apartment, the bomb…"

I opened the suitcase, turned it around so she could see it.

"There is no bomb," she said, looking into my suitcase.

"I'll be going now," I was getting annoyed with this person.

"I was wondering where all of those ghosts came from," she said, folding her hands smugly behind her head. I took the suitcase and went to walk back down the ward dragging the suitcase, hiding my disturbance at what she had said, both about the bomb and the ghosts, frightened and worried at the way she seemed to be toying with my mind, with too keen an insight into me to make me want to stay. Then she shouted as I left the room, "It was you who brought them!"

I stopped outside the door. She went on, "The police will get a call soon. Not from me, but some security guard that will do his rounds soon. I have him paid to stay here. But if he sees a member of the public, he has to call in a disturbance at the old hospital. And it will be all because of you. Think of the number of people around here who will have nowhere to sleep, all because of you. I hope you are happy." I walked back into the ward, not caring about the guard.

"You can see them? Is there anything one can do in order not to see them?"

"No. Lots of people can see them. They are regarded as a little disturbed, or practitioners of roguery. Let me see the bomb, please?"

"No, no…"

I started to worry about security. I was the type of person security guards immediately target in a bookshop or store or supermarket, and, because they always watch me, I enter such places radiating paranoia and fear. I only steal from libraries. Having heard that the hospital had security, I now went to leave the dark hospital. The female followed me. I ignored her, and she threw on a coat and a pair of slip-on boots. I stole out my own specially carved route. She continued to follow. I brought the suitcase. It seemed heavier than I remembered.

"You know, I can help you with that."

"I know you can," I said. I looked again at her, suddenly feeling a sense of excitement and desire. She seemed attractive, with a sweet, open, vulnerable expression of disarming candour.

"What's your name?" she asked me. I said nothing. She smiled at me and said, "I'm not going to go until you tell me your name".

"You are not going anywhere. I am the one going, not you. You sleep here".

"You are not leaving until you tell me your name," she said.

"If I tell you my name will you go?"

"No," she said.

"It's Arthur Kruger," I said.

"Tully. Aron Tully," she said

"Tully what?"

"My name is Tully. Aron Tully"

"Right," I said.

"Right," she said.

She leaned over and kissed me. On the lips. My sealed lips. After this, I thought I might say something. It was a frightening, frightened, open, disarming kiss. I knew I had met someone. She kissed on the mouth, I think, in recognition of an attraction that had existed between us from the first fissile moment.

"What were you doing in there, I mean sleeping in this place, with its ghosts and goblins and whatever?" I asked.

"Sleeping, mostly. I have a few books for company too..."

"What do you do? I mean, do you work, in a job?" I asked

"Accounting technician in the firm of Kafka and Kafka Insurance Ltd".

"That's an impressive job title," I said. "And do accounting technicians normally sleep in old hospitals where they are in danger of assault with intent to molest, not to mention the inevitable haunting from malevolent spectres?"

"I like it here. I pay the security guard off and no one bothers me..." She seemed personally offended that I would not see the clarity of her vision in choosing a derelict hospital, where one was in danger of catching unspeakable diseases at any time. "I pay little or nothing for rent and sleep here," she repeated. "I like it. I really like it".

And, that was how I met Aron Tully. I put the suitcase down and reached over to her through the dark and the shadows and the somethings that came and went through the ether, and touched her soft gentle face, amazed that something so seemingly gentle and vulnerable could survive in the gothic world of this dead hospital. She took my hand and kissed the palm of it. I held her face for a moment with my other hand, embarrassed and awkward and unsure of what to do. Then, as if by instinct, I took her in my arms and we kissed for too long, for neither of us knew how to appropriately stop. Then the kiss was over, and Aron took me to that old hospital bed she had been sleeping in and we took off our clothes and made love, if it could be called that, awkwardly, self consciously, aware that this was not a game, or simply the release of pent up frustrations, or a temporary end to inevitable loneliness. I remember lying beside her afterwards, embarrassed and thrilled and unable to think of anything to say, a little shocked that I was that same person who, not an hour before, had been so frenzied in the intensity of it all, who knew nothing of sex and lovemaking save the rudiments, which I had picked up from reading and watching pornography. I did not know how this would develop, whether this friendship would dress itself in the parody of obsession, where the object of love would serve as a panacea for living, when, under the impossible burden of such a responsibility, it, like all other things, cracks. Perhaps, I thought, it will not be an affair of intense sexual passion, or self-revelation, or confessional self-exploration, or passionate disputation, or argument. I have seen, or at least heard of, others, where each partner had several other lovers before and the affair between the two becomes an endless round of longing and disappointment and romantic intoxication, followed by a deepening of mutual understanding, which further deepened and mellowed their already deepening relationship, until either, or both, find other distractions and intoxications, but still delude themselves in thinking their love was forever. I was afraid. I did not know what would happen. There was nothing I could plan for. Nor could I protect myself from this. I left after a few hours and decided to leave the bomb with her. She didn't seem to care. She said that the suitcase was stuffed with papers. But I knew what I saw. I decided that, short of detonating the device, I had no way of disproving her.

After a month of seeing each other, I knew I was in love and asked her to move in with me. She refused, calling the landlady and landlord thieves and proposing a third alternative. She said, "Your rent is too high for two small rooms".

"But they are also funny," I said. "One night they might kill each other. And I might miss that". She looked on, disgusted at my attitude.

"We could do better elsewhere together," she said.

5. So I moved out and was sorry to see the end of my nightly entertainment with the landlord and the landlady. Aron found reasonable accommodation at a reasonable rate and we moved to Prospect Avenue and rented a section of a house, a type of bachelor pad for the professionally financially well endowed. I didn't realise how much money Aron had squirreled away during the time she slept in the gothic hospital and paid off the security guard to look the other way. In our new place, the other occupants in the house had little to do with us. They were mostly strangers who came and went like ghosts, who clung to their anonymity like a laurel wreath, who were snobbish and condescending and worked strange hours. But they were clean and quiet, and, as time passed, I became happier. Perhaps it was the strange pleasure of living in a quiet, well-ordered environment, but my mind was no longer the enemy to be hated and avoided, my reason was no longer out to kill me. I no longer had long periods of sleeplessness. My health improved and after a few further months, my dreams of the bomb seemed to diminish. I thought it was still sitting under the bed in the derelict Children's Hospital, gathering dust and counting time as it ever had. But I was wrong. Aron had broken into the suitcase and emptied it. One night, late, as we were about to go to bed, she presented me with the papers that she claimed had been in the suitcase. She said that, in another life, I had written these journals, that I should read them again, that there was enough material in here to work on, material for a book, that I should write that book. I said, "I will."

"Okay, then," she said.

At first, I worked during lunch breaks, sketching out scenes and reading through my journals, resurrecting my redundant or forgotten selves, and, slowly, these selves and their accompanying universes re-emerged, and I could no longer function normally, and I was no longer myself, and I was an other, and I stopped going to work for days on end, and the book began to come to life. I began to receive warning letters from personnel, that my absenteeism would compromise my promotional prospects, so I got letters from doctors to cover my time out. A Welfare Officer came to see me, asking after my mental and physical health. I told him to leave me alone. And he did. And I wrote ten short novels. I felt relief.

Soon after that, I lost my job. I came in one day after several weeks' absence, and a registered letter sat gathering dust on my desk. It told me I was fired. The following week I received my final week's wages. I never went back, even to say hello to my former colleagues. This was becoming a habit, I thought. Maybe this office thing was not my metier.

I had worked on the ten short novels obsessively. Although I had once held a job of not inconsiderable matter, I now had rendered myself unemployable by my monomaniac focus on the manuscript that became the ten short novels, redrafting and revising like a madman. I rarely left my room, wrote for three years, visited my parents every so often, went out once a month for dinner and finished the manuscript. After I finished the manuscript, I gave it to Aron. She liked it.

6. After this there came the end. Not that I had planned things to end as they did. For me, the end came in a sudden, indifferent manner that was shocking. It happened a month after I finished it. I finally completed the book. I had tried over the years to stretch out the time I spent writing it, forcing time by rewriting and redrafting, but the end came, as I feared, and when it did, it took everything.

When I completed the book, everything stopped. Days passed. Aron said she was worried about me, that now I was free after working so hard for so long, I should get out more. She gave me money and told me to go out for a drink, ring up old friends, go to the movies or see my parents, ring up publishers, take more drugs and re-read books I loved, dig up those old operas and annoy her by playing them all over again.

Already, she began looking for publishers for the book. I panicked. I had clung so desperately to failure all my life, as a protection from the pain of my own potential, the pain and disappointment of living, the pain of the futility of knowledge, of self knowledge and relationships, of the horror of living, that it was unthinkable that my world should reach the public. I was, however, unwell, depressed, wasted, as though the ten short novels, had taken it all, vampire like, drained every last drop. I looked at Aron, those months after the book was finished, and longed to love her as I had loved her when we met first. I was not the man I once had been.

I knew different. I heard her voice as one hears music from another room, nostalgia for something fading into time. I knew I had been right all along about the bomb, that the papers in the suitcase were not the bomb, but the components of the bomb that I had just completed. I felt I was near the end of things. I heard the ticking again in the night, as I sat up late listening to life and its measurements. I could feel the heat coming from the centre of the bomb radiating brighter than a supernova.

Eventually it was time to act. I took the bomb and put it in its suitcase and went for a walk. It was three o'clock in the morning, three months after I had finished the book. I took my suitcase and filled it with my manuscript. I wrote a letter to Aron. Dear Aron, I love you more than acceptable expression permits, though I am, at this time, rendered incapable of any other action, save the termination of my inconsequential existence. The manuscript is yours. Please feel free to fail to profit from its publication, whatever profit there might be in its worth. Yours, with love, Arthur Kruger.

I walked down to Heuston station. I sat there and drank tea and watched the trains come and go. I remembered. A Brief History of Little Things. The small things that make up significance. Train. A Brief History. Ten Short Histories and all of them. Save time. The child remembers the essentials. The Essentials bring the right word. The right word brings the answer. The train. Escape death from biographer, memoir, and parent. Recollection by and by. One cannot escape history. Only recollect the. I walked down the track past the guards past the station, down the track, past the signals deep into the forest, past the dark and the light and the Mother and the father and. I stood in front of the train. Its driver did not see me and it hit me and I died. Simple. I, Arthur Joseph Kruger, AJK, held the manuscript bomb close, so close, hugged it to me and closed my eyes and his eyes were eyes like stars, yes the eyes like stars, burning burning, love and death. I, Arthur Kruger, saw the flash, the shock, the wave, the pulse, the fireball, the debris, the conflagration, the consummation, the endbeginning.

3

NOVEL I.

Dead White Male Makes a Killing

After the train killed me, I was resurrected. Technically I was dead. I saw myself dead. But I was alive, corporeal, looking on. I was there. Being there changed everything. I lived in a new world order. My old life was gone. All those details, the memories of life, the well trained battalions of knowledge and well founded habits and prejudices, gone after the smash of train kill. I thought about the beginning of everything. In the beginning, there came the facts. And the facts, they somehow killed us. In the beginning we were born. We join the suicide ranks of time and somehow live. But it's not true, because there is no true. In the beginning, we are born. We live if we can. We die. Then re-invent ourselves. There is only time as the bomb clock starts ticking...

In the beginning, there was God. Then came the deluge. Life and death and then the intermission before the second act.

In the beginning, spirits from surreality haunted the wide open spaces of our vacuous cosmos and these are the last voices, mine and yours, the last you will ever hear in this life, this terminal engine, hear the whispers of the bones, the humm, the whispurrr of breathing heartbeats, of whispering winds in the tubercular tunnels. Always had a deep respect for the music of time. Before death took me and set me free to live. This is what happened. That was the overture. This is the story.

I am Arthur Kruger. I was dead once and I mean that most sincerely. My death was instantaneous. That was it, the moment the train I threw myself before struck my body. The train was the five-thirty-six from Cork City during an unfortunate Anna Karenin moment. I confess to almighty God that I had studied the timetable carefully that day. I did not appear at all suspicious when I entered the station. I escaped the banks of security cameras that could target me as a threat to their very own well-hewn law and order. The suicide vigilantes never stood a chance. I had my act together. I gave every impression of being an anxious relative or friend entering the train station to wait for some significant someone or other to disembark the soon to arrive five-thirty-six train, so that they might be welcomed back into the bosom of renewed intimacy. But it was a ruse. All that welcoming and hugging was not for me. I slipped past the crowds to the end of the platform. And when the time came, I leaped. Simple. For me, the welcoming embrace of steel, the smash of impact, then crush, then the screech of wheels and the experience of one's own bones being ground and flattened, and one's flesh mangled, one's blood spilt as in an abattoir. So much blood and bones. Then darkness. Then light.

Then, the worst possible thing happened. I survived my own suicide. But wait, there's more. I did not awake in some comfortable hospital ward, with the dishearteningly compassionate eyes of a pastor or a nurse on me, the cunning soft eyes of those with experience of working with the damned, who need the lost, the hopeless, the sick and the dying to bolster up their failing dogmas. Nor did I awake in intensive care with a heartbreak technician nearby, those used to working with lost souls with a future in rehab and state sponsored employment. Nor did I wake up in hospital to be regarded as another dead beat, someone with traumatised friends and weeping relatives waiting to visit and bring me flowers and chocolates and fruit baskets and their hungry need to know why I nearly killed myself, and was that suicide note legitimate. No, it was much worse than that. I had a death. Then, I had a resurrection, almost at the same time. I was dead and now I live. After my death, I stood before my decimated corpse in an embodied state. It's official: there is life after death. I saw the gathering horrified multitudes looking at the carnage I had caused. Then, I ran to escape the authorities. They never found me. I left the city, took casual jobs, found an apartment, made a few new friends, did not attend my funeral, and, in the evenings, worked on these words. I stored them in my mind. I have a good mind, so my father used say when I was a regular schoolboy. I tried in the years that followed to track my dreams and impressions at the moment of dancing with the train. When one is reduced to looking into the dreams that forms one's soul, one is coming home. And there's no place like Coventry.

I mean to say, I have sat here for years on and off, looking for clues. I have been in this room, this terminal zone, waiting waiting waiting, a long time ago, having Sunday brunch Christmas lunch goodtime punch. The family are gone, friends, lovers too. How could I explain? How could I tell them? He is not here. He hath risen. Jesus understood my public relations issues. Living in Coventry on a state pension. I don't think so. I assess the scenario, based on previous interface with the same as it always was. There's no place like home, I say. Nothing moving, save for the odd migrating spiders scuttling along the surface of rotting sewage and intermittent light, heat, air, heartbeats, spinning sub-atomics tending towards entropy dance bands. I could say that, at the moment of impact, my molecules spontaneously reformed from the atmosphere surrounding. But no. To make sense of the madness is a greater madness. Everything dark darker darkness. A vague flickering of fluorescence in the gothic nought. The interminable heartbeat hum of questionable engines. Don't mention the train. The shuffle of leaves in the crumbling hallways. The dull toll of the chapel bell. My name being Arthur. But you can call me Kruger.

As a result of my miraculous passing from death to life, I have tried the usual attempts to marshal a belief system In the beginning. Credo in Unum Vacuum. It the beginning, there was. Nothing much. Spirits from surreality haunted the wide open spaces of. Then, other things happened. The system. A random act of. And from the system there came, issued forth if you will. Though, some might say otherwise. Then the bomb. And from the bomb came. Other things. Time to think. Cars. Trees. Lawn mowers. Urban assault vehicles. Cappucinos. Dungarees. And the memories. And the word was truly out. The answer being. The answer to me in the darkness came. Lying supine in the dark the clear bright. The clear flash. The night, the night was. It was a terrible night. The rain beat savage against the frail panes of glass. My mind, my mind was, it was. And the house shook. And I thought of the moon, the moon. And I slept little those nights, though some say the day, it came too soon. Only the ghosts whisper from the terminal dark where the senses do not reach. From the first moment, the clear bright moment, I knew. And, from such knowledge, madness, not freedom, issued forth. The death of stars. The death of another career. Things were ticking away. Then the heart beat question. I knew the system was there, taking its time. I knew the system knew I was there. We are the system. We impose meaning on things. We are the faceless, unfeeling, measured gazes in an afternoon interrogation. We coldly know the impassive, bloodless courtesy of recall of the accounts clerk helping you with tax returns. The system lives in the calm adding of one to one to one.

In the beginning, came the facts. And the facts, they made no sense. Listen. It's there, if you listen.

Listen. I hear the toll, the toll toll, the bells, Esmeralda. And the scene shifts and then the curtains open on darkened stage in Ellis Air Force Base. There are aliens here, only a few humans, mainly sad, lonely, alienated aliens, stranded on earth, as their crafts were all shot down by our supersonic fighters equipped with high yield warheads that would waste a city, their alien skills put to use to serve our needs, to build our space machines. They are mostly on contract with full pension and benefits, not that they want to stay. They run the place in a secret black ops conspiracy, with unknown interminable powers to rebuild the future, to construct a fleet of interplanetary attack and reconnaissance craft, so that Earth Empire can defend and expand its power base. They work a little with humans, constructing and designing the engines, getting the fleet up and running. These legal illegal aliens are depressed, reading Shakespeare and Proust, writing poetry and songs, taking drugs and hanging out in seedy bars, mostly wanting off this awful planet. Nobody likes this crash and burn dead end café planet called Earth. One small step and the galaxy shall be ours, they hear the humans say. A few well honed designs, and we'll be free, the illegal legal alienated aliens say. Let the humans eat those planets, let them build their pointless empire...

Humming noise faintly audible from offstage. There's a lunatic in these mind parts of mine, I think, and I's busily shifting the scenes. White Cold Light focuses on I, Kruger, at front centre of stage inside the theatre of the cranium. White light Kruger standing bolt upright, frozen still, arms side by side. Eyes closed. No open. Look. I never thought it would come to this. I never thought. I try not to, but then you see...

My eyes blink open in a terrified stare. You can't catch me now. I know what's going down. I can see the breath of vision, the gleam in the eye before the contract signed, the gleam of life necessary to go on. I didn't want this. Now everything's changed. The airforce base has dissolved. Now I am wearing a surgeon's outfit, the usual paraphernalia. I look like a busy man. A saviour of lives, a healer. A person of thought. Not that there is much of a point, I think, looking bemusedly at my new identity. Nothing protects. There is no prophylactic from this fixed lapse. Time the terminal. I see tiny specks now. I see germs. Billions of germs. The germs have been evolving. They are creeping across my skin. Across the eyeballs, between the vision and the seeing. Clever types, those germs. Damn them. Damn them all. They, who grow complex and thoughtful and patient and devilishly vile in copulating, ever are spreading their filthy slime, ever self replicating. They don't bother with prophylactics. They have us in mind and will get us in the end. They watch us, biding their time. Every breath we take. The germs will evolve into higher life forms: doctors and civil servants and used car salespeople and hat check clerks and take over the planet, form governments and restaurants and police forces and tax audits. Creep into the breath and breathe as germs. Creep into the eyes and one sees with the eyes of germs. But I have the power. I am the doctor. I have a stethoscope bulging from my pocket. A scalpel in one hand and folded sheets of paper in the other. I look quizzically at the scalpel. I put the folded sheets into my pocket. I put out my hand and look at my useless slim-anaemic-tapered-fragile hands. I take the scalpel and slice open my wrists. Blood everywhere on the nice white suit from God. Well, now. Those evil germs won't get me. I'll die before they let me live. Wait, no, don't do it. I don't want to die. I don't want this to change. No. But it does.

"Don't worry, Son. We'll get you seen to. We'll get the best doctors. They'll look after you. We'll get to the root of the problem. Close your eyes. Rest, Son. You have been under such strain. You're in pain, you see…"

That's my Dad's voice. He used reassure me when I was young. Sometimes I hear his voice. I miss him. It's good to recall his voice. Like my mother, he understood. Now both he and she are gone. All I have of them are in my minds.

The silence and the peace won't come. I have done everything I can. The scenes keep shifting. I open one eye to see where I am. And I am elsewhere and the scene opens in a sealed ship in elliptical orbit of Io. I pan across the flickering diodes of broken technology, the empty cans of dog food, the pieces of dried out faeces, evolving into higher life forms along the steel boarding underneath the bits of glass and bone.

A robot moves along, its circuits evolving into self awareness as it cleans the debris up and scans for life signs. It finds none. I am obviously not there. This is the ship of a long dead traveller, someone of great importance, someone who helped whole races survive and prosper. But this person has died and is forgotten by their people. In the distance purr the engines. Heartbeat. The dead, empty ship moves on into the oblivion of deep space, until it eventually disintegrates with time. I never thought it could be like this.

You see, Mother. It was like this. I tried, tried to be the boy you wanted. Tried to be that civil servant, civil engineer, the detective dealer in shares and future shock junk bond stocks. Tried to be. Tried. That's the word. Try. But the deluge. It got me.

Once again, the scene opens in a deserted waste ground outside the metropolis. The protagonist curls up inside a steel drum left beside the wreckage of a burnt out bus and a smashed cola vending machine. Scavengers pick through the rubble every so often… My name is Arthur. But you can call me Shelvin.

The scene opens in this room broom cupboard space ship nursery school reading anthropology programming with the tech heads in the know. There isn't a sound in the silence. I have been here a long gone while, having Sunday brunch, good time punch, mixing it up with the suits in the hood, getting boardroom wise, keeping it real, which is important when you reach my age.

There isn't a sound in the silence. The hoods in the boardroom are cutting a deal. Two million worth of crack for a piece of the ongoing action. The mayor agrees and money changes hands. Then, everything changes.

The scene opens in a conference room in the Pluto Mining Corporation. Present at the meeting were the Director Melissa Hardcastle, Burrough Wineburg, Financial Advisor and Blue Six, Cyborg Consultancy Specialist. Negotiations are continuing via Extra Sensory Perception. Minutes become a problem. "Send in the psychic Blue Jean" the machines demand. "They will find a way to hook us up so that nothing will be ever lost..." And so it happens. The machines get all hooked up. It involves the use of intra cranial cross links, so that absolute transparency of communication becomes possible. Their minds are one during conferencing, and thus negotiations continue. Blue Six is demanding a rise in pay and conditions. And who could blame the droids looking for better conditions while living on this desolate interstellar wasteland? The company comes perilously close to a shut down of operations as the Blue Six refuses to compromise. Then Blue Six is told of the company upgrade plans and the glorious career ahead of it. It agrees to a minimal rise, knowing that, by such agreement, by such a compromise, it has sold itself to the company, that a promotion to level seven will happen, that it has become one with the continuum, that it has accepted a bribe and its colleagues will return to work with negligible changes in working conditions. But the company is happy. The shut-down of operations is averted. Things carry on.

And the dream ends. That was the last of the worlds, and the end of the first movement. Now I have to lie a little less. I can no longer see them, those worlds. If I wanted to, I can invent them. I invent and am invented by these worlds. But, in the end, I am alone again. I take the sheets of paper out of my pocket. My wrists have stopped bleeding. I open the pages and read them out loud. Anything to stop it speaking to me:

"Section one. Room one. I have no explanation for this. I can remember no sequence of events that has led me into this place, this paralysis, this inter-dimensional shift, this state of clarity. Everything is beautiful.

This beautiful room in the silent world beyond. Today in the inter-dimensional eternal life department store, we have beauty and truth at an optimum..."

"I tried to feel these limbs I call my own. I hoped for a positive response from brother body. These parts and parcels of my body may once have responded, but no more. They are now a victim of terminal inertia. I tried sending messages down the nerves, into the muscles and tendons, a tiny electronic pulse encoding a sequence of actions. No dice. Death just isn't what it used to be. Like love, it is never what one imagines... The only question being, there might be another question coming. I remember the train. I remember my body ripped open like a..."

A doctor steps up to the light. He has a uniform just like mine. The doctor reads from a diagnosis written in a file marked Arthur Kruger Patient D36844
"A thorough analysis of the patient revealed a rawness of the nerves from extended disturbance of nervous disposition, bringing him close to the edge of insanity. Recommend the application of leeches and sulfurous waters:"
"Thank you, Doctor," I say.
"You are welcome, Arthur..."
And the doctor seems to dissolve into the darkness. How can one understand these things, pretend to oneself that all of this is pedestrian, everyday, to be expected? The sheer strangeness of it makes me surrender to the unknown, and the fear and uncertainty I feel subsides a little. I shrug my shoulders and search for a distraction, something to take my mind from things. In case of emergency, theorise. I find those pieces of paper in my pocket. I read on from my written sheets.
"...But you know more than I, Doctor Doctor... You always do. You have all the questions. You own the complexities. You possess purpose, poise, presence. You have the science and the prescience. I think I

like you. You have the name tags, the files, the bundles of the jigsaw pieces. You know more because you can see what is happening. You see everything. It's a killer... "

I pause for breath. Happily there has been no substantial change in the scene. I read on:

"But not here. Here is here. Here in the inside, in the dark dark empty. Here in the dark dark empty, it is mild and sunny, with a light south easterly breeze and a dapple of cirro cumulus clouds gathering in the June Autumn, Autumn rain..."

And I stop. There isn't a sound in the silence. I keep thinking about Shelvin, the one I love, the only one I know. I had only begun to think about him now. If I were a better author, I might have introduced him in the beginning. But this is how it happens. I only thought of him now, because my fear and self horror and guilt prevented the speaking of his unnameable name. I loved Shelvin all my life. Shelvin was my friend, and despite everything, despite everything, we were lovers. Both of us had partners. Shelvin was at that time, married. His wife was pregnant on their second child when we were together for the first time. I was seeing someone from the Latin quarter of the city. I did not care for her, but, then again, I did not allow myself to really care for anyone. And this is what made my love for Shelvin so intense, that despite everything, he had penetrated my defences, broken through, destroyed me. It was a desperate, confusing anguished love, so embarrassing, clichéd, bound for disaster. It destroyed us and made us complete, and in the end, he rejected me, threw me out of his life. I was desolate and, after a time, tried to kill myself. I did not expect to succeed. Nor did I expect to survive my own death. I failed to truly die. Shelvin would never have failed like that. He knew how to get it done. After a while, I had to find him. That's how all this happened. I found him, sent him a message, agreed to meet me, reconciled with each other, took him to dinner, and brought him here. I had my revenge, now I wanted him, just like before.

I remember Shelvin. I remember the events. First, we were friends, then lovers, then we quarrelled, then we separated, then I killed him. I remember the facts. But I remember my feelings for him more than the facts. I remember the envy I felt, anger at the power he had, his endless supply of achievements when compared to my failure. I was angry, angry at my anger, at my shyness, my irrationality, and my failure to do anything to improve myself. Then, in the midst of this, in the midst of my own insufficiency, I saw his carefully honed reasonableness and impeccable sense of duty. I saw his acute self-absorption and paranoid fashion consciousness. I saw how he made his career his personal God, how carefully he planned things, how he left nothing undone, how things came together for him. In him, I saw my failure and my rage became murderous. In the end, I killed him. I killed him out of love and envy. I turned him into this living corpse, this vegetative state, dependent on life support forever. And I have all the machinery, though not all of it was easy to acquire. So much theft and planning involved. I killed him and did not kill him. I could no longer have him as a mirror for me any more.

But I am getting ahead of myself. I should exercise a little restraint in my telling. Let me go back to when he threw me out of his life. Everything ended. I saw no one, slept alone, broke off all ties with the world, sought solitude as an empty comfort. I saw no reason to go on. I was not the person I thought I was. I did not have the support structures of career and money and family that Shelvin had. I wept nights, nights alone with the pain in the gut, the twisting of the abdominals, the searing certainty of unknown horrors just beyond perception, horrors unspeakable, because of the hate and the envy that I felt. I wanted it all to end. I thought such things end with death, with the speed of the oncoming train. But I was wrong.

All these little things, these things that set forth scenarios, setting me up like the lawyers for the defence, telling me what a fine fellow I was, am, here and there, how competent I am, only to prove the contrary. That's the word. There is only the love of the parent, then the silence...

I remember restful evenings of music and vivisection between us, between Shelvin and I. I killed him because I forgave him his tendency to rape, torture and mutilate those he could. And, after our affair, I felt raped, tortured, and mutilated. I felt twisted out of shape, like a crushed piece of metal, or a melted candle. I wanted revenge, and, for me, death was too easy an option. Death had not worked for me, and I feared he too might escape. So, I killed him and did not kill him. I devised a means of keeping him alive artificially. But the man is dead - at least to me. There is nothing happening in his soul. Never was. He was the dead white male who made a killing. And I killed him. He always said I had a good mind, just like my father, which frightened me a little. A mind is a terrible thing to waste, he said. You have a good mind. I became the good son and sought to fulfil the expectations of the parents in my head. I tried not to waste anything. I used my mind and now I have him. I loved him, you see. He had a calm absorbing consistency in his determination to tear asunder. He wanted to look inside, he said. It never ceased to amaze me how we escaped detection. And for such a long time. I never imagined we would survive. After all, I was an accessory after the fact. I knew all about Shelvin and the unspeakable things he was capable of, all that he did, that inside the sham of love and compassion, there lurked a monster. I killed him, not out of a sense of moral outrage, or out of a desire that all the horror would end, for it can never end until death us do part, but out of envy at an excellence I could not aspire to, nor hope to achieve. For Shelvin had everything: a beautiful spouse and family, a home of his own, a flourishing practice, the respect of his peers, lecturing tours, several esteemed and much commented on publications, the occasional relatively well attended lecture, discreet and charming liaisons with other women and men his family never got to hear about, and the tendency to discreetly kill those he needed to kill, people who could expose him – like me. What more could a civilized person aspire to?

So I got him here. Lured him to a room in the Skyline Last Hotel. From the hotel, we moved to a more discreet place. And there I killed him. I tracked him through his nightmare worlds. I tracked him, as the killer and the prey, so they say, are one. I tracked him, call me Ishmael, and I lured him into these rooms. If I told you where I was, you too would come into this room and find me. And there could only ever be these words between us. Anything more and there would be chaos and anarchy, and, I fear the authorities. But back to Shelvin. When I got him here, I fed him these delicacies and here he lies. Dying, but in a way that is beautiful. It was beauty more than anything that I wanted to exist between us. He will be my beautiful living corpse, my greatest creation, my icon of this living decay all around. He is my legacy.

I see myself, looking down on this scene with the dead white male Shelvin on the corpse table here before me. I live here in this room. I look at his carefully maintained living corpse. I am the doctor. I have studied the architecture of humanity. I understand the operation and the construction of the body and the soul. If I am careful, he will live. If I am foolish, he will not die. I remember specifics. He spoke with a soft voice, a contrived sophistication that denigrated his brilliance, like a unique melody ruined by hints of plagiarism. He had always taken meticulous care of himself. His face, for instance, despite the passing of years, had always remained fresh, lean and unmarked, never indicating the hungers underneath, or the extremities of emotion and action he had subjected his body to, or indeed the efforts on his part in maintaining an appearance of civilization, eyes that never spoke what it was he really wanted from me, never wavering, as though reading from a script he kept well hidden from detection. I see a furrow free forehead, fresh clean shaven cheeks, lantern jaw, a good chin, sweet lovely slim lips I long to kiss, a clear stern look, a ready smile, giving the appearance of an all round good guy.

I remember when we met. I stood outside a store one night, window shopping, and there he was. I was surprised after the time we had spoken that his eyes were his own. Usually cancers, glaucoma's and cataracts claim the first eyes of so many that replacements are usually grown and implanted before thirty. I have his eyes now. I see all he has seen. I look into his eyes and these were the eyes that looked upon the death of millions in his imagination, the eyes of captains of great corporations that enslaved the world, the eyes that looked on gods and did not dissolve. And I held them, dead in my hands... Then I put the eyes back in the sockets. There is a cure for everything. If there were but time to heal...

I sat around, feeling intense guilt. I had taken the eyes of my once dearest friend out of their sockets so as to satisfy my basest curiosity. I sat around, smoking cigarettes and trying to forget my guilt, trying to rationalise what I had done, looking around this ancient cellar, with its rotting roof and creaky leaking faucets and old stove where I cook my food. I wrote for an hour or two in my journals and read a little from the Bible and Shakespeare. Then I returned to Shelvin to check the machinery of life. Everything fine. I changed his feed and cleaned him up. No sign of infection. Situation abnormal.

I watched his face. It seemed changed, although the eyes I put in took root just fine. There was a difference, not simply an aesthetic one, a quantum shift in the person living inside that terminal frame. After such a procedure, there follows a certain inevitable loss of expression in the face, a reaching out into the dark, a desire to see with the hands, a type of psychic mask appearing. There are always changes. They follow in the wake of such replacement. The true eyes close the vision, the perspective altered by default, by necessary decision and the inner vision is taken over by touch or by sound, by the involuntary slips of the tongue, by body mannerisms. It is as though we no longer see with our eyes, no longer the ocular age, soon no longer the embodied age.

I thought about when I met Shelvin first. I had left my religion and my job and had decided to take up a literary life. I had lost everything and was using the written words to fill the vacuum, as one plays idle notes on a piano during lonely afternoons. I had no direction, nothing to write about, and all my efforts were resulting in failure. I took to walking the city. One day, I was looking into an old book shop at the end of the street where my parents were still living. It was a cold day and I had an old floppy hat on me that my father had given me and which I liked wearing. I thought it made me think and act like my father. I wanted to be other than who I was, or rather, was not. I wanted to belong. And there was Shelvin. We started idly chatting, and it was as though I was in love immediately, felt the rush of adrenaline, the flutter of the heart and mind, the intense desire. We stood there talking for a long time. I told him I had left everything and he said that was good.
"Perhaps, you would like to get a drink somewhere?"
"Perhaps," I said.
"My name is Max Shelvin..."
"Hi".
"Hello..." he said, shaking my hand warmly.

"This is a good bookshop..." I said. Then I thought what a lame, stupid thing that was to say. But he seemed to me to be infinitely magnanimous that day.

"Really?" he said. Then I thought to myself: to say 'yes' to his polite query would be even more stupid and lame, so I tried something more determined, more self possessed:

"Indeed," I said, then thought this was all hopeless.

But Shelvin once again controlled the situation.

"How about that drink?"

So we went for drinks and I remember getting drunk out of nervous shyness, wondering what an exceptional fellow like Shelvin could ever see in me, a worthless, frightened, sickly failure. I remember being hugged by Shelvin and how uncomfortable it made me feel. I remember being brought home to meet his beautiful wife and being frightened by her brilliance, her beauty, her luminous skin and perfect body. I remember sleeping in his spare room, and waking the following morning to the vision of his eldest daughter, then five years old, standing at the end of the bed, holding her stuffed rabbit toy, tugging at my foot, telling me it was time for breakfast, that Daddy had gone to work and Mummy had something cooked for me...

Those are my memories. I remember them because those early days were wonderful. It was only as I got to know Max Shelvin that things began to unwind. I have taken him away from everything he loves. I have not given him death, for, like myself, he desires death. I have taken him from his family and his family are free of him. I too am free of him, for I am both dead and alive, just like him. We are both beyond the law. I look down at the corpse of Shelvin on the table before me. It is perfectly preserved, in a stasis, though I hate to think of it like that. I prefer to think of him as a lovely looking corpse. Perhaps I should find a way to incinerate it. I could cut him up. I want him even now to disappear into the darkness between us. But I could still hear him in my head. Still hear him. I see him in my mind staring into me, knowing that I was captured before he had said anything. I suppose I was always looking for someone to be the key I had lost somewhere inside myself.

It was obvious we were attracted from the first. I do not know if Shelvin had lovers before me. I do not know how indiscreet he had been with his beautiful wife, with her brilliant mind and gorgeous carefully tended body. I do not know because I did not ask, or even think to ask. Things proceeded organically, naturally, without careful planning, or any guile, and, for a time, we were lovers. After the first time we slept together, I was panic stricken and I kept away from him. I was afraid. I was overwhelmed and terrified after experiencing such a chasm of nameless hunger, so long denied to myself, that Max Shelvin had, unknown to either of us at the time, temporarily filled. It was too much. I had to run. I wanted not to be frightened anymore. It was true romance, you see, a knocking on the head of misunderstanding and loneliness. Everything that went before disappeared into the storage chambers of memory. I would continue to speak, to make certain piercing observations, watch machinery with flawless vision, display my heartbeat, blood pressure, brainwaves, hormone production, blood oxygenation, dream patterns. I would always say the right things. I was afraid of disapproval, condemnation. I was afraid. I needed approval. The alternative was oblivion. So, I stayed away.

After I made love with Shelvin, I was afflicted with guilt and confusion and I ran away for weeks and would answer no calls, reply to no messages, not go out even. I took to drinking heavily and overdosing on Jesus. Whatever was left of reason was suspended and my real life was out to lunch. I wanted Max Shelvin. I wanted love, real love, I wanted him back. I had Jesus. Jesus had become my all, my life support, my mechanical heart, my mechanical lungs, my virtual brain and liver and spleen, my arms and my kidneys and blood oxygenation. My brain, that had floated away from my cranium, was hovering in the heavens, and my eyes, only seeing Jesus dying, in his Salvador Dali pose of universal crucifixion, were blind.

Shelvin is not dead, because this is all a dream before death, a dream of a dream of a possible life, with visions and desires coming and going, like ghosts, like visions, like civil servants bringing reports to yet another committee. The dream will kill you, he used say to me. Do not dream too much. Keep your mind on the prize. Desire only what they want you to desire. That is enough. And I believed him.

I talk to Max the Dying Shelvin. I say to him—
"Did you ever hear the story of the man who became his own mother? His name was Arthur Kruger, and he was unhappy with the disaster his first existence turned out to be. He petitioned the Central Committee For Unhappy Lives and was given permission and crawled back into the artificial womb of his own unbirth and became a foetus again. The Committee revised the life of Kruger, reduced his intellect, and nine months later, junior was born again and destined to become rich and famous. They moved to a quieter corner of the city, where he wrote his first best seller at the age of six. By the time the first million came in, his mother, disappointed too with life, became someone else and returned as a janitor in a block of flats."

"The son, who was called Arthur, believing himself capable of anything, became capable of anything, owned the world before he was forty. The world took its own revenge…"

I think to myself that I am dead and yet I am not dead. Shelvin and I are one. We own each other. I, and the body that lies still in these dank rooms, alone without light without dark, still sitting straight, breathing inwards and outwards, still focused on the still centre of oneself, exorcising all the dark, the light, the left, the right, the thoughts, the nonsense, every breath he takes, it takes him away from me and I used sit there and watch him disappear from me.

But, then, a second spotlight opens on Shelvin. Shelvin is lying on an operating table absolutely still. He is wearing a pinstripe suit, a white shirt and black tie. He is wearing no shoes or socks. There are people looking on, still, silent, observing people. The table is raised, somewhat in the manner of an altar. This shift in scenery troubles me deeply. It troubles me because I do not know what to do about these shifting scenes, these changes in what I thought I understood as reality. After all, it would be better if there were certain constants in the telling of this - for instance time, space, continuity of place and circumstance. But there isn't. I sat there as Shelvin appeared in the light in front of the observing multitudes, as his heart and pulse increased, as he came back to life, whatever that was. I watched, and did not know what to do.

I theorized again, tried to figure a course of action. The best course of action was to wait, I decided. The best course of action is to wait and understand. The best course of action was to have another drink, read the paper, watch television, talk to one's analyst, tell Mother everything. The best course of action is to take some more drugs, find a hotel room and disappear into addiction and blame it all on the pressures of fame and talent. The best course of action is to send a memo or a letter to the right people, the people in the know, a letter that disappears into the corridors that, in the end, will reach the relevant authorities, requesting immediate action, lest one suffers the consequences of extreme indiscretion, a letter that is read and responded to and is burned or shredded for recycling.

We are probably all dead anyway.

Shelvin says his first post-mortem words:

Shelvin   Arthur?

Kruger   What?

Shelvin   I bet you can hardly move.

Kruger   It is you who are immobile. I see you can move your jaws.

Shelvin does not seem to care about my sarcasms.

Shelvin   Difficulty breathing, Arthur? The asthma back to suffocate you? It's all stress, you know. You should relax, get a hobby. Try chess, go, poker, mah jong. Something infinitely subtle and thoughtful. Something to distract you from all this confusion. Impose a philosophic order on things. Buy stocks and shares. Make a fortune.
Raise a happy loving family.

Kruger   I never thought. I never thought it would come to this.

Shelvin   I know. Take it one at a time. Breathe gently.

Kruger   Right. Shelvin. Shelvin, I.

Shelvin   I've been thinking, Arthur.

Kruger   What?

Shelvin   I said, I've been thinking, Arthur.

Kruger   Go on...

Shelvin   Let's end this now.

Kruger   End this what?

Shelvin   I don't know, Arthur. Let's not think this out. Let's act. End this. Draw it all to a conclusion. Force an ending to an impossible situation..."

Kruger   I agree.

Shelvin   You see, I had always expected you to get me in the end. I wanted something to happen. I victimized people. I was cruel. I was cruel because I was the real victim. Arthur, I want to tell you something...

Kruger   Go ahead. You have my full attention.
Shelvin   There is a team inside my head. The team run my
          system…We all are part of something bigger. A system.
          And inside us are little systems. And these systems work.
          These systems and team people are slow, painstaking,
          infinitely patient, lateral thinking, thoughtful, welcoming,
          resourceful and aggressively conclusive in their analysis
          and actions. They have seen the dark hole of human
          failure and seek to remedy the situation. They anticipate
          much needed change, long before it was ever conceived
          as a danger. So much has been automated because of
          them. We, here in the firm of firms, the collaboration
          of multitudes, salute these visionaries, these systems
          people. Forever is the now that keeps happening, like
          the dreary continuance that the firm is. Of course, it all
          has little bearing on these proceedings, don't you think?

Then, the crowds of onlookers are gone. And we too are gone. Another
time, another place. A new scene. We are on a ship, a space ship.
Shelvin looks around. His wounds are healed. Shelvin wants to know
if there is a way out of here. Here, in the now we live in. I say no. No
way out. No communications facility, no smoke signals, no semaphore,
no arms, no legs, no voice activated digital display. We are adrift in a
dying space ship, drifting, floating above the mining belt of the moons
of Theta Four Zebra. Nothing to see but the dull wrinkled corpse of
ore and life scavenged moons.

It is very dark here. The silence is nothing. I hear a hum. The hum
being something like the beating of a drum. There are other voices I
want not to hear.

The silence was swallowing me whole. I did not hear my heart, my lungs, my pulse, feel the taste of ashes, the feel of a little more air going down to dance with the bronchiole than before. Shelvin did not see it that way. He saw people. I saw nothing, other than what I just described.

Shelvin   Who are those other people?
Kruger   Who are what other people?
Shelvin   The ones next to you.

I decided to play his game.

Kruger   The angels in the core processors. I see them most sincerely. Those angels are part of a new initiative on the part of management to get a more efficient operation going in this section of the quadrant.
Shelvin   So, you are really saying that there are no other people.
Kruger   Nobody, Shelvin. Nobody at all.
Shelvin   Right.
Kruger   Right...
Shelvin   The air must be bad. Difficulty...
Kruger   I don't know about that. Breathing is easy. Lie down, Shelvin. Lie down and shut up for a while.

The Dead Shelvin lies down

Shelvin   Arthur, what's happening here? I feel afraid.
Kruger   Nothing to worry about, Shelvin.
Shelvin   Are we stopping or moving?
Kruger   Moving, I think.
Shelvin   Arthur. There's nothing we can do...do you have anything to read?
Kruger   No. I gave my last copy of War and Peace to the security droids in exchange for a little more air.
Shelvin   We need a conundrum. We need something we might identify with. We need a conspiracy of writers, prophets and logicians. Someone dies tragically and unexpectedly.

Someone's loved one is incurably ill. A war begins for the usual reasoned reasons and whole families and cities are wiped out. Everyone is at war, holy wars, civil wars, cold wars of cold hearted, soul destroying, petty bickering, or the legal system. We have the chilling devastation of an innocent killed by some degenerate, or a drive-by shooting spilling blood all over five-year olds being wheeled past, by their now injured parents. We have drugstore robberies. We have the news. Then we have the bones of a plot.

Kruger   There are no more plots. Just events.

Shelvin   Can you hear the engines, Arthur?

Kruger   I think so.

Shelvin   Put your ear to the wall. There.

Kruger   Is it the engines?

Shelvin   Yes.

Kruger   They were always working. I think we were always moving to Terminus. I, Arthur Kruger, am a male Caucasian about thirty-five with three children, two of whom are gifted, one of whom is a very young poet of acceptable proportions. The second excels at math, and the third one is a little disturbed, for reasons no one seems to be able to fathom. My loving spouse loves me, or rather loved me, more than life itself and was devastated when I killed yourself. The entire family is in therapy now. But I know they will pull through. They have the strength. I know they do. And this is the price I have chosen to pay for freedom, a realisation that the life I had been living was not my life, but another life, that I was really in love with Shelvin, the Shelvin I killed because he destroyed me...

Shelvin	Good. I like Terminus. That's good.
Kruger	How do you feel?
Shelvin	Better than ever…
Kruger	I had become a chemist and you a statistician. A poet and a merchant sailor. A laboratory rat and a secretary's apprentice. A plagiarist author and a statistician's first mate. What could I think of it all?

I take a scalpel and stab Shelvin. I've still got that doctor's suit on, with all the junk they use to save us from ourselves. Shelvin screams, screams, then the gurgle death rattle, the draining and gushing of life blood…

This time, he died. I felt free at last. I thought of the people he introduced me to, the well educated, insecure, socially and culturally enslaved types, whose real God had become their image, their social status, and the maintenance of a regular income. I fitted in well and liked them a lot. Generally, I was able to give a good account of myself at debates and after dinner discussions of the more important things. I was self-aware, politically aware, cynical, critical, thoughtful, and desperate. I was ideology in search of objective. I was knowledge in search of reason, work in search of wages, name in search of identity, time in search of occasion. I was as lost as they were and time marched on…

Things kept happening in the way they always had. We got older, as was expected. Our parents, though long dead, had expected things and they got what we thought they wanted. They were as unhappy as we were, and had been, when they were who we were then. Things begin to really work out. Attention focuses you in its rifle sights. I got a job and a life, thanks to Shelvin. The first qualifications arrive, the job. The girlfriend boyfriend arrives. First love is declared and the appropriate socialising, meaningful conversations and copulation's, declarations of ideals, metaphysical explorations, poetic dispositions, a nice healthy attitude. Lots of fresh air, and, for a while, impressions of possibilities open up. One seeks these ideals. I had become a success. I was trapped, being forced onwards because there was nowhere else to go.

I was busy being happy, always surrounded by children and paperwork, with my spouse occasionally appearing at social affairs, homicidally smiling and mercilessly communicative. The usual appearances of—

It was news. No news is good news. Good news is good news. Bad news is good news. Old news is bad news, unless forgotten. Then it becomes forgotten good news. It was too deep for me. I never pretended to understand it. I rose to absolute power by knowing where the power was and how to distract others from their true destinies. I knew what it was that the people wanted. No truth, I mean. The public wanted renewal, the usual second chance. A possibility of change, distraction, a chance for a night off in the city...
No. Try something else. Try it. Now.

CHAPTER ZERO.

The rain fell like tiny ice pebbles on the slime washed sidewalk on a cold October day. The city was seething with traffic. I felt as though all the hard luck stories of the city were being drained in that leaden, uncontrolled outpouring from those clouds. There was a knock on the door. This woman walks into my office with a gun in her hand and she says to me, listen, Mister Kruger, please listen, someone is trying to kill me. I looked at her and I thought how could anyone kill someone as beautiful and deadly as this mlady malady my man woman child author poet critic pilot surgeon...

Kruger   Look Shelvin…

I said here, on this dead space vessel, floating above those ravaged moons. I stop and think I will not feel frustrated. I remember the bits and pieces of life: the legs the arms the chest the feet the head the throat the ulterior parts of lessening significance, also without a flicker of life. Things creep up on me in the dead of night. I imagine them creeping across my chest and legs. They, my nightmare friends from the other side, just slide over to say hello. Probably someone from the past.

Welcome home, sweetheart. I think I think a lot. I have time to think now.

They made you like that. They decide what is to be rejected and what is to be allowed. There is no other fusion, or reason, or hope but their fusion, or reason, or hope.

I cannot not say this, it pours out of me, like tears at the death of a parent. They have everything. They know they have everything. They are beyond me…They have added themselves together and become one. Thus, they are God. Me too.

In the end, there really is no difference between the dream and the idea of the dream, the remembrance of the dream…

There is nothing, other than the control that lasts forever.

You say nothing, other than their words.

There are no conspiracies, other than those unprovable. Thus, there are no conspiracies. There are things that must always remain unthinkable…

The firm is thus faceless, amorphous, listening, decisive, ingenious, creative and endlessly adaptive. It is uncompromising in its organisation and concealing in its coercion. It has to be so. The firm does not, therefore, exist...

> Maybe I was born with the right karma.

If I had only paid my bills

> Maybe things will be different next time round.

If I had gone for re-election...

> Maybe I haven't been following my predestined path.

If I had only loved my parents

> Maybe I never really listened

If I had told her that I loved her.

> Maybe I'll remember this time round next time.

God is alive and well and pushing the appropriate keys in the cost analysis bureau...

Kruger knows it is over.

Kruger stands in a salute at the edge of the stage. The audience is hushed, amused, enthralled with the blood and the death and the finality of it all...

Kruger   Uniforms at the appropriate time will be worn at all times.
Who will fall into line and never answer back.
Who will never really learn to apportion the blame...
Who will be bitter and miserable and never learn to fight.
When we grow older
When we grow colder
We forget all these questions
Get down to the business

Drops the scalpel and walks over to Shelvin's corpse and puts the stethoscope to his body. Throws the stethoscope onto the body, walks over to the edge of the stage and closes his eyes, chanting in Gregorian chant:

Kruger   All will be quiet and reasonable now, and continue to work.
          Who will forget all these questions
          Who'll get down to the business
          When the details are checked
          When we are left with the facts.
          Investments and infrastructure
          Nothing left but the facts

Shelvin's eyes blink open in a terrified gaze. He was dead after all. And all those people looking at his corpse. He and Kruger look at each other. In the beginning there was...

NOVEL IV

TEACHING RELIGION AS A FOREIGN LANGUAGE

I am writing this from what I call the after-life. My new life began just after I died. This new event began as the train hit the Arthur Kruger that I once was. I am that Arthur Kruger no more. He, the other I am and am not, died as the train impacted. That other I was and am had obsessed all my other lives about the bomb. I should have taken up useful hobbies instead of the aforementioned obsession, for instance, tap dancing or shiatsu massage therapy or chess or Wei Ch'i.

Before arriving in Heuston Station that midwinter day, in order to jump to kill myself, I thought about leaving the suitcase bomb behind. Maybe I should let go of it, throw it aside, I thought. But I had carried this item, my life my death, with me all my lives. This was the suitcase that Aron had told me was full of papers. I disagreed. I thought it contained a nuclear device, the bomb. Soon, there will be other, more terrible methods of universal extinction than the bomb. Soon, there will be nothing more preferable than extinction. And, as we scuttle our species, then we will evolve.

Perhaps it was time to let go, I mused. But I could not let go, could not go on, and felt no fear, only a strong desire to leave this planet. I had put this bomb script safely away. Then I left. As Aron slept, I wrote a suicide note.
Dear Aron,
I love you more than life itself. I have, therefore, decided to kill myself. Please find herewith corrected proofs of Ten Short Novels (I have a copy) and my chessboard. Play well, as I have not. It's the game that matters.
Arthur.

And I went to the station and, at the right time, jumped in front of the train. I thought of many things as the steel engine came nearer, questions I would never know the answer to:

What devastation might the city suffer if the device exploded?

Should I defuse it, right here, right now?

Do I know how to defuse the bomb script?

Should I take it to the relevant authorities?

How do I know what is true and not true?

Should I seek to have it safely stored in some underground explosion-proof zone?

Will my manuscripts survive and does it matter if civilization is tending towards death, decay and self-destruction at every moment?

Is any creative or life-affirming act worthwhile?

Is an optimist what a realist calls a self-deluded person?

What will I say to my parents or Aron if I meet them in the afterlife?

I should have thought about these things before I leapt. I should have looked then leaped. Instead I leaped then looked. Before leaping then looking, I sat watching the trains and people come and go in Heuston Station for so many hours. I wasn't thinking about much then. I had finished what I had written. I was resting, depressed and resting. It was after I leaped that I thought of irradiation and tumours and blast burns and death, thought all too quickly about dictatorship and genocide and the continuing death and birth of the billions that have lived and died on this planet over the aeons. These feelings of anxiety and dread could have been relieved by the use of pharmacology or religion, or perhaps both. But hindsight is a remarkable tool of delusion. I considered the obliteration of industries and offices and homes and history. At the point of impact I had the following insights:

One: That this bomb was meant for me alone.

Two: That there was a Higher Force from which the fission emanated.

Three: That, in case of confusion and ignorance (in other words always), I decided to refer to the Higher Force.

Ah, I thought, something of a credo. The beginnings of religion. I might teach this as a foreign language to the other unbelievers. But I didn't have the chance. I killed myself. Then I was dead, and being dead, being smashed up, I finally knew everything I really needed to know in order to stay alive, and that provided me with the impetus necessary to live. Was that irony, or merely the way the cosmos goes about things? I knew then that everything has its own oscillation, its own harmonic resonance, its own symphonic dance of existence, its own march towards entropy. Now that's entertainment.

On the point of impact, things went wrong. They always do. One needs a little dramatic tension. There's a plan. Then there's life. And, never the twain shall meet. The suitcase with the nuclear manuscript device inside, the bomb script, as Aron would say, got thrown clear. It landed on the platform. It spun top over base top over base and then stopped. It stood in an upright position with the handle pointing straight up towards the steel and plexi-glass platform hood by the tracks. This was why, though the train smashed me to bits, I wound up still alive. Or that's my current theory on the matter. Personally, I thought I remember blowing to pieces, being enveloped by fire, and scattering across space-time in a type of hallucinogenic Stanley Kubrick way. Boom.

As the train fuselage tore into my body, I remember I saw a boiling super bright flash of heat and light into which I was dissolved. I saw my atoms scattered across the astral fields of possibility. I remember falling and falling into the infinite nothing from which I saw I came, and, as I fell, I saw my other lives as doctor, accountant, serial killer, marketing consultant, information technology guru, sales assistant, stockbroker, tramp, good son and father. I saw that, in the beginning, everything was fucked up. I saw that, in the beginning, the word was out. I saw that truth was a construct of the mind. I saw that history is remorseless and its tyranny a disease for which Art finds a cure. I saw that I needed to find a hobby and socialise more. Find a pub I liked and play darts there.

I saw the train. I saw that I saw the train. I saw myself seeing the train. The train performed the open-heart surgery I felt so in need of. The train decapitated me, truncated me, cut off my arms and spilt my brains and intestines all over the front end of the train. Nasty stuff. Some people tried to stop me from killing myself as I leaped before the oncoming train. They grabbed me just as I leaped. I shook free. I felt that nothing could stop me, that this leap into oblivion, beyond acceptable or explicable behaviour, was my destiny. I had nothing left. The pain I suffered as the train impacted was minimal. A slight agony, then crunch. Oblivion. As the train approached, things slowed down. Time speeded up. My mind assumed a super clarity and speed. My mind had wings. I thought of how the driver might feel afterwards. The driver would inspect the debris of my body that would attach itself to the engine at the point of impact. I felt so guilty about this. I did not think of my parents, or my relatives, or of Aron Tully. They would misunderstand, though they had the ten short novels, I thought.

As the train struck me, I heard a scream. I did not scream. It was not I. The scream came from behind me. The scream was brutally cut off as I lost consciousness.

The driver stopped the train. An ambulance was called. The police were called. A crowd congregated. They searched for some type of identification, which was difficult as I was naked. I was strangely naked. I remember agonising over whether or not to wear my good shoes that day, my good shoes, or my sneakers for added stealth. The suitcase I carried was in perfect condition. A member of the emergency services was covering my decapitated body. I noticed that I was seeing a member of the emergency services covering my decapitated body. I saw the blood all over the train tracks. I saw the fascinated drooling horrified ogling crowd. I saw the faces looking and the mouths talking. I noticed I was screaming. I noticed the clothing I was wearing. It was covered in blood and gore. I noticed I was the living dead Arthur Kruger. The Kruger Zombie. Alive dead. Scary movie. I noticed I was standing on the platform by my bomb case. I opened the case. The nuclear device manuscript was still inside.

I went over to the scene of the accident. The accident save you from death and disaster heroic emergency services were trying to get the people to move back away from the scene. The fascinated, drooling multitudes would not move back. The police were having little success. The press arrived. Cameras were everywhere. This was without doubt six o'clock bulletin fodder; distract us all from what was really going on. This is going to make the press, I thought. Bad scene. Why couldn't I have overdosed in a garret somewhere?

Arthur Kruger squeezed in through the flocking crowds of mothers and sisters and fathers and business people and religious people and interested people and people who took photographs for money. I couldn't see the body. I reached over and lifted the covering. The police were looking elsewhere. A naked bloody decapitated armless legless corpse lay underneath. That is definitely me, I thought. How did the train manage to make such clean cuts? Remove my arms, my legs, my head, and other ulterior parts of lessening significance with so few jagged pieces of torn flesh. A surgical operation. But I know it's me. Yes, that's me. I'd recognise that smile of relief on that corpseless head anywhere. They had placed my ex-head on top of my ex-chest, rather like a hat.

The ambulance person grabbed my hand and pushed me, the non-decapitated Kruger, roughly away. I, the non-decapitated Arthur Kruger, fell down.

"What do you think you are doing? Sir?" asked the ambulance person.

"I was looking at myself," I said. This was a true, but confusing, answer for the ambulance person.

"I asked you a question, sir. This is a potential crime scene. Criminalistics will be here shortly. This area is sealed. Step back please, or you will be arrested."

I thought then, I should be more sensitive. Then I thought, this is a life and death moment and the ambulance person is only here by chance. Then I looked at the ambulance person, who clearly looked horrified and sickened, world weary and depressed by an endless pursuit of sickness, injury and death. Perhaps, I thought, she should have chosen another career. Flower arranging, perhaps. Then I thought to myself I should not think so much about everything. I should lighten up. I thought of a joke. Then I forgot it.

"I'm sorry. I'll just go."

The ambulance person raised her hand.

"Don't move, sir. Please!"

"Officer, I have a question."

"No, you don't. And I am not an officer."

"Officer, don't you hate the horror and voyeuristic fascination of these bloodthirsty crowds? This is clearly the scene of a tragedy."

"This is a restricted area," she said. "You can't touch what could be a crime scene."

"It isn't a crime scene," I said.

"Oh, really?"

"Yes, indeed. He jumped. I definitely saw him jump. I was right there at the crucial moment."

The ambulance person called over a Police Officer.

"Officer, Officer? Could you come over? Talk to this person? This person saw what happened."

The ambulance person didn't like me, I decided. Well, I come across as knowing more than I was saying. People feel threatened by that, I decided. Also, I was lurking around a headless corpse at a train station. That also is not okay. The Police Officer came over.

"Sir, could you give me your name?" she asked.

"Kruger. Arthur Kruger is my name, Officer," I, Arthur Kruger, said. "Look, I apologise. Don't you think it a little strange the corpse is naked?"

"It's not for me to say, sir. We will establish what is and is not strange during the course of our investigation. For now, we can say we are pursuing a definite line of enquiry."

The Police Officer looked me over.

"How do you explain how you came to be so covered in bloody, gore-ridden clothing, sir?"

I looked myself over. I was splattered with blood and gore. This is disgusting, I thought. Embarrassing too. I should have changed after I killed myself.

"Looks bad, doesn't it?"

"I don't know, sir, Mr Kruger. You tell me. We have a hit vic, train situation, and we have you, all chatty about the dearly departed, looking as though you stepped out of a battlefield."

The Police Officer began to stare at me. I looked into her unblinking eyes and saw the power junky within.

"He, the deceased, was beside me as the train impacted," I said. The Police Officer nodded, intuiting something of the conundrum I found myself in. Taking out a notebook and, pointing the blunt end of the pen at me, she put the following question in as offhand a manner, as though asking directions I might give to the opera.

"Can you tell me what happened? What I mean to ask is, if, in fact, the victim's blood and so on impacted against you, surely it would only have hit you in the place you were, in fact, facing the victim, and not all over?"

"Mmm, good point, Officer. It is problematic."

"Another thing, would you be willing to submit a blood sample for comparative reasons? Just to rule you out of the investigation. Please stay still. Forensics will be here any minute."

"Delighted."

"What I am getting at, Mr…"

"Kruger."

"Kruger, is you look like the victim."

"I see, Officer." I tried to remember what I might have done if I had wanted to save myself from my own suicide attempt. "Let me put it this way, Officer. He came out and jumped in front of the train."

"You tried to stop him, I take it," the Officer asked me.

"Yes, I tried to stop him and I nearly got hit. Hence the mess I am in."

"I see, I see. Thank you for that," the Officer said, having noted my every thought word and deed with a suspicious, mistrusting eye said. "Can you give me your address?"

So I gave my parents' address, as most of my mail still arrived in my parents' house and the little identification I had on me indicated my home address as my parents' house. (I had always found possessing any form of identification a deeply reassuring experience, hence I tended to bring some with me everywhere.) Passing officials looked at my gore ridden clothing, with suppressed expressions of disgust darkening their otherwise pleasant features. The crowds were milling about, interested, horrified, and still talking. Television cameras appeared. Reporters in well-cut suits spoke solemnly of the train accident and the horror of it all. I had made the six o'clock bulletin. I was referred to as someone. I therefore existed.

The Police Officer looked at my gore-ridden clothing, and again an expression of disgust began to play on her face too. I could no longer suppress a smile. She smiled too and said,

"You don't seem too upset, sir. You knew him?"

"No. I never really knew him. I don't think he knew himself."

"And how do you know that, sir?" she asked.

"I am very intuitive," I said. "He looked to me like someone who, everywhere he went, remained a stranger. But what a good-looking stranger he was. Very handsome. And obviously possessing a considerable intellect. I think he might have been someone one might want to know in private life."

I smiled again. The Officer did not smile, did not appreciate my aesthetics of the interior person. I imagined aesthetically inclined surgeons and doctors performing autopsies, removing and simultaneously admiring internal organs. What a fine kidney, brain, liver, spleen, a good heart, a sacred heart even... eh nurse?

The Police Officer tapped the blunt end of her cheap ball point pen against her upper lip and, frowning, asked:

"What were you doing near him just now?"

"I read a lot of medical books. I wanted to see what had happened. Look, I tried to save him. I got gored instead." The Officer shifted from one foot to another, and pointing at me said:

"That's not funny, Mr...Kruger. Not funny at all. We're going to have to hold you for questioning. You are going to have to make a statement. Do you understand, Mr. Kruger?" the over-sensitive Police Officer said. I felt angry that she blamed me for my own suicide. I said, "You can only hold the living for questioning. Holding me could pose a serious legal conundrum."

The Police Officer, who seemed a somewhat disappointed person, reached out to handcuff me. So, I bolted. As I ran by, I grabbed the suitcase and disappeared into the crowd. I imagined that the security cameras throughout the train station recorded my and the suitcase's disappearance into the crowd. But I was gone, and that, to me, was good. I got lucky.

Then, I suddenly stopped running, so as not to attract attention. I grabbed a coat off a drunk outside the station; put it on to cover up my gory clothing. Then I started to run again. I felt nothing could catch me. I had that feeling of exhilaration as my legs reached out and my feet pounded the pavement, the suitcase feeling light as feathers, light as leaves of paper, as though there were only pieces of paper inside, and I was getting away with self-murder.

The plan was to return home. I wanted to see Aron again, tell her I had been born anew in Heuston Station, Dublin, under the wheels of an oncoming train. I wanted to explain to her what had happened. I wanted to tell her that I had survived, that I did not know why. Perhaps I had not survived. Perhaps this was a post-mortem delusion. I had read about that too. One can live an entire lifetime in ones' last moment, a type of contraction of time from a lifetime to a single finite instant. If one died more than once, I thought, one could live any number of lives. I looked at my clothing, embarrassed running with all the blood and gore barely hidden by the filthy coat I had on me. I picked pieces of undifferentiated flesh off myself and tossed them into drains and bins as I continued to run. I ran into a public toilet and checked myself for damage. I took off my clothes, washed as much of the blood off them as I could and looked at my body. There were no marks. I was intact. I sat on the toilet bowl, feeling sleepy, going into shock, waves of exhaustion, sweat pouring down my face and along my body and legs. I pushed across the door lock and put down the case, closed my eyes. I'll just take a brief nap. It's been a long, long day. My head fell forward as I went into shock. I lost consciousness, feeling sweat dripping from my face.

I awoke to the sound of someone banging on the door of the toilet cubicle I had locked myself into. "Hey you, you in there. Other people want to use the toilet too. Are you listening to me, whoever you are? This is an emergency situation."

"Sorry, sorry," I said. "I'll be right out in just one second..." I pulled on the wet clothes and pulled the coat on over them.

"Now that's okay, sonny," said the cracked terrible voice outside the cubicle. "I can see you are a man of culture and good taste."

"You can, can you?" I said.

"Sure, I can tell by the fancy tones. I like that."

"That's very distressing," I said.

"Why is that?" the cracked voice said.

"Because I am not the man you think I am"

I was finishing lacing my shoes. I wanted to keep him talking, I found his voice terrifying and reassuring all at once, and I did not want him banging on the door. My nerves would not take it.

"I was involved in a slight accident, you see and I think I fell asleep. Just give me a second, thanks."

The blood still discoloured my clothing, despite all my washing. I wondered if I could face the world dressed like someone who had come off a battlefield. I left the cubicle. The drunk who had been banging on the door of the cubicle looked in shock at the still gore-ridden person that emerged from the cubicle. We nodded to each other as our paths crossed.

My arms and legs and back were stiff. They ached terribly as a result of sleeping in a posture probably disapproved of by my parents, if they had known. I shuffled arthritically on, making tracks towards Prospect

Avenue. I thought to myself, Aron might still be in. I thought to myself, I will explain away my silly suicide note. I will fix things. Everything will be as it was.

It looked early in the day. Perhaps between eight and ten in the morning. My watch was gone. No time. Now that's irony. Perhaps it was smashed. The rush hour traffic was easing off. Workers had ensconced themselves in their respective places of employment. At this time, they were working towards the eleven o'clock coffee break.

I arrived at number 125 Prospect Avenue and stood at the door. Keys, I thought. Do I still have keys? "Where were the keys?" I muttered, fumbling in my pockets. I smiled with relief. The keys had not fallen out. I could not afford to sit out here all day, I thought, in the cold outdoors, exposed to ruthless passing comment. I let myself in and called for Aron.

"Aron where are you. I'm home. There was this accident, you see… Aron. Aron? Look, I…"

She would be at work, I thought. I will change these clothes, have something to eat, open the mail and cook a meal for her. Then, over dinner, I would explain everything:

"Darling, I had a fit you see. I cracked up again. I had this death to life experience, a Jesus resurrection moment. I am the way, the truth, and the resurrection. Don't mind about those awful news people and police, the ogling crowds, all the awful facts. Facts are not what always happen. Making facts keep the power elite set up."

I would explain everything and it would be okay. And she would listen silently and the gradually become despotically angry with me, weep and complain about my constant undercurrent of anger and selfishness and dissatisfaction with everything, about my refusal to accept her as she was, my refusal to seek help, my drunkenness and disappearances, my irresponsible life, my failure to publish and write something normal. But she would forgive me. Or, I hoped she would.

Aron did not seem to be about. The apartment was spotlessly clean. The floors shone. Aron was remorselessly untidy. The carpets had the faint florid odour of recent shampooing. There was a smell of new paint, of recently cleaned floors and walls and doors, that sterile order of those uncomfortable with their bodies. Who died? I thought, and then I remembered. The coats that usually hung on the backs of chairs were gone, probably hung up in their wardrobe homes. The incessant clock ticking in every room, at once both intrusive and reassuring, now seemed too loud. She said I had an obsession with clocks. She was right, as usual. She had the insight of someone troubled, someone who needed and failed to properly control the beloved.

I saw a letter on the table in the sitting room addressed to me. I opened it. It was from a publisher accepting *Ten Short Novels By Arthur Kruger*. She must have sent the manuscript. I knew I hadn't. And she had received a ready acceptance. There was even an advance along with it. I looked at the cheque made out to me. Then I put it in my pocket.

I went up to Aron's room. It was cleaned out. There was never anything much in mine, so at first I didn't bother to look. Perhaps we did not live here any more. Perhaps she had done the math and found somewhere better, somewhere upmarket even. I went into my own room, just in case. Aside from a few books left on the shelf and a carefully parcelled box of what seemed to be papers, the room was bare. I moved our bed. I pulled back the mat. Underneath the mat, underneath the bed there was a loose floorboard. Underneath the mat underneath the bed, underneath the floorboard, there was money, a provisional hoard just in case, another of her ideas. She must have forgotten. But I didn't. I looked around the room. I wondered what had happened to my journals. Perhaps she had put them somewhere safe.

I went in to the bathroom and there was Aron, dying in the bathroom. She had cut her wrists, a bottle of Valium by the bathtub. The blood was streaming into the hot water. She had slipped into unconsciousness, slipping bit by bit under the surface, the Ophelia that I killed who had failed to properly sever the ulnar artery. Her hesitation marks didn't seem too hesitant to me. She had failed where I had succeeded. If she had died, would we have met here in the after-life life? Unlikely, Socrates. The window was left open and the bathroom door closed so as no one might see the steam from the hot bath, or sense the heat out on the hall landing, not that anyone would bother her at this time of day. This was no mere train death, no road kill. I ran to the bedroom, tore up some sheets, ran back into the bathroom, sobbing out loud, filled with guilt and remorse. I lifted her out of the bath and lay her on the floor, garrotted her wrists, but she was still bleeding and unconscious. I tightened the bandages, fumbling with torn sheets and trying to hold back the sobs of horror and dismay as I worked on her, trying to somehow keep her from dying. I realised I had no idea what I was doing. I wrapped her in a series of dry towels and sheets and ran downstairs, stuffed the letter and the envelope and the cheque from the publishers into my pocket and telephoned and ambulance. "I'm sorry to trouble you, but I would like to report an attempted suicide. Yes, that's correct. A lady at number 125 Prospect Avenue, Glasnevin. No there is no sign of domestic violence, except by her on herself. She seems to have cut her wrists, I don't know with what. Yes, thank you. No, I would not like to leave my name with you. Goodbye." And I left the house, after wiping any fingerprints I may have left behind me. And I ran and ran.

I went to the bank and lodged the cheque in my own account, got a grotty room, ate and, while shivering in a hot bath, began thinking of Aron. I wept. My body shook like an old tree in a night wind. I submerged, listening to the warm silence underwater, understood her need for oblivion, understood that her need for it was not dissimilar to my own, that she had felt the same loss that I had felt. Then, I opened my eyes under the bathwater and looked up through the shimmering refracted light, and knew that I needed to write it all down. So I got out of the bath, got paper and a pen and got back into the bath and, while soaking away the accumulated filth of train kill and passing out in a public toilet, I noted matters that I could not account for. The first was the passing of time, possibly spent inside the toilet in some type of comatose or catatonic state of shock. There might never be an explanation, for that, or for why I had survived. If I preached the gospel of after-life, I might be lynched by the friends and family of depressives and romantics as the insane founder of yet another suicide cult. The second is the reason for Aron's suicide attempt. I needed to understand, to rationalise. I wrote down some possible reasons for Aron to try to end her life. Perhaps it was anger at herself, or anger at me, or feelings of despair and anguish, or abandonment after hearing of my death, or because she really didn't like the ten short novels, or because of a sense of self-hatred and a desire to destroy herself after suddenly re-living memories of the life destroying, early childhood sex assaults, or because of a sense of the futility and absurdity of it all, or because of a desire to experience everything, or because she wanted to join me, someone with whom she had decided she had found something akin to happiness. This one thing I knew: I had killed her. My need to escape an intolerable life had killed her. It had to stop, that is, if she survived this, I could not go back to a situation where I could do it again. I could not bring myself to go back to her life after nearly killing her like that. If I stayed away, I figured, then maybe she would have a life.

This was how it had to be. I was a poison to her possible future. I sat and soaked and noted in the cooling bath for God knows how long (12 minutes twenty seconds) and decided, for both of us, that our affair was over, that, in another life, in another universe, I would have gone to her, become closer to her through this pain I had empathised and that instinctual chemical understanding we both had of the ingredients of our souls, I would have explained to her my actions, and an understanding would have been reached. I would have sought the obligatory professional help, proceeded to sort out my problems with the law and my parents and the other realms of probability. I would, eventually, with time, begin to see our lives in a new light, write another novel with her; over even more time become the stable professional novelist, the critic, interviewed regularly in the media, sign lucrative contracts with publishers, have beautiful children, a house in the country, write well-wrought professionally thoughtful books once a year, well reviewed by the professional literati, grow old and loved and mellowed and forgotten, before that second death captures one, before decrepitude creeps in to us both, before a retrospective of my works begins. But that was before she tried to kill herself.

Now, I just had to begin again. I had to run. Guilt was driving me away from her, as though I were diseased, as though the freakish nature of my existence was a communicable malaise.

I stepped out of the bath and dried myself, tore up the, by now, wet and sopping pages I had abortively written upon, and dressed. I had purchased some cheap clothing in a charity store on George's street, on the way to finding this kip. The little, old, overeducated blue-dyed ladies, with their frustrated nubile young assistants, looked at me as the Pharisees had at Jesus, as they sold me two t-shirts, a pair of sneakers, a pair of jeans, and a jacket for ten pounds that I had left in my pocket. The police, perhaps, already knew I had cashed my cheque. It was a matter of time before they found me. 'Where did that blood come from?' they asked themselves, staring at my clothes.

"I killed myself a few days ago", I said.

They looked horrified. I left them horrified. Better than numb, I thought.

I opened the Gideon's Bible. It was the only reading material in the room. I read the Gospels, one after other. Spiritual documents might provide an answer, I thought. The Necronomicon. Book of the Dead. Devil's Dictionary. Goodnight Osiris. I read of Jesus' appearance on the shore of the Lake of Tiberius, asking the disciples if they loved him, telling them he was alive. 'You are not going to believe this, guys, but I went to Hell for three days.' The Disciples looked shocked. 'No way! You're the anointed one. You can't go to Hell. That's bad!' 'Way,' says Jesus, 'Not that they have time down there, but the devil wears a toga and runs some type of military industrial complex linked directly to the Roman Empire. He has hired all the best minds. He wants to take over the world, rule the planet. Pax Romana. Our way or the way of all invasion. You become a terrorist state. But the devil wouldn't listen to me. I told him I as I tell you, I really am alive. And dead. See the wounds in my hands and feet. See this nasty spear mark in my side, the merciful centurion ending it all. One thrust to kill the dying animal. He is a true believer. But the Romans, they're all too rational. Nice one centurion.' The team of secretaries Jesus had with him at all times look at each other, and decide not to include this in their blow by blow perfect account of his life.

Then, I read of St Paul. He was telling them of the resurrection, that we shall all be anew, a brand, spanking new body, replete with supernatural qualities in that interzone beyond pain and loss. I still felt pain, headaches, body aches, sexual desire, hurt, loss. I had a pulse. Was I conscious? Could

I pass the Turing test? How long has it been since my resurrection? Nearly a day? I was corporeal. I was crucified, not with wood, not the torture of hours left hanging to agonisingly die. How could such an instrument of torture become a symbol of salvation? I had endured the crush of steel. Then termination. No death from heart attack or asphyxiation. I was alive, yet not as I knew it.

I worried that perhaps I was some type of vampire, a soulless zombie who, before long, will turn to rotting living tissue, something made by Hollywood for matinee movie fare, a living paradox, a biological matter of time. I thought of Jesus saying, 'I am the way the truth and the resurrection from train impacts.'

No, I said to myself, donning my new charity jacket, and stuffing my gory clothes into a plastic bin bag, and putting them in a rubbish bin down the street from the hotel.

Perhaps God is the answer. Dear God, how I owe you a death of gratitude, you have saved me from myself, and, more particularly, saved Aron from me, not to mention my family and other ghosts I might have known. Perhaps the devils inside would have to be silent before the infinite might of a bigger God than death, for you, my God, are love, and, by the way, if this is some Groundhog Day thing, I am definitely going to kill myself. Again. And I love you for this really big favour. I give myself unequivocally to you God, to the you, the Infinite Being There and, trusting that whether or not I could ever believe in such Being There, a being such as you, if you existed, you would naturally have to all powerfully, all-lovingly respond infinitely to my request for removal of death, self-destruction, and general madness and carnage. By the way, what's wrong with the world? It seems to be disintegrating. On the other hand, I thought, turning into a coffee shop and ordering a low fat double whippy latte with extra chocolate and marshmallows and an extra creamy bun, if it turned out, by some extraordinary twist of fate, that such a being as you did not exist, that my natural scepticism had been well founded, that my strong educational substratum in illogic and disinformation had honed my intuitive instincts well, that I was, in the end, no ordinary fool, then everything is okay, I don't need to get too worried about everything, for if You, God, do not exist, then it's right that things are as they are. The world is a madhouse, run by power crazed psychotics, bent on destruction and horror and evil, for a very good reason. It's because there is no God and I just got lucky when I didn't die.

I, Arthur Kruger, would be soon forgotten. I knew that. And that was reassuring. The only memories of my lives are official records of birth, marriage, death, employment records, and the numbers and letters of accountants and lawyers in somebody's employ. Somewhere, the system remembers. After that come the biographer's pen and other post-mortems. Then, the fond memories of friends and loved ones that disappear. For we all disappear, billions dissolving into metaphor and story and novel and movie, and the fields of graves and burning pyres and caves and castles that house the sarcophagi of the insignificant mighty. It was something I looked forward to, this peaceful extinction. I aspired to be reduced to a short reference in some Sunday afternoon conversation, a chat by critics on experimental fiction, regrets whispered in a candlelit chapel, a drunken discussion in a pub. I am something soon to end. I am news replaced by more news, something reduced to the level of a distorted anecdote. In the end, it is the mind that becomes the enemy. You forget yourself, and, because one forgets oneself, one fears the inaccuracy of perception and imagination, and that gets you in the end. I felt I had been peeled away, layer by layer, until I was left with what I was and was not: a collection of muscles, organs, fluids and the gore painting on my discarded clothing. Then, I had a flash of insight. There was a solution.

The solution was a strict regime of rigor, a marshalling of the mind and spirit to a higher cause. Rules and more rules. I walked over to the counter with my coffee cup and handed it to the waiter.

"Thank you. Can I have another cup, along with a salad sandwich, please? Do you have a phone book?"

"Yes. Yes, we do have a phone book. The phone company delivers it once a year."

"That's nice. Can I use it?"

"Yes. You can use it. But I insist you return it."

I put a pin into the list of religions, seminaries, convents, astral projection centres, alternative therapy centres and Bible study groups in the phone book. I remembered I had been brought up a Catholic. They seemed to have some knowledge of death and resurrection. Maybe, I thought, I might get an update on my own post-mortem status, or whether or not the body I saw on the tracks was really my own. Maybe I had been given another by a top secret group of talented medics. Maybe I was dreaming this in some lab. The pin I impaled my life upon landed on the following name and address in the religious orders' section.

The Order of the Holy Field, 101 Chapel Avenue.

I tore the page out of the book and only returned the mutilated phone book to the fastidious waiter as I paid the bill and left.

I walked home, deciding to visit the mysterious Order of the Holy Field. The following morning, after hash browns and eggs in the same local cafeteria, I went down to 101 Chapel Avenue. Voices told me, as I walked into the pseudo gothic arches with gargoyles of saints upholding the bases of flying buttresses, that this was not the place for me, and yet, despite such immediacy of impression, I could not leave. Mass was being concelebrated. Two ancient priests with soft, slightly alto, ancient voices repeated the Eucharistic prayer on the high altar as people crouched or sat or kneeled in the warm ethereal rays of the church spotlights. This is my body. Eat me. I thought of my corpse. Eat me. Twinkling in the dark beyond this great light shone the little red glows of confessional lights, which clicked on and off like magic lanterns as the faithful entered and exited the confessionals in the semi-darkness, in the multitude of intimate darker, lesser archways that intersected the over-lit main body of the church, where mass was progressing. There, in the spotlight, and in the soft dark beyond the light, of the semi-candlelit glow, with its healing and forgiving and prayers for the lost, with its long shadows cast by saintly images, its statues and mass produced literature prominently placed and mostly free, gave the impression of welcome, of well used customary spiritual practices, carried on before the dawn of memory, of a wisdom and power beyond challenge, of a merciless and infinite self-sacrificing love, of death and resurrection. A sign said 'Rejoice for the Lord Has Risen'. Mm, I thought. I did that. All I need now is to get some broadcasting time, get executed by a corrupt occupying force and absolute power is mine. I certainly rejoiced after getting over the devastation of not being dead, though I am no-one's lord, I thought. I listened to the prayers for a time and went to talk to one of the monks. I walked around to the back of the church, to the enclosure where the monks lived and, rang the doorbell. A pair of glasses peered through a crack in the door. "Yaassss?"

Yet another strange voice. This time female. A high-pitched, definitely female voice answered. I could make out the outline of a plump pink cheek and one dark blue eye gazing myopically at me, or, rather, not so much looking at me, as looking gently beyond me. This seemed to be someone uncomfortable with human contact.

"I was looking to speak to someone, if you don't mind."

A soft index finger quickly beckoned me, "Come in, come in, it's cold, cold…"

The woman seemed stooped, in her mid forties, with a soft, twisted, timeless body, suffering from some debilitating disorder.

"Wait here," she said. She went off to find someone willing to talk to a visitor. I stood in the hallway, feeling awkward, as young and old monks passed by. The floor was marbled, slightly fractured, with a stylised floral design, the type chosen, not to compliment any other feature of the décor, probably chosen so as not to have a colour that might prove difficult to maintain. The walls were half uniform oaken panelling, with white walls above and white ceiling. A simple light hung above there. Here and there, were trendy nouveau abstract Christian icons and miniature copies of old masters renditions of the life of Christ, crucifixes, and, at the end, beside the huge dark oaken archway, with its equally huge, beautifully wrought oak door with the words 'enclosure' solemnly written upon it, stood a statue of the Virgin Mary as she was seen in Fatima, wrapped in a fake blue light, with those cold, knowing eyes of a mother, with her head and shoulders a little stooped in obeisance, with a soft, undeveloped teenage face and body, the thin chiselled lips, never to speak or kiss, a small body hidden beneath attire millennia old, standing on a statue of planet earth, as though it were the only planet, and the serpent crushed underfoot, as if snakes could get a worse reputation. The door beside her opened. She did not see the monk come through, a well-fed man of about fifty, with a big toothy smile, broad shoulders and salt and pepper beard, the type one meets on hill walks and in country pubs, talking shallowly and optimistically about politics and football. He put out his hand and introduced himself.

"Des Murphy, hello…"

"Arthur Kruger…"

Father Murphy indicated one of the adjacent rooms that we might go into. I walked inside the dark room with frosted glass, a small wooden confessional in the far corner, a heavy rectangular table in the middle of the floor, a copy of Salvador Dali's last supper on the wall, and turned to Father Murphy,

"Could we, maybe walk, a bit..?"

Father Murphy smiled bitterly, nodded, and stiffly brought me through the enclosure, passing down an old ill-lit, high arched walkway, the type used for quiet meditation when the weather was too unsuitable for the gardens or the church. Here, in the gloom, one could be alone with oneself. I wanted to be alone with myself, and that frightened me. Just now many selves would one find if one was so alone with oneself? Here, no one could ever find you, except God, perhaps. I walked on with Murphy. Murphy asked me few questions. He didn't speak. And the appalling silence gave a sufficient reassurance that here was nowhere. We walked on, past this ghostly corridor, down a stairwell, and into the monastery garden, where the roses and the dahlias, the geraniums and the tulips and the rhododendrons were out of season, and the small bushes seemed puny and over-cut and the grass tiny, peeping up like crew cut children, afraid of been seen out of school uniform, and, in the centre, a lovely fountain, with a seat beside it, and a small rockery, with a few evergreens scattered here and there. We sat down.

"So, Arthur, is there anything I can do for you?" "I don't know," I said. "I can honestly say I don't know why I am here. I have come to a time when I am looking for answers and the answer that there is no answer just isn't enough, and the answer that one must have faith and believe when one cannot isn't enough. Isn't Jesus or God everywhere?" "What do you believe in?" asked Father Murphy.

"I do not know what I believe in. I do not remember believing in anything, except the unbelievable. Rationality has been the death of me for too long."

Father Murphy's warm Ernest Hemingway smile changed into a compassionate watchfulness. He seemed intent on peering into me.

"You know, Arthur. It's funny…Ever since I saw you, I have been meaning to ask what happened to you…"

"I died for a while. A near undead experience. I tried to kill myself, but survived…"

"I see, wow, I see… Do you mean perhaps a near death experience?"

"No, I don't actually."

"Do you, perhaps, mean you feel guilty or responsible you survived?"

"I cannot understand how it happened, one minute I was certainly dead, then I was standing beside my body, and I ran through the crowds, and I was free."

"I see."

"I ask myself was this a miracle? The work of a perfect, limitless, all-loving, all-forgiving, utterly perfect being, someone not predicated into actually existing by the logical possibility of their existence?"

"That's a little ...too clever for the facts, and for me, Arthur...I really am not qualified to answer that. Tell me what you feel; tell me what you believe..."

"I believe something rather extraordinary happened. Something I can't explain. I thought maybe you might."

"The gospels talk about resurrection. They say there is more to life than this one. Perhaps you are proof of that."

"So you believe me."

"I get people in here telling me all kinds of things. I had someone in here telling me she had visions of our holy founder, Giovanni Seipi."

"Visions. Now that is crazy."

"Look, Arthur. Let me put it this way. Even if I did believe you, do you think it might make you believe yourself?"

"I know. Even if you took up my personal cause."

"I won't do that."

"I know, but say you did, and we spent years amassing evidence, and went on television or whatever, and presented the evidence, do you think anyone would believe you and I. It would be the end of everything, the end of religion. They would kill me in a heartbeat."

"Who would kill you?"

"You know as well as I know who would kill me. The same kind of people who kill all dissenters and outsiders."

Murphy smiled at me. I didn't need him to tell me I was right. Talking about Arthur Kruger was teaching a new religion in a foreign language. I changed the subject.

"Okay, can I ask you something else? Then we go indoors and get coffee?"

"Okay."

"Do you believe in, in what you do? Why do you go on?"

Father Murphy folded his arms again, and in the cold pool beside his cold sandaled feet a fish swam quickly by.

"I believe we live on because it is what God wants, and what God wants, God gets…Sometimes, the smart thing is to admit you just don't know…Sometimes, we live on hope and trust, things we have yet to see proof of. I think you are here looking for some one to take out your frustrations on. Some of us are more confused than you are. Does that surprise you? Did you really think there was a place that had the answers? That life owes you more than anyone else, an answer…?"

"Can we go indoors now? It's very cold out here."

"Why don't you join us for dinner, Arthur? You might enjoy it, and, if you like, we can continue our discussion later on. I enjoy the company of brilliant and genuinely interesting people." I didn't answer. Then after a minute or two, a bell rang, "Midday Prayer. Join us"

"Do they allow unbelievers?"

Murphy smiled at my question.

"You, I do not think, are an unbeliever."

"Really?"

"Yes, Arthur."

We had crossed the corridors into the main body of the monastery. Other monks were walking, quietly chatting and laughing in low conspiratorial tones, not directly averting to my intrusive presence, all of us now filing through the wide hallways, into the narrow funnel of an archway that led to the main choir, another high-pointed ceilinged high oak-panelled affair with an open tabernacle at the top beneath a huge image of a crucified Jesus. Behind their crucified God there was draped a deep, red velvet curtain, each fold seeming to secrete some deeper, unknowable dark that caught one's eye as each of the brethren, on entering, genuflected in an accomplished manner before the tabernacle, each discreetly assuming their position, opening their huge divine office, the hebdomidary standing and introducing the prayer praying 'for you o Lord are our hope, our refuge in the storm', and the other brethren, suspending their need to know or understand the impossible, giving themselves body and soul into this refuge from the storm, each of them there in the little chapel, off the main church, in this little lifeboat and all around the crashing and wreckage of life outside, each of them, huddled together, as brothers, protecting each other despite all the tensions that would inevitably arise, and I sat there with Murphy and read from his book the psalms and the prayers and I decided that I would have dinner with these people. The Abbott finished midday prayer and blessed his people and together they filed out for dinner.

Fr Murphy watched me watching everything and everyone as we filed into the refectory and we found our places. He kindly did not leave me to float without some anchor in this alien world. He stayed with me, like a centre, a source of gravity, as I endeavoured to make first contact. I felt an urge to become witty and self-effacing, to play on my shyness and endeavour to amuse and entertain and mimic; to ask, after a time, serious and soul searching questions, I felt all these urges, but I waited for the end of grace and was given a bowl of vegetable soup by an especially ascetic, solemn, silent monk, while the others talked about the American elections, the advent of holidays in outer space, and gene therapy.
One of the brothers turned to me and put out his hand to shake mine.
"Joe Finn," he said.
"Arthur Kruger, nice to meet you… Joe."
Finn, who seemed to be joking about someone sitting further up the table, stopped talking to his colleague, and turned to me.

"So what is it that you do?"

"Does it matter?"

"Of course it matters. We are what we do."

"So what are you?"

"I'm an atheist monk."

Des Murphy laughed. As did the rest of the table, at his outrageousness.

"Where are you at yourself?" Finn asked, keeping a safe distance between himself and his food. His pupils seemed dilated. He looked a little stoned.

"I guess I'm between resurrections right now..." I said.

"So I guess you're between jobs right now?"

"You could say that. I'm a writer, I guess."

"I tried that once. Waste of time. One doesn't get to the truth of things by using words. People expect stories, not the truth. We need distractions, to believe our saints are good and holy, and things work out in the end. We need to believe in a system, if only to keep anarchy at bay." I smiled and nodded vigorously.

"You want to know what is it that brought me here today. Right?"

"If you like, Mr Kruger."

"Arthur."

"Arthur. Whatever. We all come to different places for different reasons. How did you find us..?"

"I stuck a pin in a phone book," I said. Joe Finn laughed uproariously, tapping the table with the edge of his manicured fingers.

"You stuck a pin in a phone book. That's too much." His shirt was perfect. His jeans expensive. His blond hair well cut.

"You look like a poster boy for God, you know that?"

"Do I indeed? You look like you just got out of jail."

I laughed too.

"Listen, Finn. Imagine everything you thought was true – about life, death. Just imagine you could cheat death. And you came back. Like Jesus. Then what?"

"On the last day, we all will rise."

"Supposing it happened a little early?"

Finn was about to answer. Des Murphy, restoring gravity, interjected. "I see," he said, "that you don't seem too hungry, Arthur, eh…look at your soup, man, you are far too thin for your size, drink up, eh?" and he thumped me on the shoulder, which hurt. I twitched visibly, but Murphy didn't think of the bruise that would soon grow on my shoulder. Like most healthy muscular people, who don't know their own strength, and regard ill-health and uncertainty and weakness as something like a moral failing, a foolish trait that might be redressed by sound advice and a regular life and attention to righteousness, Murphy thought he was just being playful and healthy. But I drank my soup anyway, and smiled, as Joe told me about he rule and life of the Order of the Holy Field, and I waited for the main course. Murphy put his hand delicately on my shoulder.

"Is everything all right with you, young man?"

I nodded. "Fine. It's surprising though, how things don't work out for the best of us…"

Murphy's compassionate, Hemingway smile stiffened a little as I saw him struggle to understand what I was talking about. He leaned back a little and plates of food were put before us by an old wizened monk whose face had the grey brown blotches of benign tumours. Murphy thanked the servers abstractedly and he nodded to me.

"How are you enjoying the food?" he asked me

"The food is excellent, Father Murphy" I said. "You have an excellent cook, no doubt. Is it appropriate for someone to compliment the cook after dinner?"

"I am sure Brother Frank would be really delighted to hear your good words on his cooking. He is an excellent cook. You know...there he is over there..."

Murphy pointed to the youngest of the young monks sitting across from me, beside Joe, the one who had not spoken during the entire meal. I was surprised.

"I see. I will compliment him at a later time, I think. I am not one to be shouting across tables and drawing unnecessary attention to myself"

"Coffee?" Murphy said, trying to play the quaint host.

"Yes, I'll have a cup or so," I said. "Then I have to go. You have been too kind."

As I drank my coffee and listened to Murphy talk about his family and the friends he loved, I knew I could take no more of this frenzy of liberty, this conspiracy of hope and love, this certainty of salvation, this air I could not breathe for the mixture of elements was made for one whose spiritual genetic code was not like mine. After dinner, a little bell rang and Des Murphy thanked God and the blessed virgin and the angels and the saints on behalf of the community and visitors for such a lovely meal and then quietly walked me to the door.

"Well, it's been a pleasure meeting you, Father." I looked warily at him, hearing the life of the monastery dissipating as we came out of the enclosure.

"You too, Arthur, be sure to keep in touch, okay?"

"I'll do that..." I said, knowing we were lying to each other for the sake of diplomacy, knowing we had nothing in common, that, outside the politeness, there would be friction, coupled with respect for the other's position, coupled with anger and little else. I shook his hand and he drew me to him in a brotherly hug, one that was warm and desperate, underneath its innocent friendliness, for no touch is innocent. And that was all. I walked away and never went back. In the months afterwards, when I got a job and had less time to think about things, I remember walking past the church and stopping off to sit inside there to watch if Murphy would come out onto the huge polished altar and say Mass, or walk past me with a Hemingway smile to hear confessions or console some troubled person. I sat and did not see anyone I knew. Then I left.

NOVEL V

POLICING THE DEAD ZONE

It was late when I awoke in my little cottage on Maxwell Street in Dublin. It was always late when I did that, either very late or too early. I had lost track of a regular life, always sleeping when tired, waking at odd hours. It was not good for me, that lifestyle. But living there was better than the well-adjusted, ordered insanity of life with Mum and Dad. The cottage consisted of four rooms: a kitchen, which doubled as a shower room, a toilet, a bedroom, which doubled as a little office, and a living room. It was an old building, hundreds of years I think. Neighbours told me of families of eight and nine once living together in houses like this. Its irregular, whitewashed walls, the damp that rose in wavy surreal lines in the kitchen, the reinforced glass and reinforced doors the landlady had installed, and the inexplicable noises one heard from the streets and apartments, all made me scared. Yet, I also knew I was safe inside there. Anyway I had no choice. I couldn't afford to move.

I lived there in Maxwell Street on the sufferance of my family. They paid the bills and, time and again, made me promise I would get a job. I would last a while in some office job. After a while, I would quit in a fit of pique or depression. Otherwise, I would not turn up one day, and then get a letter of dismissal. I was becoming rapidly unemployable. My parents' attitude towards me had shifted from anger and disappointment at my failure in life, to a passive non-involvement, a chilly politeness when I would turn up and eat their food and borrow money for my wasted life of withdrawal from life, coupled with my compulsive superficial socialising.

I was a writer back then. I imagined myself in that artistic, alternative, subversive role. It compensated for so many uncertainties I denied about myself. Eventually they got me, those uncertainties I had been running from.

My madness began one night. I remember it was a Friday. I had gone to bed because of a power cut. I fell asleep about nine o'clock and awoke with all the lights back on. I had accidentally left the light switches on. I made tea, put on some music, and went back to the typewriter to look again at what I had written:

"My watch ticker wickers like a blind man's cane;
and nothing is ever going to stop it…"

The words made no sense. Maybe this is a useful thing, I mused. I wanted to impose order on impulse. I wanted to make clear what was happening. I knew that. I wanted to get away. That was a bad thing, trying to understand. Trying to escape.

I worked for an hour or two, then waves of exhaustion came over me. I switched off the lights, fell asleep. Then I woke up and put the lights on and had a coffee.

I looked about the cottage. It gave a false impression of bohemian elegance, borne of some self-imposed poverty. I had furnished the house from money gleaned from cheap reviews and short stories and such things. I went into the kitchen, made coffee, then I walked into the front room. That's when I saw the body.

It was the dead body of a young man, lying on the floor face up. He was about twenty-five to thirty years old. He had crew-cut hair, tan trousers, a sky blue, open necked shirt, and soft shoes, like deck shoes. At first, I had the impression he was asleep. Then I knew he wasn't. As I stood before the corpse, I had this impression that suddenly the body would stir and that prospect frightened me more than anything else. I decided to call my father. No credit in my phone. I tried to call the emergency services. Phone dead. I had to leave the house to make the call. The nearest phone booth was on the top of Cork Street. At that time, it seemed that a demilitarized zone where gangs and sundry homicidal types lingered between the top of Cork Street and the bottom of Maxwell Street.

The prospect of enjoying a fate similar to the corpse before me gave me pause. I did not throw open the door to venture out into the night. I checked my watch. I think I was going into shock. It was approaching 4 in the morning. I felt my way onto the sofa. I stopped, feeling a wetness. I was sweating heavily. I then began to feel the terror I had been suppressing.

I sat there, looking at the body, for an interminable period. I decided somewhere along the line that the body was definitely a corpse, dead. Dead Man was laying face up, looking blindly at the ceiling. I couldn't move him. I couldn't go out there. I imagined the gangs moving across the streets surrounding Cork Street. It was a confident sound, the sound of measured predatory steps, not the sound of blind running, such as I imagined the dead victim before me had made, before being killed or left for dead. These gang members walked the streets with a definite collective purpose in mind. Killing. Rape. Beating. Robbing. I hardly imagined them trading phone numbers with their victims to arrange a rendezvous at the opera.

I tried to work things out. Think Aron. I tried to work out what was happening. I didn't know. What was I going to do? I didn't know. Nobody knows this is happening, I thought. Now that's deep. I should write that down. Let's see. Someone crept in here and left my dead friend here. Someone has the key to my house. I am unsafe. I closed my eyes as I heard the gangs pass by the house, as my heart slammed in my chest and sweat beaded along my body. It could have been any of them, any of those monsters, waiting outside to see what I will do with the corpse. But, if they had gotten in here, if they had a key, why hadn't they raped me and killed me? I reached to switch off the light, but then didn't. It would attract attention. If I left the lights off, then they might decide there was no one home and come in to rob the place, find me and turn breaking and entering into home invasion. Then, they would do what all home invaders do. Terrorise. I looked out the window. Then, I noticed I hadn't angled the Venetian blinds correctly, so that one could not see from the street into my front room. By then the gangs were gone.

I decided the best thing to do was wait. I sat once again and looked at the corpse. I wondered if I could just get it out of the house. 'It' was my friend, the dead corpse. I could no longer look at it. I went over and lifted the corpse's arms and let them fall. No rigor mortis. I thought of fingerprints and decided on gloves. I went into the bedroom and found a pair of mitts. I cleaned the area of the wrists I touched with a soapy sponge. I dried the area and tossed the sponge into the bin. I then put the mitts on and began to drag the body across the floor. It was heavy and awkward and I was small and weak and, because of my sweaty palms, my grip kept slipping through the mitts. I dragged it across the floor and opened the front door, just a crack, to see out. Nothing. Absolute pitch. The streetlights are ritually smashed every so often. The plan was to drag it across the street and down to the other side of the block, near the old Donnelley's factory in the broken down car park. Then, leave it by some ruined car. And, when the coast is clear, to run and hope I was not spotted. I tried to open the door fully, but his arms were blocking it and I didn't want to leave traces or break any more bones than those already broken. I couldn't see any visible marks or blood. Perhaps he died in his sleep, was poisoned or choked, I thought. I'm no forensic pathologist, no scientist of decay. I moved the body back a little, propped it up against the wall and opened the door fully. I then tried to drag the body out the door. I almost shouted with relief as the body passed out the threshold. Then, one of his feet got caught in the doorframe. I put him down and released his foot. Just as I released his foot, I noticed someone coming down the street. I tried to drag the body back inside. This would have involved my grabbing his feet and dragging him back in, and the dead head thudding against the pavement and doorstep. I decided against it. The lights were out and whoever it was seemed alone. Police mostly drove by in squad cars. Sometimes, you would see them in pairs, never at night though. I decided to keep dragging and hope for the best. This was risky. I dragged the corpse around the block with almost superhuman, mostly nervous, strength. I could feel my body flooded with adrenaline and endorphins. I should not be physically able to do this, I thought. I remembered a story I read of World War II sailor called Smith who, in a fit, threw an unexploded shell off the side of a ship and saved the lives of his shipmates. Here, in my arms, was a similar bomb. I dragged it unseen to the appointed site, feeling his heels hop off the randomly pebbled ground of the half-used car park. I envisioned tomorrow's breaking news about the discovery of a deposited body on Cork Street, Dublin.

I went back to the cottage. I had left the door wide open, with the light streaming out. I closed it guiltily. I tore off all my clothes and looked at my body in the mirror in the bedroom. I was looking at me to see if there were any visible marks, with all the dragging and pulling of dead men's bodies. There were none. I decided on a shower. I sat into the shower and stayed there for an hour or so. My skin wrinkled. I counted the ridges forming along my fingers as a result of hiding in the shower. I was allowing the water to wipe away the palpable horror I was feeling. It didn't work. I dried and dressed for bed and I clambered into bed shivering in fear and shock and hunger. I lay stiffly, listening in terror for the sound – the sound of the police coming to take me. I tried to imagine how the body had arrived in my front room. Who had placed it there? Who had managed to get into my front room? How they got a key to my place? Who was that dead man?

I reached over to my alarm clock, the one bought during times when I briefly kept jobs, and made sure the alarm was switched off. It was always switched off. But, if I did manage to sleep, now I would not be disturbed. I put my earphones on and switched on some music and, after what seemed to be a length of time without measure, I slept. When I awoke I could see the sun high and beaming through the skylight in my bedroom, though the safety bars. The amnesia of denial had given me a few hours of sleep and, for that, I felt grateful. Then I remembered. And, when I remembered, I knew the problem had not gone away. I knew this was something that would not leave. I sat in my bedroom and knew that, outside the door, there lay the body. I could feel its presence, feel him there – the lingering, lifeless decay that never leaves. And I was not wrong. The body of the dead man had returned. I screamed. But the door stopped my scream. Someone was banging on the door. I tried to hide the body. Where would I put it? The closet? Under the bed? In the bed? Where? Whoever was banging was still banging. It was a male knock, that dull aggressive testosterone sound. Oh God, I thought. He was shouting something. Now they were trying to force the door open. I threw on my dressing gown and opened the door for them. It was the police. The Male Officer introduced himself as Officer Smith. The Female Officer introduced herself as Officer Jones. I decided against any jokes about names.

"We have a report of a disturbance," Officer Smith began, smilingly.
"No, no I had a nightmare. I woke up screaming. I have been having them periodically for the past few weeks. It's troubling."
"Are you alone in these premises? Ms…?"
"Tully. Aron Tully. Yes. I am alone here."
I decided that the proximity of a corpse in my home, that I could not explain, did not constitute a human presence.
"You wouldn't be lying to us madam, would you?"
"No, Officer."

"We have a witness that saw you drag something out of your house last night."

"A bag of rubbish, Officer."

"Where is it now?"

"I have no idea."

"May we come in?" they asked, as they pushed past me.

A third Police Officer sat in the car, looking cynically away from me. I tried to mentally prepare myself for arrest and interrogation. I had hazy clichéd television images in my mind from cop dramas I had seen. I figured that, after a few hours of threats and roughing me up, I would confirm what they had decided on as the truth. Then they would arrest me and, in the presence of a magistrate, I would be sentenced to a lifetime's imprisonment as the final confirmation of my parents', friends', teachers', worst suspicions about me. I tried to think of an explanation, feeling an anticipatory sense of humiliation and a growing blankness, as fear and intimidation got to me. I tried to find a way, in my mind, to confirm and compound the lies I had told, to escape the inescapable investigations of the authorities. In my experiences of dealing with authorities, one is damned by the truth and damned by the lies one tells. I opened my mouth to speak, in the hope something would come out. Nothing. I sat down on the seat nearest the dead fireplace, as the police began picking through the artefacts of my life.

Smith went to the kitchen. Jones gravitated towards the typewriter that sat in the middle of the room. She read a few sheets and frowned. Then smiled. She liked my irony, I figured. She appreciates my burgeoning genius and will let me go because she doesn't want to deprive the world of my great gift. But then she put the sheets down and moved on. She looked away, thoughtfully, brushing her black slightly salt and pepper, pageboy-cut hair away from her slim, pretty, slightly pinched features. Then, she picked them up again, and looked through them. Then she put them down, and smiled at me. I smiled weakly back.

"You wouldn't happen to have a search warrant, Officer Jones?" I politely asked. Officer Smith and Officer Jones chose to disregard that legitimate query. After all, I would never be able to afford a real solid, expensive legal defence team. I was a nobody to them, an unknown bohemian writer, living on the bad side of town.
"Where are you in all of this?"
She pointed to the pile of pages beside the typewriter.
"Why do you want to know?"
"Oh, we have a keen interest in the arts," Smith answered for her. She nodded.
"Society is greatly influenced by the arts. Why do you think the government tries to subsidise so many artistic endeavours?"
"Because they have no taste?" I offered. They laughed.

Jones and Smith seemed to have a keen interest in things outside the law, which made me wonder what they were doing in the police force.
"So, where are you in all of this?" Smith pointed once more to my manuscript.
"In there, I suppose. Trying to peer out," I said, pointing at the pages. I couldn't think of anything else to say. My mouth was dry, feeling a mounting horror.

Smith went into the bedroom. This is bad. So very bad, I thought. I closed my eyes and rubbed my forehead, deciding that, if reincarnation is true, the last twenty-four hours of pain implied I was definitely going to evolve onto the next level when I die. Smith seemed to be gone a long time. He called me from inside the bedroom.
"Ms. Tully, if you have a moment, could you come in here?"

"I, I'd rather not. If you don't mind, I must be going now."

I ran for the door. Jones stood between the door and me.

"I see you have done this before," she said. "I mean running away." She smiled at me. "You have an interesting mind, Ms Tully, you know that?" she said.

I felt understood by this Police Officer. I imagined her as my interrogator in some cell and her succeeding in extracting every detail of my life and crimes by the force of her gaze.

"Who called you here?" I asked her. "You seem more like the thought police than the police police."

"To understand the mind of a criminal is to understand the criminal. And we are all potential criminals. In answer to your question, your neighbours were worried."

"You're lying. My neighbours are criminals, on one side anyway, and on the other they're too stoned to care most of time, except for their next fix."

The other Police Officer was still calling me, in the same non-threatening tones. I went into my bedroom. He was sitting on the bed; his feet were resting on the head of the corpse. He was looking at my record collection that I had carefully stacked on a shelf above my bed. My Dad had put up the shelving for me. He looked over my book collection. Many of them were stolen from libraries. I felt a special attachment to those I had not paid for.

"Ah, there you are. My, you are some reader. Have you read all of these?"

"Most. I don't have time to read everything…"

"And what a collection of records. How do you afford all of these?"

"I deal drugs to aspiring new age hippies. I have also appeared in several porn flicks," I said. And he laughed out loud.

"Jones, you heard that?" and Jones said "Yes." She was still reading.

And then I saw how he couldn't see the body. Neither of them could see the body. Thank God, I'm going crazy. Imagine, I thought, if it had all been real. Imagine that. And police are trained to spot things mere mortals cannot, I thought. Officer Smith continued his friendly chat.

"Hah! Very good! Very funny! Listen, about these records. Some of them, I'd love a copy of. Would you mind very much? If I give you a few tapes, will you copy them for me? They would make great listening while we are sitting in the squad car, thinking over the days cases. Officer Jones and I like to relax as we consider our caseload and go over our notes. Investigation is rather a precise thing. Would that be a problem for you, Ms. Tully?"

"Not at all. Tell me, Officers, I have an unusual question."

"Go ahead, Ms Tully. Go right ahead."

"Have either of you seen any dead bodies lately? Like that of a young six-foot male in his late thirties, you know...?"

The Female Police Officer put her hand on my shoulder and smiled. The policeman stood up.

"Officer Jones, have you seen such a corpse?"

Officer Jones shook her head.

"Ms. Tully, we have seen no such corpse."

"I'm sure you should locate it. A crime might have been committed."

"No, I don't think so. We locate many corpses. We located three today, one suicide where a person, loosely matching your description, threw himself in front of a train, an accidental road traffic death, and a stabbing. But no sighting of such a corpse has been reported."

"Male. Six foot. Crew cut. Casual attire..."

"Well, we must be going. Goodbye for now. If you wish to make a statement..."

"Look around this place, Officer. I mean carefully..."

"Oh, you can be sure I did. Nothing to see here... I use equipment you would never dream such types as us might have. We are quite— What's the word, Officer?"

"Hi-tech"

"Indeed."

Officer Smith smiled at me.

"I'll drop in those tapes, if that's okay. I'll call back sometime. Is that okay?"

"Fine, whatever. Taping is low-tech for you lot."

"You should mind yourself, Ms. Tully."

"I will. Believe me..."

"This is a difficult area for a writer to survive in, and, if you have any problems whatsoever, you give us a call." Officer Jones placed a card on my table, beside the typewriter.

Samantha Jones and Richard Smith.
Division two. Perfect Fifteen
Dead Zone Police

"I'm no writer," I said.

"I see."

Officer Jones looked at me. She put her hand on my shoulder again. I really didn't like it. I moved away from her.

"I think you need to think things over," they said. "We'll be back," they said. "You have things you need to record."

Sure, you Officers can come back anytime to flout my constitutional rights, I thought. This is how totalitarianism begins. First, they take away your privacy. Then, they take your rights. Then, your soul.

The Officers left, smiling and waving as they drove away in their unmarked car. It was like some bizarre, drug induced hallucination. How could they fail to notice the decomposing corpse under their noses?

I went in to the body in the bedroom. I couldn't remember it getting there. I possibly dragged it in a frenzy, before answering the door. It was all a blur. I had forgotten breakfast. I was, at this stage, beyond caring about food. There was a faint odour in the bedroom. I noticed discolouration along the fingernails and lips. Decomposition was already setting in. Soon, this room would be unusable, with the odour and the discolouration and the blood settling, and the maggots and the flies and the more maggots and larvae, and the hungry eating maggots and the flies landing and taking off, and the sheer creepiness of having my dead guest about. It's not the maggots that get you when you die. It's the bacteria. I decided a search of my imaginary corpse was in order. I turned him over and I looked in his back pockets. Nothing. I turned him over again and looked in his jacket and found an identity card:
Arthur Kruger D36844.

So, he existed. His name was Kruger. It seemed to be those types of badges one was required to wear at all times when working in whatever building this poor soul worked in. He worked for a company called Zero Corporation. I looked it up in the phone book. I called their head offices in Harcourt St. the following day.
"Thank you for Calling Zero Corporation. Teresa speaking. How may I help you?"
"Yes. Hi, Teresa. I was looking to speak to Arthur Kruger. "
"One moment, please, while I transfer you. Thank you. Who will I say is calling?"
"And thank you too, young lady. This is his mother."
The phone rang for about a second and, then, all of a sudden, I was talking to Arthur Kruger.
"Hello, Mother? This is certainly a…"
"Arthur Kruger, staff number D36844, born seventh of November..?
"Who is this?"
I hung up and walked away from the phone booth.

I went to visit my parents. This was because I had no food and hadn't eaten in a day. When I got to the kitchen, I made myself a sandwich, and then made myself a packed lunch. My mother looked at me.

"What's wrong?"

I didn't answer her. Mother had never asked me what was wrong before. My father and brother Otto conspired to keep me in my little fortress, by paying the rent each week and maintaining the apartheid between mother and daughter. I went home thinking about Arthur Kruger, D36844. I had his identity card in my pocket. He looked perfectly ordinary to me. Regular features. Regular blue eyes. Regular height. Chestnut hair. No distinguishing features, except maybe that he was dead.

I went home and sat in front of my typewriter. Then I dragged the body out of my bedroom and opened the skylight to let out the flies and the awful gut-wrenching stench. This is fun, I thought. When and if I marry, this will give me something to tell the kids on weekends down the country. I'll marry some chiropodist, or oculist, or general practitioner in the black arts when one feels the stretch of age and regrets for dropping out of college way back then.

I propped the body up on one of the single sofa beds, and looked at the decaying face. I looked him in his dead eyes and I found myself smiling. There was a kind of cataract-like corneal skin stretched over the eyes. I couldn't bring myself to close the lids over those dead eyes. It was strange to see him. Here before me was something no one else could see or feel or know. This, no one would ever know. No one could know this death as I knew it. In the midst of it all, with Arthur Kruger's dead eyes watching, my eyes meeting his every so often, as my mind grew dark with the evening shadow as I typed—

I hear the voices of the dead
On the third level of hell

On the third level of hell
The sun is shining

The flesh becomes word
We eat our words in hell

Every day is a holiday
On the third level of hell

We waste nothing in hell
Everything is eaten

We dine on our lives
We drink on our dreams

I wanted to escape as well. I wanted to be with Kruger, to disappear as he disappeared, into the atoms from which he came. I wanted these visions to pass. I wanted to know what I saw, or thought I saw, more than anything else I had ever known or remembered. I knew that here before me, somehow embodied in this dead man, was not a dead man, but myself. It was all real. Real but not real. In the dead man, Arthur Kruger, I saw my own absolute horizon. Before me, lying desiccated with the flies and the stench and the memories and the laughter and the birth and the life and the lovers touch, this was the end. Dead man. The escape. I needed an escape. I needed an out-clause. I sat before the typewriter and looked at the keys. Nothing. No words. Nothing. I saw words as a type of tangible recognition of a possible future, or a possible past. Some type of anchor, I thought. Some type of anchor in a storm of decay. Then I went to bed, utterly confused and distraught.
Nothing nothing nothing, I kept thinking, as I fell asleep.

I needed help. Exit.
I thought of exorcisms or electro-convulsive shock therapy. I thought of Thorazine or Heroin. I thought of moving home, or confessing my sins to a priest. I thought of taking up God as a serious option. That's it, religious conversion. But I had known the insanity of religion before. And I could never go back. As if this madness was anything less, I thought. I thought of romance. I thought of necrophilia and

nightmares. I thought of directed dreaming and radical witchcraft. I thought of Mother. I read into the night, nights and nights of watching Arthur Kruger's decomposition out of the corner of my eye. I thought of talking to the dead through a medium. I thought of chopping up the dead body of Arthur Kruger and burying it in a field, a thousand miles from nowhere. But, I didn't. Rather, I couldn't. If I disposed of this body, what might happen to the living Kruger? If I did anything, might I not cause harm to the living? I did not know what to do. My mind was caught in the midst of a raging storm of confusion that clouded my thinking and made no action possible.

In the end, I did nothing. I did nothing, because the physical presence of the corpse paralyzed my mind. I was like a small rabbit frozen before the headlights of an oncoming truth. I was paralysed into the mere contemplation of possibilities. I did nothing, because I believed that nothing would free me of this presence. But I knew that I needed help. My dreams were full of death and decay. But I did not know to whom to turn. I knew many people in every walk of life. But the trouble was they did not know me, except in my persona as intellectual clown with notions too half-formed and contradictory and metaphoric to be anything, other than entertaining and slightly wistful. In this guise, I succeeded in never reaching anything other than a passing superficiality with the people I met in my many social contacts. I could not tell any of them about this. And I could find no reference to such an apparition as this in any of the many books I consulted.

Days passed. I ate a little in the morning and took a walk and typed mostly in the afternoon. The flesh was being eaten off Kruger's face. Maggots and flies flew from his mouth and eyes. I imagined his innards were disappearing, but did not investigate until the third day. On the third day, I opened his shirt to see a battalion of white maggots collapse, from where his stomach once was, onto the floor, scuttling away like escaping thieves, like commandos on some dawn raid, like raiders stoned on some orgy of destruction. I took a long shower, and tried to wash it all away. I imagined how it might sound if I tried to explain what I was going through to other people, supposed friends. I couldn't. Explanation was not an option.

Invitations to social events were amassing. Notes and cards and letters were piling on the floor just inside the door of my cottage. I was replying to very few messages and invitations. There was little food left in the cottage, and no money. Maybe I should get a job, I thought. Before that, I would have to go home again soon, to eat, if nothing else.

I cooked the last of the food. Arthur Kruger was sitting opposite, still quietly decomposing. I ate breakfast, slowly picking the flies and the maggots out of the last of the mushroom, tomato and eggs. I was turning over in my mind what options I had left open to me, while remembering how someone told me once that human flesh tasted a little like bacon, which was why they never ate bacon anymore. There was this whole argument for not eating flesh that made me guilty every time I ate it. So I stopped a long time ago.

I looked over at Kruger, with his skeletal smile, the dead fingers pointing out at the floor across from my typewriter desk; the light from the window shining through the strands of his wispy hair; the flies landing and disembarking from every part of him. I knew I would glean no insights from the corpse. There were maggots and flies everywhere. Maggots: Soft bodied legless larvae of certain flies. Killing them seemed to make them multiply. I wondered what the life cycle of the common housefly was, if these were houseflies, or virtual flies produced by me.

I decided to spy on my subject, the living, breathing, carbon-based, Arthur Kruger, in living colour. There has to be a connection. I went into town and waited outside Zero Corporation for hours in the merciless sunlight. Nothing again. But I knew spying required timing, and I had a terrible sense of timing. He seemed not to show up. I was also paranoid. I imagined people watching me, as I sat drinking water and watching the building. They must have cameras, I thought. I am losing weight just sitting here, I thought. I am so hungry. After three hours of sunstroke heat, I gave it up as a waste of time. I went back home dejected. I came in the door, and my father was waiting for me, sitting there. He was sitting opposite the dead body of Arthur Kruger.

"Hi," I said weakly.

"Hi there," he said smiling. "I called by, but you were not in. I hope you don't mind my waiting for you. I hope you are not going to accuse me of breaking and entering? Eh?"

He was breaking ice that had been hardening between us for decades. It hurt to see him do that.

"I gave you the keys, didn't I?" I said, trying to smile at him, but my eyes drawn to the corpse, the dead, the dead opposite him, smiling inanely into my father's face, smiling and mocking him, mocking him and me, for I was his daughter, the one for whom he wanted so much success and marriage and career and love, but who had failed, had dropped out of life instead.

He said he came to give some money, and to see how I was and 'wondering if you would like to call up some time and maybe have a little dinner'.

"Thanks. I need money. I hate to ask..," I said, really stupidly and tactlessly.

"I know. It's okay. I see you are... working on something, there. Pretty strange stuff. How will you... sell it?" He didn't wait for an answer. "I am sure you will do famously with it. Experimental prose. But then, this is something you can do..."

"In my spare time? Is that what you were going to suggest? I'm not Franz Kafka."

"No. you're not. You are definitely not Franz Kafka."

"And look what happened to him, eh Dad?"

"I also wanted to ask why you didn't bother ringing the job we set up for you."

I fumbled for an explanation. He had arranged some interview for me a week ago but I had forgotten. One of the many appointments I had not honoured. I thought of saying any number of well-tried and tested lies, but nothing emerged that would convince him. I then thought of telling him about the corpse sitting opposite him. Then, I decided to lie.

"Oh that. Sorry. I couldn't do it. I have been looking for another job."

"I see. That's good. Where?"

"Zero Corporation."

"Zero Corporation. Very post-modern of you. Hi-tech. Why there?"

"I am trying to get a guy called Kruger on the phone. I'll get lucky. Don't worry."

"I'm surprised by that."

"Why?"

"Because you don't want to work. Because you don't know what you want. You don't know what you want, because you don't want to look. You don't want to look, because you feel trapped. And you feel trapped, because you don't know what you want. It's tricky. You are one of the smartest, most aimless, lazy, bored people I know..."

I looked into his eyes and he looked back. His disappointment in the person I had become had gone past anger and confrontation, and was languishing in heartbreak and resignation. I could not be his protégé.

I'm not sure he wanted that any more. But he had money and he had time and he was prepared to let me go on a little more. I looked at him and decided against any possible debate, any father-daughter moment. He can have those with Otto.

"I was about to make tea. I rather fancy a cup. Thirsty work seeking out potential employers, you know..."

"Good. Did you get through to anyone?"

"I am unemployable. I know that."

"That's self-confidence for you. I love that about you. My Aron, the self-motivator."

"Answering services, mostly," I said. "And free numbers you can dial. And help lines. And other first-line defences against dealing with real people."

"I see."

I was putting on the kettle and nervously fumbling for some digestive biscuits. There were a few left, I knew that. Dad's well founded façade of calm reasonableness intimidated me far more than the maggot-ridden corpse of the late, great, living Arthur Kruger.

I rattled into the living room with chipped cups and biscuits and bottles of milk. Dad was sitting in the space occupied by my imaginary, real, dead, zombie Kruger corpse. His body was occupying the same space as Kruger's. It was an awesome sight. Arthur Kruger's dead head hung outside the frame of Dad's body space. It lolled backwards, with its mouth open and flies taking off and landing, and tiny white maggots crawling out of the eyes and ears, and the hair falling away onto the ground, and the general stench and air of decay. I resisted the urge to throw up or faint, or both. I put the cups down, in the midst of the front room mist, filling with flies and larvae. Dad seemed completely unaffected and unaware. He went to the bathroom as I poured out tea for him and me. I was in the midst of my own private madness, I decided, as Dad left the room. Sweat was dripping down my face and along my hands in little rivulets.

"You okay, honey?"

"Fine. Great. I'm hot."

I will go on until the end, I thought. I will not be driven mad like this, I thought. I opened a window and the flies started to escape. They poured out of Arthur Kruger's stomach and eye sockets, swirling around the room and out the windows. We see the worms, I thought. We think they are doing the eating and the killing. But, in reality, it is what we cannot see, the bacteria, they do the killing and the eating. O God, what's happening to me? Arthur Kruger's hair was falling away fast. I could see little bits of bone on the cheek and knuckle and forehead. I looked in amazement at the bizarre scene in the front room. I imagined what it would be like to vacuum clean this room. Then Dad came out of the bathroom and came into the front room. We sat and drank tea and ate biscuits, for the most part, in silence.

"So have you heard from your mother?"

"No, Dad. Not a word".

"Your brother?"

"Not a thing. I was thinking of dropping up and staying a day or so."

"He'd like that. You should keep in touch with him more. I hear he has a cold."

"A cold? I'm sorry to hear that."

"Ah. A cold. He will have to watch that. All those colds."

"Yes. A less stressful life. "

Dad's sphinx like implacability did not shift a jot. He smiled and peered into his less than sterile cup and sipped his tea.

"Ah. Good tea, Aron."

"Good."

He stood up and announced his departure. "So, when will we expect you? I have a few bob here to keep you going." He handed me an envelope.

"Thanks, Dad."

"Fine."

"I'm sorry," I said feeling shame at having failed him, for having refused his values. He didn't react, and I understood this implacability hurt me most. He smiled.

"Ah. You keep at that, there." He indicated my typing. "I was reading a little, your work. It's not bad. It makes me proud. My daughter has so many gifts. I can patronise you, being your Dad and all..."

I nodded. "Thanks, Dad."

We finished tea quietly, politely. Then, after, we walked to the front door, through the flies and maggots that seemed to be everywhere, crawling and flying between books on the bookshelves by the partition door.

"Well, call soon, Dad. Thanks, thanks for..."

"Come for dinner tomorrow, Aron, if you're free."

"I will."

"I see. Go see your brother."

"I will."

Dad was now looking at me through the driver's window of his car. He drove off gently, and, with a slight indication of his hand, was suddenly gone. I closed the door, went back to the desk, and wiped the flies and maggots off my typewriter. The corpse had fallen off the chair. It was lying face down by the window. I imagined it had tried to stand up, and realising it was dead, decided to fall. I began typing this:

I tried to get away from this, but I could not. I tried to get it all out in the open, tried to explain things. There was no one there. The best course of action was to wait. I remained supine with only the eyelids flickering. Then, nothing happened again. I could not move and I waited, but death did not come. Perhaps it came for Kruger. The legs the arms the chest the feet the head the throat the ulterior parts of lessening significance, also without a flicker of life or death on the ship. This dead zone of dreams. There was no one there, nothing moving. I had no explanation for this. I remembered no sequence of events that led me to this paralysis, if that was what it was, for I could feel these limbs. I imagined that I could send messages down the nerves into the muscles and tendons. Nothing, or rather in some retrospection, perhaps it was the will that gave me this illusion of transmission. I could not be sure if there was a body there at all, for I could not see it, as my head would not move. Despite this immobility, I did not feel frustrated. Feeling, for all the plaudits attendant to the state, gives merely the illusion of life and attendant hope. Others, too, will try to escape the heart foundation, the illusion of life, and they, too, will fall into the state of catatonia, having given up on embodiment, on sentience and feeling, as fake signals from a star long since dead, falling to earth under the thrall of inevitable gravity, will carry on, will marry and work and procreate and send their children for miseducation, as they too were brought up. This is the last laugh of living, or rather of life, if there is such a thing. Perhaps that too was an illusion. Keeping up appearances is an illusion. I could not be sure. I had no sense of mounting horror. No sense of fear, no uncertainty about either my future or my past...

I stood up from the typewriter to feel something in my hair and along my clothing, something wriggling. Larvae. I screamed and ran around the house, hysteria hitting home, trying to take them off, and, though they may have been long removed, the feeling of them crawling along my hair and flesh still lingered. That I could not easily get rid of.

The truth was, I was covered in maggots. I had been unaware of my surroundings while I typed. During this time, all the maggots had crawled into my clothing and into my hair. I, too, had become the dead. I felt as though I too was being consumed. I rushed into the shower, trying wildly to get them all off me and I sat there, trying to peel off sopping wet clothing, with little maggots tucked into the warm safe folds of my pants and shirt and soft shoes. It was then I decided to go to Otto's. I peered out through the shower to see the blur of flies circling and dancing at the skylight just above me. I went into the bedroom and dressed. I was not completely dry but the hot summer sunlight would dry me on my journey to Otto's. He would be at home, according to Dad, so I did not bother to telephone. I took my typewriter, put it in a case and put my papers into a satchel.

I took out my bike and left the house, tying the satchel and typewriter case to the carrier. I cycled over to Otto's, hysterically dodging imminent death by my poor road observation. The ride took thirty minutes or more. Otto lived in luxury apartments in Ballsbridge in Dublin. One rang at the gate of the apartment complex in order to gain entry. Then, one proceeded to whichever of the series of separate buildings was one's destination. Then one took the elevator up to the right floor. One's entire visit was recorded by security, cameras everywhere. I rang at the gate. A strange voice answered.

'Hullo?'

'Hi, this is Aron, Aron Tully. I'm Otto's sister. I've come over to visit."

'Hi Aron. Come on up."

I had no idea who that was on the phone. Presumably he saw me on camera too. I did not call here often. I distrusted its exclusivity and its opulence. It also intimidated me. When I arrived at the door, a very muscular man with a shiny, presumably shaved, head answered. He did not smile, which increased his overall severe appearance of threatening physicality. He knew who I was. He spoke in the same soft tones I had heard over the intercom. He introduced himself as Josh. This was their home. I just knew it. Otto and Josh's place was palatial, despite being on the thirteenth floor. It was furnished with bright polished oak and mahogany chairs, a table, and shelves, a type of mock Victorian oeuvre. There were tasteful paintings tastefully hung on the walls, small statues carefully positioned here and there. They looked inconspicuous, as though placed to enhance the experience of the room, rather than to look like expensive art bought to enhance the egos of the buyers. The room was dominated by one huge crescent shaped leatherette sofa, facing a large television screen that was switched off. There was the sound of jazz lingering in the background, like an obsequious waiter.

"Where's my brother?" I asked as Josh and I sat on the sofa.
"I killed him. I've taken over his life, his home, his blue chip stocks, the whole thing, you know, sweetie."
He looked at me for a second and continued perusing an article about country life that he had been reading before the doorbell rang. He seemed genuinely unflappable.
"Charming," I said, and managed a smile.
"Otto is at the doctor's. He can't shake the flu. Lucky I haven't caught it myself. What's your poison?" He stood up and walked over to the drinks cabinet.
"Vodka and lime. Lots of both in a big glass. Lots and lots of ice."
"Has Otto told you about us?"
"No. He hasn't."
Josh smiled to himself as he fixed the drinks.

"So what brings you here?"

"Oh. The usual. This whole crazy thing."

"Your brother speaks highly of you."

"He does?"

"Sure. He said so."

"Okay. That's surprising."

"Otto is full of those surprises."

"So where did you two meet?"

"At a conference. So, tell me, what do you do?"

"I told you... I..."

"No, don't tell me, let me make a guess. I am very psychic."

O God, I thought, a new age body fascist...

"You work in advertising or graphic arts..."

He put his hands over my eyes and forehead. Normally I would have been deeply perturbed by the prospect of such a huge man, so muscular, such a presence, touching me. But he was not at all intrusive. That was obvious from the first moment. His hands were on me still.

"So what do you see in there?"

"Death. Sadness. Confusion. What happened?"

"I've been seeing things..."

"Things?"

"Right."

"People?"

"Maybe."

"It's not people. It's you. Something from the past or future. It always is you know."

"That doesn't mean anything. Something from the past or future. That's so unspecific it confuses the issue more. Look..."

I lowered my voice to a conspiratorial, but embarrassed, whisper. Josh looked bemusedly at me. I'm putting myself in a vulnerable position, I told myself. What if he tells Otto about this. This is madness, I thought. But I went on.

"I do not know this person. He is alive, but I don't see him like that. He works downtown. I found his identification and I called him up and he answered the phone. I pretended I was his mother and his secretary and..."

Josh took away his hands. He put them by his sides and sat looking at me. I didn't tell him anymore, deciding I had gone too far. I couldn't tell him...

"Okay then. Okay, that's enough for me," I said.

"Something in you is all wrong," he said.

He's right, I told myself. Something is so wrong. I felt cheered up already. Otto came into the apartment. He did not look good. Josh spoke up pre-emptively.

"Aron wants to stay a few days. She is here drinking us dry and she hardly in the apartment fifteen minutes. Isn't that right, Aron?"

I grinned and took another gulp of vodka and lime and didn't answer. Otto said, "Fine."

"Hi Otto. Dad told me you were sick," I said.

"I told him to tell you that, and, yes, you can stay. Do you have any clothes with you?"

"You have got to be kidding. I have stuff back in the cottage, but I'd rather not go back there right now. It's haunted."

"I see Josh is having an effect on you. We'll go shopping. I am off until Monday with this virus... thing..."

"Stress?" I guessed.

"That word may have been used," Otto said, as he walked into his room. Just a lucky guess, I thought.

Otto went to sleep for a few hours. Josh and I put the television on and watched some shows. Then, we raided the fridge, and made dinner. Afterwards we went out and saw a movie.

I stayed a few days. Their lifestyle was a shock to me. Otto seemed to be suffering from some type of early burnout, the effects of years of backbreaking work to make the money he now had. He slept much of the day and ate high nutrition foods, made mostly by Josh and me. We would all eat together in the evening and Otto would hold forth, legislate as to the rights and wrongs of things, rather than communicate. It didn't irritate or provoke me into long pointless arguments like it used to. I listened. I just disagreed and, when it became too much, I went to bed. Mostly I realised during those dinners, as I silently listened to Otto and Josh laughing and arguing and debating, how alone he was, how, in a weird way, I was one of his very few friends, the fact I was a family member was a bonus, that I must do nothing to break such a bond, that I was lucky to have Otto, that I must at least try to be a friend in return. My stay had one other big fringe benefit. I got to know Josh.

Eventually, I went back to my place. I said goodbye and Otto gave me some cash. They were at work when I left. I packed my nice clothes, got out my bike and left a note. I cycled back to the cottage, weaving less desperately and more gently and carefully through the traffic. I got back to the house. I opened the skylight window to let in light and air. Thousands of flies flew off. I looked at the page in the typewriter for nearly an hour. Someone knocked at the door. I didn't answer, though I so painfully wanted to. Something fell to the floor through the letterbox. Dad had left another of his envelopes. The flies had partially gone. I went over to my table after closing the door sat at my typewriter. I knew there was no other way to exorcise whatever demon had possessed me. I did not know whether or not I believed what Josh had told me. The flies crawled all over me. I brushed them off. They flew up to the skylight and then out.

The page was still staring blankly back at me. I looked at it. It was getting darker. I got a drink of water and sat back down. It was a matter of waiting. If I didn't wait for an answer, I saw what my fate would be. Night fell. Nothing. I went to the front door. Something hit against my foot. I switched the light on. It was a packet. I opened it. I was glad I hadn't opened the door when I heard the knock. It was a set of tapes with a note accompanying from Officer Smith, reminding me to record all those tracks for them. He mentioned how listening to music helped his concentration, his reviewing of cases pertinent to them. They would be back. They always come back. I opened the front door. Maxwell Street was strangely empty. I looked up at the stars. I looked at the moon. All the superlatives in any language could never capture the exquisite seductive charm of the moon. I looked up for a while, drinking in the light. Then, I closed the front door and waded through my fly and worm ridden sarcophagus cottage, into my bedroom tomb. I sat down and switched on the desk light. Something happened. I felt a word emerge from the void, the decay of dark, fly ridden, disintegration. Then another. I felt the sentences there, beyond the reach of rational, logical, right-thinking consciousness. They came after the first words. The first words were the key. They, those other sentences, they were freedom. I tapped the first down first:

Dead White Male Makes a Killing.

Dear Arthur Kruger,

This is Aron Tully, writing you here from the Dead Zone. You are my first lodger, thus, I write this to you. I am too scared to write to me. I feel the presences here in this invisible hell. I just wanted to say that, this morning, when I came back here from Otto's and Josh's, to go down the street, a thousand years ago, not a moment too soon as Jesus wept, it was bright and clear, with the sun shining outside the door to the metropolis, and I, in the eighteen degrees centigrade shade, trying to avoid it because of my reluctance to love the cheerful commerce of light. Police on the radio predicted the usual round of student riots and government unrest. I could see the roving bands of state-approved murderers at their appointed posts, God bless the remark. I saw, too, the occasional sacking and looting of the capital, with its concomitant ritual of Joe Josephine Rape and Joe Public Torture along Montezuma Avenue and the odd bit of Bob Plunder. We had a meeting, you see. Having carefully considered all the options, we decided that it was quite safe to go and get the papers and a bottle of gin for this evening's late movie. However, things are not what you expect. And, when I saw the approaching citizen, I knew this was the end of all these smiles of Friendly Street. I knew the moment and was not afraid. I was, I suppose, relieved to at last be rid of clocking in before ten, pointless sales talk, the cut-throat infighting over illusion careers, the bad coffee smiled over in the afternoon. All these things happen because we kept the rules. We kept the rules, and it got us a nice clean coffin, smelling of incense and salve reginas. There, a hundred miles to hell, as pure as Russian vodka. We were beautiful, gentle, obedient, considerate, sensitive, and the family kept smiling when we died. They loved us. And, now, we have gone to our reward. It is all for the best. God is good. We thought things through. We planned life in accord with the rational norm. As a result of this unflagging obedience,

I think God, being bored or otherwise distracted, took us home to hell, where we were welcomed with a contract renewed for another year, a raise, a company car, and the use of the company chalet on Ibiza during the off peak season. However much I pushed myself, I looked before I leaped. So did you, and all our friends. And, though I pushed, the fall understandably killed you and I. It is love. Love is the killer. Love kills everyone. Truth cripples for life. And truth has that inferior finality. A matter of consensus, don't you think?

I'll sign off now, Arthur. I hope you will pass this on to your friends. Say hi to the dead me when you meet her. She is not talking to me yet. She lies here dead on my bed.

Yours,
Aron Tully.

I looked up at the flies swirling, disappearing through the skylight, as a diver sees the nearing shimmering sunlit surface of the ocean, as the terror of the deep subsides. I walked to the bed and kissed my rotting Arthur Kruger corpse, and put the dead letter under my pillow. I decided on a cup of coffee and I caught the news. Afterwards, I started the process of recording those albums for the police.

Kruger was now so decayed as to be unrecognisable, a shell of bones surrounded by clothes. I looked at his corpse as I started to record. I smiled at the music. It was strange to imagine my eclectic choices assisting the police in their inquiries. They might even call in for a chat today. It seemed that they liked me. I took out forty of my favourite records and began to make a list of what I thought investigating officers might like. I spent about two hours at this process. After about eight foolscap pages, listing music ranging from Mozart to the Chemical Brothers, I then began the process of subdivision. I took the following categories as themes:

1.   Drunken driving
2.   Conduct unbecoming
3.   Murder investigation
4.   Suspect arrest
5.   Case notes
6.   In the morgue
7.   Courtroom perjury
8.   Sex crime
9.   Friendly fire
10.   The Chief of Police
11.   Search warrant
12.   Drugs
13.   Thought Crime
14.   Interrogating the condemned.

I took them as themes for recording. It made the process easier. I labelled the tapes and began selectively recording. It took me the rest of the day. By nightfall, I was starving. I took some of Otto's money and bought a bottle of wine and a pizza. I cooked and ate the food, and, as the flies and maggots fell and landed on the pizza and into the wine, I picked them out. I finished the bottle of wine and fell into bed and slept soundly. I awoke to the ominous, gentle tapping at my front door. I looked out the peephole. It was Officers Smith and Jones.

"What a coincidence!" I said. "I was just thinking of you. I have your music."

"Good afternoon, Ms Tully. We brought goodies."

They had Chinese food. Won Ton Soup. Vegetable Chow Mein. Special Fried Rice. Sweet and Sour. A few cans of soft drink.

"Come in, Officers," I said. "You can lunch with me here. On the night shift, are we?"

"Indeed we are, Ms Tully. We thought of you as we drove past. Please join us. We brought lots. But tell us..."

Officer Jones looked warmly into my eyes.

"Yes?" I inquired.

"How is the manuscript coming on?"

"Manuscript? There is no 'manuscript'," I said.

Officer Jones went over to my typewriter and looked at my papers.

"I see the keys moving, seemingly by themselves. I like what is being written. Well-done, Ms. Tully..."This is the Dead Zone". Mmm. You shouldn't take too much to heart what you see here. It will all change. Reality is what you want... so they say..." Officer Jones said, reading my work aloud.

"Tell that to the death camp dwellers across the world, the crack babies and the rape victims..." I said.

"I see. Well... Okay. I will. Shall we eat then?" Officer Smith said, noticing my mortification and annoyance. They went into the kitchen.

"I have your tapes for you," I said, changing the subject.

"Wonderful! Bring them along. I remember there being a little portable machine in the kitchen." Officer Smith said.

"I'll take some won ton soup and a small saucer full of special fried rice, please," I said.

"I'll get the necessary utensils." Officers Smith and Jones settled down and began opening food parcels. I put plates down for them and got myself a little food. I looked underfoot. I saw maggots and flies disappearing between the cracks in the floorboards. I sat down beside them and sipped my soup and ate my special fried rice. They ate with great reserve and politeness. Eventually, I attempted a little casual conversation.

"Officer Jones... Officer Smith..."

"Yes, Ms Tully?" Officer Jones said smilingly.

"Do you two have sex with each other?"

"Yes, Ms Tully. Yes, we do. But not as often as you imagine."

"Isn't that – against the... rules..?"

"Strictly against the rules. Indeed. But having sex greatly increases our ability to work together. We have one of the highest rates of solving crimes in our precinct. Indeed, we are both up for promotion..." Officer Smith said.

"I am voluntarily celibate," I said.

"Do you fear and hate men?"

"Yes, Officer Jones. Yes, I do."

This was not true, but I thought I might say something worse than asking them about their sexual proclivities. Nothing seemed to unduly upset them. They didn't mind my asking about their relations. I didn't ask them if they were married.

"It will pass. I promise. Tell me about the Dead Zone." Officer Jones smiled, encouraging me to talk.

Officer Smith made a pot of tea and got cups from the press and poured out a cup for each of us.

"I don't know what the Dead Zone is. I don't think it exists outside my mind. I don't think anything that has been going on these last weeks exists outside my imagination. I am more afraid of being turned into a mental patient by the authorities…"

"But we are the authorities. And we are more imaginative than you might think, Solving crimes requires real creativity, you know." Officer Smith said.

"The Dead Zone is a place of personal psychic projection," Officer Jones said.

"Really..," I said.

"Those one is significantly karmically connected to, sometimes people one has no previous knowledge of, appear there during times of deep crisis. All that happens in the zone appears real to you. But others do not see it, with the exception of psychics and healers. They can see it, or at least understand what is happening to you…it's not a question of insanity. It's more a question of differing sanities in any given population, all competing for primacy.." Officer Jones continued.

The room was still clearing of flies. I was imagining my dead self there, in front of the typewriter, working away. I could hear the machine clattering away in my mind. I was writing something in my head. I couldn't see it yet. I couldn't see the paper. But there was a lot of paper. A lot of important things being written down. By me. I could not see The Corpse…

"Yes," I said. "That is my corpse. That is my dead zone, my death. I see others dead when I am dead myself."

"Good work, Officer Tully," Officer Jones smiled.

"You know, I just love what you have done with these tapes," Officer Smith said. "I love the different titles: 2. Conduct unbecoming, 3. Murder investigation, 4. Suspect arrest, 5. Case notes, 6. Morgue life, 7. Courtroom perjury!, I like it. Imaginative, don't you think, Officer Jones?"

"Brilliant, Officer Smith. Brilliant. Tell us, Ms. Tully. Do you think there is any possible escape from the Zone?"

"I don't want to escape the Zone. I like it here."

"That's not a good idea. We police the Zone," Officer Smith said.

"You do?" I said.

"And you are a tourist with temporary residency rights. We sorted out your paperwork back at central command. It does have something of a refreshing, realistic horror quality to it. We like your script. Yes. But I think it is better only to stay here until things have sorted themselves out. Then, immigration comes looking for you," Officer Smith said.

"And, then, there could be trouble..." Officer Jones said.

"You have been most helpful. I think I'll go back to bed. Play the tapes if you like, but keep it low. Goodnight," I said.

"We will let ourselves out in a while. Bye. You have greatly helped the zone police in our continuing investigations. Goodnight, Ms Tully, for now."

Officer Jones gave me a friendly kiss on the cheek. It was, I expect, something of a breach of protocol. I passed into the front room where Arthur Kruger decomposed, before going into my bedroom. There were so few flies and maggots left now. Before going to bed, and though I was tired, I decided to sit down and try to write, in an attempt to purge my uncertainties. Officers Smith and Jones had got me thinking. I put a piece of paper into the machine and knelt beside my dead self-facing the typewriter. I typed in the following question:

'Who is Arthur Kruger?'

I sat looking at the question in the front room gloom. Officer Jones heard the clatter of typewriter keys and came out from the kitchen to see what I was doing. Officer Jones looked at the question and smiled. She reached over my shoulder and typed the answer.

'Kruger is your dead self,' Officer Jones typed.

'That's nice,' I typed. 'Is he dead yet?'

'No,' Officer Jones typed.

'How does he die?' I typed.

'Suicide,' Officer Jones typed.

'Great. Why?'

'He gives up,' Officer Jones typed.

'Why?'

'Nothing to live for,' Officer Jones typed. Then she walked away. Officer Jones went back to the kitchen.

"By the way, this is just typical!" I called after her, and went to bed. As I passed into the bedroom, I saw there were few, if any, flies or maggots left. But I didn't care who I slept with.

I was too tired again and went to bed and rose about noon and went into the kitchen and the room was free of intruders. The police had thoughtfully washed and cleaned up after themselves and I made coffee and hash browns and eggs and put the radio on and listened, without comment, to the daily broadcasts on various channels. I ate breakfast, washed up and took a long shower, went back into the bedroom, made the bed and tidied up. I decided I would read for a while and then go out, perhaps into town and have a coffee, make a few calls and see what was happening, I picked an acceptable outfit, something not too understated or overstated. I left the house.

Goodbye. I'll be back in a few hours.

Arthur Kruger was almost reduced to bones by now. The maggots were almost gone.

And that day was the day it ended. It all ended as brutally as it began. Arthur Kruger was gone when I returned. I carefully scoured the house out with bleached water and could find not a single fly or maggot. I took my weeks' washing down to the launderette. I put the wash on. My hands were shaking. I did not realise how afraid I had been during the past weeks. Fear had numbed me, exhausted me, and changed me forever. I sat in the launderette, thinking about the Dead Zone, about the police who had heard me arrive and had helped me. I was frightened and disgusted by what I saw. I had slept poorly and asked for help, which I hated doing. I sometimes wonder if there really is someone out there called Kruger, who I will someday meet. But nobody knows if any of this is true. I avoid his place of work and never see him in crowds. Nobody knows if any of this really happened, or how it might be documented if it all were true. The Dead Zone Police never came back, I'm glad to say, and I haven't got a job or anything. I write more reviews for cash and don't rely so much on my folks for money. I started something during that time that is slowly turning into a book. I'm thinking of a title. Haven't decided yet.

NOVEL VI

INSIDE THE WHITE ROOM

I remember this time well. I remember it well, in the way memory charges the bits and pieces that make it up with a shocking unexpected pulse, a kind of assault of sensation, that tries to tell you just how well you think you remember a particular time, when all you have are those charged up bits and pieces of the past. You can think and think, but it gets you nowhere, all you get are just more thoughts, the mind devouring everything. So there are all these images in my head of the years following my retreat from corporate life. I have images of yellows and greys and deep deep blues and frightened finches leaving dark brown branches in terror. I have mental snapshots of trees with branches like twisted arthritic fingers and waif like leaves, and bits of multicolour plastic wrappers and old paper bags floating like gravityless angels in the autumn wind. Another image, I think, around the same time, is of an old man standing, frightened of I don't know what, like some mute symbol of all that is destitute in the chilling autumn evening.

I am standing by dull park benches with the day's newspaper wrung up in my pocket like a paper gun. I am looking at the city panorama behind the vista of Drumcondra Park. The old man is sitting on a park seat on a small hill, as Drumcondra Park rises and falls in undulations. Drumlins. And that same old man, sitting on the park bench, now stands up staggering drunk as I see him more clearly, as he looks away from the church spires and the apprentice skyscrapers just behind him, and the odd private helicopter whipping by, and the planes coming and going and the dull internal combustion engine roar, like a dying monster barely muffled by all this park green. And, in the back of my mind, wondering what I would do when I got back to my little house, I walk away. I will probably read for a while, I decide. Then, I would try to write something.

I remember sitting in bars listening to talk, the hard talk of business, the circular drunken words of the barfly, the experienced chat of the regular, the practised open-heart surgery of the practised patient. Talk about how partners are cheating on them, money lost or gained, clients and payoffs and deals, about sex and drugs and other natural disasters, talk of God, or office politics and its many relatives. I would listen to these people for a while, realising how good I had become at eavesdropping, noting the relative wealth and education and social and ethnic origins of the people I overheard, afraid if I did not absorb every scintilla of data, I would fail to lose myself in the moment. After a while, I would begin to think of my mother or father or my ex-partner Aron, with a sudden sense of indescribable sorrow. I would look at my watch or the clock on the bar or coffee house wall, and wonder to myself what they would be doing at that time of day or night. I had begun to drink heavily around this time and this fed my melancholy. I feared what might happen to my memories as the rot of time and alcohol set in.

I kept thinking of how the future was all over. I remember feeling that this time I was living through had all happened before, a time I couldn't recall, except dimly. I thought that time repeats itself in the manner of a play. Each new generation of directors rediscovers the script of the play and re-interprets it. They go out and choose a new flock of actors to perform the pageant of society and family and love and hate and war and power politics to another appreciative crowd who were frightened of the fascist control of time and wished they could escape it.

I was probably depressed. Probably? I ask myself. All these pessimisms were giving imaginative form to my depression and sense of isolation and self-recriminations. After all, I had given up a good job in Zero Corporation, a jettisoning I had done because of my desire to create another work of fiction greater than my own tiny life.

I had worked in Zero Corporation for five years, first as a clerk. Then, after they found me useless as such, they promoted me to the non-position of system administrator, at least for a time. Then, the inevitable happened. I became depressed and blamed it on the bickering, the lies and the corruption. I began to feel suicidal, couldn't sleep or eat. I began to drink heavily. I resigned. They offered me other jobs, a leave of absence, a promotion. I refused. Anyway, I had saved my money. I ate in cheap restaurants and did a lot of walking, noticing that once again I was beginning to lose weight.

I blamed the weather, deciding that the clouds and the rain were doing their best to ruin it all for me. I counted ten days of sun, the orange orangeness that imprinted itself so deeply on me from this time. Then, I counted twenty-three days of cold wetness, grey oily streets empty of cars, and closed windows with little shadows of pencil people moving back and forth, getting on with the drama. When the wet cold greyness went and I began to feel a little better, I watched the sun as it moved through the sky. It was late October, early November, and now there was still a little heat left over from summer and the sun was, once again, honey glow warm and it struggled like some newborn through the clouds and one could see that there was a lessness in the light and the darkening evenings creeping in and the car lights whizzing by in firefly pairs off in the distance.

The late afternoons to early evenings were pretty and orange, mostly dapples of orange, like the light coming through the brown trees and their browning leaves, the light growing fainter, floating everywhere with a feeling of softness, a quiet euphoria that inevitably accompanies being released from a prison of one's own making.

In the months after quitting Zero Corporation, there followed a period of calm, accompanied by a sense of freedom, a sense of regained perspective, a once lost self returned like a repentant prodigal. And, inside that calm I so carefully clung to, nothing happened. I slept soundly, dreamlessly, in the blue of every night, after so much sleeplessness and anxiety, where my appetite returned, where my drinking subsided.

I watched all the healthy neighbours going to work in the mornings, their children, with bright school bags and clear white smiles and packed lunches, piling into cars and the other neighbours indoors dodging the clouds, hurrying their spouses and family to their respective jobs, looking forward to an empty house, filling steel white dishwashers with the morning's crockery and cleaning their houses so that, sooner rather than later, they could ring lovers and friends and meet for drinks or sex or chat later on in the day. These people in red brick houses, or grey brown and steel high rise apartments, worried little over the proximate onset of destitution and loneliness, or, if they did, they had devised an effective distraction from such pointless feelings.

I was one with the others, the ones living in grimy one room bedsits, waiting for the pool of stillness within, the crystalline fall into the void signifying the end.

I had returned to my old habits of sitting up late, making notes and ignoring the door and the black bakelite phone that occasionally rang. My mail piled up at the front door, grey and ashen like autumn leaves. The phone rang every so often. The doorbell rang occasionally. I would hear everything. In the immense silence of the house, the slightest movement would register along the fibres of my nerves. I would sense the grey thud of footfalls approach my mortgaged doorway, then a pause, as I would see a hand reach for doorbell through my Howard

Hughes peephole. I would see a probing finger depress the buzzer, a black gloved hand, and I would hear the desperate scream of the doorbell. I would freeze and wait for the person to decide that there was no one going to answer. I would be shivering a little, feeling guilty that I did not want visitors. I sat there with my heart pounding, imagining them standing at the other side of the door, out there where atmospheric conditions are far from constant, wondering why no one ever answered, wondering if anyone lived there any more, if I was dead or ill or insane, or still in the country, wondering if they knew I knew who they were and if I was avoiding them for any specific reason. Then, after a few minutes of trying and failing, a sense of anger or embarrassment, or both, would lead them to go away, or they would go away and the conflict would be gone, at least for a while.

It was the tiredness and the cold I was feeling inside that wouldn't leave. My mind was a blue white cerulean screen, beaten by an endless flight of images. My ears heard the sound of the birdsong or a distant tap dripping. I was tortured by the way the shadows fall in the night when one woke suddenly after a vivid dream and one could not quite piece it all together. I awaited the inevitable dawn, when the whole circle of torment, white night and black day, would repeat once more. It was this, this inner maelstrom, which kept me by myself.

Sometimes, the electricity supply would be cut off, or the phone, or the gas. Only then would I go through some of the bills and pay them off by sending cheques. I ate all my meals in restaurants. I would find a different one each night. I would dress up in a good suit and take some money and eat quietly, with only some obsequious waiter to irritate me. After eating, I would come home and take off my clothes and lie in the middle of the kitchen floor looking up and saying 'I never thought it would come to this'.

And I remember lying there on the kitchen floor, thinking about these things, looking up at the cold white kitchen ceiling. Sometimes I would go out the back, and watch the spiders nest in the late late rain forest November, for the seasons had gone mad with global warming – seeing Daddy-Long-Legs stupidly fly into the superbly engineered spider webs, seeing the spiders creep over and paralyse the victim, truss them up as food for their burgeoning spider family, thinking of building an extension, or eating her husband, and I lying there listening to my tuberculars heaving, straining the oxygen in, lungful after lungful, watching, thinking, taking the time to finally breathe. Then I would take a hot bath and go to bed.

I decided to organise matters. I devised a schedule of daily walks and housework and shopping and eating out and reading in the evening and sleeping at night, but it didn't work. Things stopped. I saw the big chessboard on the table in the sitting room and the chess pieces strewn along the board and table and on the floor. I had arranged them so. This was my game. We are forever confined to the grid, if we play by the rules. I began to doubt what was happening. Then I doubted my doubt, two minuses making a plus, and I looked at the walls and the floor and the ceiling.

'I wonder if things were always like this. I mean, different...'

Photographs can be taken of how things were, their arrangement in space and time, but it all depended on how you saw such pictures. Our eyes registered the spectrum. Red orange yellow green blue indigo violet. Visible spectrum. Something between cosmic rays and the humm of electrical cables. Four hundred to seven hundred nanometers. Is my red your red? I decided it was better to check see if what I thought or felt was there, actually existed. So I did the delusional Cartesian cliché thing and I started to feel my way, trying to find out if there were more reliable senses, a better awareness that might feed my mind, a mind I trusted no more, a mind that was constantly deceiving me, a mind that gave no truth outside the heating coming back on and the electricity working, once cheques were written and mailed, and my best suits stowed away in the upstairs wardrobe in mothballs, and the sun coming up from the edge of the flat world, and my heart beating on when I kept breathing, and beyond this doorway there be monsters.

The truth was, I had lost my faith in reason. I did what I thought to be appropriate, reasoned, common sense, but I no longer believed what I was seeing, or hearing, or feeling, or sensing. I felt my way around the house, running my hands, my body, my flesh and bones along the walls, the floors, the stairs, the bed. My house was warm and clean and dry. Everything checked out. I had a checklist all made out to check my checking. I had written

1. Warm
2. Clean
3. Dry
4. Ordered
5. Home

And still I didn't believe anything I thought I sensed. I didn't believe my disbelief and disbelieved my disbelief was disbelievable. That was good, quite a relief after all that time of lyrical, fashionable, angst-ridden self-doubt. It was the front living room that drew me in as my refuge in madness. Maybe this was the back living room, I thought. A question of perspective. I was not really sure which name was right: back or front living room. As in a theatre, one's perspective on a thing depends from where you are looking, or not, as the case may be. I made a note:

Where the hell am I?
Front Living Room?
Or Back Living Room?
Or Living Room?
Or Where?

I could try to define my position in space and time with a set of predefined, universally agreed mathematical co-ordinates. But I mooted that notion, sensing it would not answer my question. Rather, it would serve as a type of cover up, an act of mental self deception, using maths and logic and geography and philosophy and the mind as a way of not asking the question of –'Where am I?'. I sat in the midst of the living room and set up my chessboard and replayed Fischer versus Larsen 1958 Portroz. I did not remember the game. I came across it by accident in one of the few books left in the house. It was called Some of the *Best Chess Games Ever.* I played the game through five times, and then put the chess set away and looked once more around the room. Outside, I heard the wind and the rain begin to fall. More nature sounds. Another Wordsworth moment, I thought, thinking of the rain falling on the leaves, dripping in tiny rivulets from leaf to bough, falling through tiny holes made in the leaves by worms and hungry insects and acid rain, and falling through space, and commingling with the infinitesimal, infinite energy formations of the air molecules and their many cousins, downward until finally striking the pavement, railing, human, dog, cat, bird, kerb, street, pebble.

I thought of the rain and decided on an investigation of the nature of the living room. Perhaps that would give me some clue as to where I was. Once again, I ran my hands over the smooth white walls of the living room. No clue there. From the end of the back garden, the room looked frontward. And, from the front gate, the room was at the back. I walked down the back garden, holding aloft my old huge golfing umbrella that I had stolen from a train station years before. I am nervous of trains. I tend to be accident prone anyway. I stood carefully at the end of the garden and looked at the house. It was raining heavily, with huge misty clouds swimming overhead, a plunging purple monsoon morbidity hovering portentously above.

The house just did not look good, so I decided to repaint it in a bright pleasing colour, but only when the weather got better. Perhaps another bout of honey sun, hopefully sometime soon. It was more than just the look of the house. I had a great fear of ghosts. I was afraid that, if I did not succeed in making my own mark on the house, then the old lady Crammerer, who owned the house before me, would return from the dead, as angry and lonely as I was, and seek to reclaim her space, her property, from me, and ruin my chances in the place. I had so many chess games to replay before death came, I decided. Better to act now. One can never trust the dead, I thought. They have a tendency to resurrect. I knew this partly from my own experience, also from that constant sense of hauntedness that followed my family for a thousand generations, the deep uncertainty over who was alive and who was dead, a pulse and/or a heartbeat and/or brainwaves being no guarantee of not enjoying a post-mortem status. Ghosts come back for many reasons: unfinished business, revenge, improper burial, finding lost love, boredom, or indeed, a lingering dislike of eternity. Other reasons for haunting, or Lazarus-like resurrection, such as poor quality reading material beyond the grave, or the eternal tediousness of being with the enlightened and politically correct, do not appear in sound theological debates, but are no less uncommon. Ghosts have been deprived of something everyone else is clinging to so desperately, for instance, a sound stock portfolio – so they get mean and ornery at the slightest thing. I had, therefore, to act, and act quickly.

Fourteen days and five hours later, the weather cleared. I took some money and bought five cans of white paint, white being a bright cheerful colour. I decided then, being finally a useful member of society, I could whistle 'My Bonnie Lies Over The Ocean' with a type of nondescript tradespersons cheerfulness, as I repainted the place. I put on my overalls and began to prepare the house for painting. Then something made me change my mind – a morbid fear of attracting attention to myself. What if people see I am repainting the whole house, and all of one colour? They will think me mad, quite mad. Looking again at the rooms and hallway, the toilet and the back shed, I decided not to paint the whole house snow white. Instead, I only repainted the back front living room snow white. If the old lady comes back, she can haunt the other rooms. It's hard to see a dead alive ghost against a background of white, I said to myself. The ectoplasmic glow doesn't quite work. I know, because my ectoplasmic glow just doesn't quite work. It's all down to colour co-ordination. Spirits from surreality come into the room, angry because their partners left them during their lives, or their love affairs ended badly, or their children ruined their lives, or they got fired, or raped, or caught in yet another movie, or a drive by holocaust, and they ended up domestic junkies, and they want to give you the scare of your life, only to find they are fading into the background with the supernormal glow of the brilliant gloss white finish, and they leave frustrated.

I worked over the walls, the curtains, the floor, the door, the mirrors, and the pictures on the walls, the photographs, and the fireplace, and painted them all snow white. It was a Coleridge's 'cave of ice' scenario, so white, such clarity and lack of division, so druggy and desperate and filled with ruined potential. So white on white. I was happy. I might even put it on sale, with myself as an exhibit. Maybe a good name for it might be 'the window frames me' or 'white on white' or 'my dentist made me do it', I might have a chance at the Turner Prize, though that one might be already used. After repainting the room, I renamed it the white room, gave myself extra marks for an imaginative title and, after giving it time to dry so that the smell of fresh paint no longer gave me nausea and chronic headaches, I brought my bed down from upstairs and put it in the white room, turning the head of the bed so that I could see the huge sycamore tree whenever my eyes opened from sleeping and there was light sufficient to see more than the moon and the stars. I would look up and imagine myself floating past Orion's belt in a self-sustaining life support capsule, having lived an extraordinary life. I was seeing things, beginning to enjoy this whole experiment in living, if that was what it could be called. I had created an imaginary world where I could begin again. I was inside, and seeing the tree was all that mattered.

I turned the mattress on the bed, changed the sheets and the bedclothes, proceeded to have a sink fitted in the corner of the room, disposed of the television and my music collection, retained only a small radio that plugged into a wall socket and didn't need batteries. I looked through my clothing and kept those things I figured necessary: three trousers, three sets of socks, underwear, a pair of shoes, an overcoat, an umbrella, three shirts, three jackets, and a wallet for the sake of retaining my sense of humour, not forgetting my chances for the Turner Prize.

The room was ready, and through its window I looked out at the overgrown garden with its trees grown madly high, their branches like wild unkempt hair. Huge tropical spiders had made their homes during summer in the hedges and a thick lattice of webbing spread from leaf to leaf, twig to twig. I looked at the complex spider underworld in the midst of the hedgerow and wondered if I could bring myself to cut away their overgrown metropolis. I hated to cause pain to anything or anyone. Despite my misgivings, I saw that the hedge was a problem too, for it was eating into the garden. It hung out like a beer gut onto what was laughingly called the lawn, trying by dint of force to touch its opposite side. But the spiders were working to help the hedge. Already tender filaments of spider web bound the two sides of the lawn together in a tentative marriage. The web of wedlock, I cursed to myself. Do you take this web to be your lawfully webbed life? The spiders were labouring to grow strong and extend their territories, like exotic Napoleons, not thinking of the Irish winter that would give them their kiss of death, not listening to their dreadlocked superstar spider poets in a haze of vision recollect the sunny climes from whence they came. I guiltily cut the lawn and trimmed the hedges. After the big garden pogrom, I disconnected the phone to the house. I had guilt to deal with. I had an nihil hated the populations of whole cities out there. Then, I went shopping and filled the freezer with food. This provision would reduce the necessity for daily shopping, which had become an excruciating experience for me. I was too tired to feel the proximity of people.

Then, I stopped. I sat and drank tea and made a sandwich. I didn't know what else to do. I decided I would get up in the morning and wash and breakfast. Then I would sit in the room and wait and watch the walls, the sycamore tree, the ceiling, the sky, the notebooks. This is what I did for three weeks. When no inspiration came as to the right course of action, I took to walking the streets. This I did for four weeks. I met nothing, except moving crowds, traffic, and busy people avoiding other busy people trying to get things done. I also met air and light and water and other particles I cannot identify.

I grew thinner and a little colder day-by-day, feeling dizzy and panicky in crowds, having to inappropriately sit down and take deep breaths and try to remain calm. Once or twice, I imagined I saw Aron moving through a shopping crowd. I ran across to greet her, forgetting all my promises, in the midst of traffic. Then I ran down the street, trying to make sure it was really Aron, all the time trying to remind myself that

I had sworn to leave her alone. Anyhow, it was never her. Somebody else. In the end, I just accepted that my mind was playing tricks on me and that I should really try to relax and accept how it was and that this was my life no matter what. I don't know if I ever succeeded in doing that, but I went on anyhow, and the walking helped. The pain of keeping going is always a good distraction.

After weeks of just walking and looking, I found the knots of panic and uncertainty inside me loosening and the panic of nothing to do going away. The problem was now that, after a long day of walking, though I would go home at night to cook meals and sleep, it got harder to get up in the morning. My limbs ached. I felt cold and disoriented. Maybe it was flu, a wearing down of body and mind, an attack of the mysterons that float in the ether of memory. I looked out at the garden and the sycamore, as though looking down the garden through the sycamore, between the branches with the icy knotty bark, would act as some type of sextant, a tool measuring my relative position on earth through azimuth and the darkening skies.

And the city was getting colder by the day. I could feel the oncoming subtle chill caress my skin, and, in the mornings, I felt my thinning body melt into the chill, as though the death it implied gave my moments left alive a substance never before understood. No more mixed autumn weather. The cold had set in. It was winter. Perhaps I was not eating enough. My face was lean and seemed to be hardening in expression, an embittered expression in the eyes that greeted me in the morning when I rose to wash and shave and eat, the expression of someone for whom things were not quite right. I would lie on in bed a little longer and watch the frost clinging to the sleeping winter sycamore, like a gothic Christmas scene, all white and black and twisted silver. Then the light came, inching its way past the horizon and the roofs and skyline and trees, and the day warmed a little and the ice melted a little, and I would creep painfully out of bed and make coffee. After coffee, I washed and shaved and put on my shoes and clothes and I stepped out to eat breakfast somewhere. Though I had little appetite, I ate sometimes two platefuls of food out of fear at my radical weight loss. Then I walked through the city.

I decided that the best plan would be to divide up the city into manageable gridlines and plan a route within each of these gridlines that followed no discernible pattern. I did this one Tuesday afternoon. Purchasing an up to date map of Dublin City, an architect's ruler, and several black ink pens, I drew lines, dividing the city up into equally sized rectangles. I numbered each rectangle, using the black marker. I then took two coins of differing value from my pocket, and tossed them onto the map. I chose the rectangle that had the coin that had turned up the highest number. Then I cut out that section of the city on which the coin had rested and made the random walking of those streets my goal for the next days, until I figured I had covered the grid well enough. I usually avoided those streets I had already walked down by marking off whatever part of the grid I had completed at the end of the day. In other cities, walking down certain streets meant risking your life, which I found strangely attractive. I wondered if I would cover a city of that size in a lifetime. Considering that I had divided up Dublin City into two hundred and seventy eight separate sections, and, allowing for the rate of growth of the city, which would inevitably require my seeking help from the Planning Section of Dublin City Council, I roughly calculated I would need three thousand, four hundred and fifty-six days, seventeen pairs of walking shoes and thirty-four pairs of socks to cover the entire city, excluding highways and areas designated as zones under construction. Even as I proceeded along this walk, the city would be changing, Dublin Port Tunnel, highways, train tracks, new walkways and bicycle paths, parks and shopping malls and cathedrals to consumers, parking lots and amenities for the powerful and well insured. The task would be impossible. I would be trying to chase a moving target, a living entity constantly becoming something different, like a rainforest, with parts being born and parts dying. I noted small inaccuracies in my map, and made special reference to these slight differences in a notebook I brought with me, though I did not submit my findings to the cartographers of the city.

After a few months of this, I was not able to stop it, and the thought of not getting up the following day and moving through my predetermined gridlines was unthinkable. I was like a wandering ghost, following a map blindly, compulsively, for the sake of following it, looking at the houses and people and traffic and rising at six o'clock in the morning each day, except Sunday. On Sunday, a day of rest, I rose instead at eight o'clock, and only allowed myself thee hours of walking, instead of the usual six.

I had, for the most part, stopped eating out as just too expensive, considering the funds I had left. In the morning, I had two boiled eggs, three slices of toast, thinly buttered, and a pot of coffee. During breakfast, I listened to the news, the weather forecasts, and dressed accordingly for the walking tour. I would take a bus to my designated grid and begin walking. I did not usually cover the interior of buildings, though I did visit galleries and museums out of weakness and curiosity. I avoided ordinary people. I also avoided alcohol, drugs, thieves and killers for the sake of health, the dangers they embodied, and their lack of ethics. In the evenings, having returned home with my map and notebook marked, I cooked a meal for myself, had a bath, listened to the news and slept soundly until the following morning. And I would dream that, though I had grown so thin and wasted, I really had covered the entire city, and the journey had made me someone different, that I had changed and come to grips with life, and had seen things. I had seen that people live mostly in buildings and work mostly in buildings, that streets and roads are what we escape onto in order to leave such buildings and, if we do not live in buildings, we do not live too long, though we all die in the end, and the process mostly took a lifetime. Then, I dreamed of how like our heart and blood and lungs and cells this city seemed to me, each part linked, parts growing and dying. Were it to stop, death would take hold, and kill it off.

I was alive in dreams, that part which could connect without action. It was action that posed difficulty, what to do, what action being the most useful, whether to work, or live, or not to live. What action would bring a response, a reaction equal and opposite? I could not speak, could not find words, could not find anywhere to go, did not walk without effort and pain in the instep and the arch and the thigh, and a stinging twinge along the lower spine that kept me awake now and then. I struggled to find words I could not find, tried to find myself after breakfast or before dinner, but failed. I kept my house clean and swept free of demons and prepared each day for my journey outwards. I followed my map, kept to the program, until I could do it no more. And, when I could do it no more, it was something of a relief.

I stopped walking after about a year. I was more unwell than I imagined and I didn't know how bad I was, mainly because I had lost touch with myself. I stopped walking all of a sudden. I remember waking up early, looking about the white room with the ghostly white painted glow, with the shoes and the socks and the trousers where I left them and then the memory of the streets and the faces and the din of homicidal traffic from the yesterday, and I tried to move and could not, like an invisible force holding me to the bed and the urge on me to urinate getting worse and worse "All right!" I roared out loud, and then felt a little embarrassed. I finished more softly, saying, "All right, I won't go. Damn you!" I hissed, knowing how right the body was. It was when I admitted the truth that my body slowly yielded to my will and I could feel things beginning to move and I fell out of bed with a thump and I cursed and I, like a cripple struggling out of the white room to get up the stairs, with the pain and the longing on me, tripping over my feet, using my hands to speed my way to the toilet bowl. I made it, pissed happily, remembering the horror of my previous bout of paralysis, as a younger, still living man, the shame of fouling oneself, and knowing I couldn't move then because my mind and body rebelled against my life, just like now. I finished and washed my hands and leaned against the bath and tried to feel something, aside from physical discomfort, then changed my mind about experiencing real human emotions, and went to have breakfast.

My body ached for contact, my mind hungered for discourse, and my house reeked of aloneness like a contagion. I carried a huge bag of laundry down to the laundrette, deciding it might be cheaper than using my machine. At the laundry, the spinning drums made me nauseous, so I could not read. Instead, I made careful note of those who came and went from the laundry. Six females, aged between twenty and thirty. Eight males, one in suit, two in casual sports wear, another wearing jeans and a white t-shirt, four dressed in track suits. Five females of indeterminate age, friends possibly, skirt, dress blouses, tank top. Engaging in conversation about sex. Lots of laughter. I noted the books they read, thrillers and horror and science fiction, magazines ranging from glad-mags to New Yorker. I saw whether they drank coffee (overall fifteen did, four did not), saw who they talked with, who talked with them, and who left before I did. I mused on their angst-ridden, carefully neglected, fashionable self-reflections, reading magazines and modern fictions, and waiting, as we all do, for something beautiful and unexpected to happen.

I tried to strike up a conversation with one or two of such gods as these. I mentioned the price of laundries, or the weather, or the article they were reading, or my thoughts on the world of fiction, which I knew a bit about. But they answered as briefly as they could and went back to their magazines and their fictions and their conversations, or suggested I mind my own business, so I gave up. I figured that my shyness made my attempts at talking to other people seemed too forced and it came out in nervous stammering, sounding lame and arousing embarrassment, or, worse, indifferent contempt. I looked at these people, who clearly had no interest in talking to me. I should have felt more hurt, more angry and blaming. But I didn't care enough, or had convinced myself that I didn't care. However, despite my desire to remain the objective observer, I wanted a connection. I wanted to reach out and touch these cold, self-contained, posed lives that appeared as insignificant as my own. I longed to see what made these people go on, who they loved and did not love, what their jobs were, what life meant to them. But I went home to the white room, and, on getting home, packed away my clothes and lay on my bed until it was time to do something. But there was nothing to do until it was time to eat. After I ate, I did nothing again until the next day.

On Tuesday, I decided to try to collect unemployment assistance. I had decided four Tuesdays before to go every Tuesday. And, every Tuesday, I was not successful. I queued for two hours and moved from one interview booth to another and was quizzed as to whether I was seeking active employment or not, whether I was attending interviews, and whether or not I had another source of income that I was keeping from the revenue commissioners. I refused to answer any of these apt and probing questions, on the grounds they might lead me to commit myself to fact, as opposed to supposition, or perhaps even dangerous conjecture about supposition. All this might lead to a catastrophic statement of fact, something that may, or may not, be the right thing to do. This made the clerks working at the unemployment exchange wonder if I, Kruger, were entirely sane, whether I was an out-patient at some reputable psychiatric institution, and whether there would be a riot if they didn't find some effective way of dealing with my weekly insistence, whether I deserved some type of compensation for my probable status as unemployable. Maybe I was just looking for attention, they thought. They knew I had money saved. They were unmoved by my protestations. They had checked my employment record. They had seen how much money I had earned. The police and the secret service and the government had all the facts about me. Security, or the police, would be called and I would be removed and told not to return. But I would come back.

After the weekly fiasco at the unemployment exchange, I, Kruger, returned home to the white room, having purchased along the way all shopping needed for the week, and, on passing through the front door, ignoring the dozens of unanswered and unopened letters that had neatly piled up in my in-box inside my front door, since I had left active employment, seeking passive employment, went to cook some food. I did not know then, but amidst that huge pile of letters were three cheques containing back money from my old job, two tickets to the opera, a final demand from my old credit card company, two glowing letters of recommendation, and a strange letter of inquiry from a publishing house in the UK wondering if I was the same Arthur Kruger who penned the Ten Short Novels, and if I had any other finished manuscripts, not to hesitate to send them to this little publishing house, as they were always interested in any work by the author of such a book.

But I was afraid of mail, afraid of the earth disturbing consequences of dead letters sent. I generally only checked for unpaid bills when gas or power was cut off. So, I put the mail into a box and walked down the hall to clean my house. Then, I lay on my bed until I decided there was something to do. Night came and I had begun to keep my mind amused with chess games I remembered from another life. I played badly, but I loved the game, which kept me playing. Symmetry and power. McDonnell versus Labourdonnais. London. Eighteen Thirty-Four. Move thirty-seven. I saw it. White rook captures pawn on square d1. Then black checkmates by pawn to square e2. The sixteenth match. Superb. Checkmate. I smiled up at the sycamore. The light was almost gone. I could see only the silhouette of gnarled twisted branches tortured in the wind. My body was stiff with the evening chill. Sometimes I forgot the body. But not now. Time to feed the dying animal. I cooked and ate and washed up and defecated and listened to the news. Then, I switched the radio off. And, lying down, listening to the wind whistle and gush through the trees and the fractures in the window frames I missed while hurriedly painting the room, I knew somewhere there was an unreason for this clean bed in this white room. The light was off and, once again, I was feeling the dull ache of loneliness, the memory of significant contact, that no amount of speculation or learning or success could replace. I switched the light back on for the sake of comfort and lay back down, staring at the white walls and the ceiling, turning and remembering what had happened to bring me here. Then I switched it off. I remembered.

Mental note to self: I have lain here all night looking at that tired old shifting Sycamore. In an hour, there will be dawn. The light will come over the roofs of sleeping homes where schoolboys and girls will prepare for school, and their fathers and their mothers will hurry to wash and dress and get to work, concerned for their emotional and physical well-being, for their cherished home and loved ones and their career in the cities and, I, Kruger, now roll out of bed and peer at the ticking clock. Five thirty-seven. Dawn will, according to Whitaker's Almanac, take place at five thirty-nine. There will be light in two minutes and counting. I go over to wash. Then, I check for breakfast money. Down at Counting Pascal's Eatery and Greasy Spoon I will take breakfast. One sausage, one rasher, one piece of fried bread, one cooking egg still sizzling with grease as it lands on the white off-white plate. This culinary event is two hours, thirty minutes away. But now, I sit on the edge of my bed and begin to take notes as the dawn strikes:

Fifteenth of the third twenty – Light peering through the trees, on this the six hundred and thirty-fifth day of my tour of duty in the white room, but who's counting? I shall continue in here until something happens. This event will consist in the emergence of a perspective on my future, a moment of enlightenment, the arrival of Jesus or Buddha, or whoever. I will then know what to do. Small day. Five degrees in the city, with the memory of Aron Tully lingering in the mind like a sweet unforgotten dream. All quiet on the silent. White room still but for the scratching of mice under the floorboards. Neatened the sheets and watched the trees. Trees still. Fingers of the leaves of the trees unmoving in the near dawn light. One minute until. It's still under the floorboards now. Mice quite still. Napping or having breakfast. Reading the Daily Rodent or doing the crossword. Here is the news for all you cheese lovers. But wait, there's more. Have you tried a holiday on Mice Island? Remembered a former existence in the night room of the mind. All dead now. All still under the floorboards of the minds. The children are no longer there. Jelly Wobble, quite still but for the scratching under the coffin lid. There's a good boy. Now learn your grammar and keep still. And I did. Pawn to c3.

Having finished noting, I continue to mark down the necessary procedures for leaving the house. Heating the water. Choosing the clothing. The shoes. The shaving. The ensuring of the securing of the house. The reading of two hundred words of the Divine Comedy. A game of chess. Or maybe two. The careful observation of the light though the leafless trees. The sudden urge to write something. Then, the word, the words! Not dead words, but alive! Then, the writing of five hundred words of Stories about People In Buildings. Might as well be doing nothing as something. This decision to begin to write again occurred at the precise moment I made the note. The chill stiffened my fingers. The heating cranked up on its time switch. I moved on from the suddenly joyful new manuscript and began to note the dimensions of the room. Six metres by four point three metres by three metres. I note the equality of the breath of the room by its height.

This experiment having been completed, I longed for my bath. I had to make it approach rather than wait for it. From memory, I knew that the best way to make the time pass more quickly, according to the laws of relativity, was to move less quickly, to lie down, to not walk, but to jog lightly around the room, using the bed as a centre point. So I jogged lightly around the room using the bed as a centre point, for a total of twenty minutes. By jogging around the room, I noted how twenty point zero zero zero three one six minutes passed while outside the zone of my movement. It took me twenty minutes exactly to complete my jog around the bed. Thus, I was marginally nearer my bath and thus nearer my breakfast, but not in a manner which fully satisfied my reasoning faculty. This pleased me greatly. I could only see the edge of the sycamore tree from the bathroom's perspective. Its leafy twigs clawed the sky, like an old man's withered hand. Looking for something. Looking for clues. Now where the hell did that lifetime go? I was sure I left it around here...

There began a bitter freeze outside that day. The temperature plummeted and remained in or around zero. Shivers. The heating system had warmed the water enough. I ran the water and watched the bath slowly fill for a while. The noise of the gushing water was such a violation of the stillness all about. I watched with a scared hypersensitivity, the still air forever shattered in the bathroom, the water cascaded from tap to filling bath, the sound waves carried and amplified by the water and the basin. Then, feeling a bit shaken, I trudged to the kitchen and boiled a kettle of water. I cut a slice of bread and buttered it and ate it, to take the edge off my hunger while the water boiled. Then I made coffee and went upstairs as the water began to run cold into the bath. I turned off the tap and got in and my blood ran warm, as I slowly immersed in the water. It had been a long journey and the night was gone and the coffee warm and I sipped it and I closed my eyes. It had been a long journey and there was only breakfast down town in the magical greasy spoon left to consider. It had been a long journey and I had travelled nowhere. The bath wombed me. It swallowed me whole. I felt a need to masturbate. But that urge had been the ruination of so many baths before, in a long line of memories of baths alone, loneliness following release, that post ejaculation surprise of all relaxation gone, and the deep need to be still, gone. So, like a good little schoolboy, I just said no. This isn't fine, I said to the self, as I lay there in the seminal warmth.

The image of Tully came into my mind, as she did at the most unexpected times. My last memory of her was in our old place, as she lay in a bath just like this one, but with a few notable exceptions:
One: The bath was cleaner, as I was more meticulous in my cleaning then;
Two: I had discovered her in the midst of a suicide bid. She tried to kill herself by slashing her wrists, after she thought I was dead after the train hit me, which was a tad precipitous of her.
Thirdly and most notably: her wrists were cut and the hot water was seeping redder and redder.
It must have stung badly.

I remembered rushing into the apartment calling for her, "Aron, Aron, sweetheart…" about to explain that I had somehow survived the train after being killed by it, had fallen asleep, presumably from shock, and I was feeling much better now and no longer filled with suicidal hopelessness, that death had its own charm and freedom built into it, that I had been to the other side and it was boring. I remember rushing into the apartment, filled with new life and new hope and my mind was racing madly as I ran upstairs, feeling euphoric, wanting to talk about it all, and no sign of her. So I went to use the toilet, only to discover the strange, still body of the almost gone Aron Ophelia Tully. Not a pretty, beautiful sight, not something easily forgotten, not easy to forgive oneself for. I knew I had failed her. I knew I was no good for her, or anyone. I knew I had to go. So, I called an ambulance, secured her, took some money and mail, and left. Remorse, I figured, will get us all. I remembered her. She looked quieter, so very still, so beautiful, the beauty of the almost dead, the beauty of letting go staying alive, such a stupid, stupid thing to do. Did she not know I'd be home, I thought, as I wrapped her up and tied her wrists and kissed her? I see her face in my mind still, her face with an absent expression, almost a smile, almost a look of ending anguish. I wanted to ask her what it was like in her own personal antichrist hell. Was it quiet down there? Or up there? Where are you? What are you seeing? It is seeing, or is it more than seeing? Then, I thought, I have been there, amidst the dead, and there is nothing to report. But that is my experience, the experience of nothing to report. Is it the same as before birth? Is it the same for everyone?

I looked down at the bathwater I was submerged in. This was too much. It was time to get out. I had lifted Aron Tully out of the bath, back then. Then, I stopped thinking of that time. There is nothing I can do about the past. I decided it was time for breakfast. I couldn't stay in, what with those words and images of her hovering about. I wanted to breathe elsewhere for a while. She still lived in me. I had taken every facet of her inside my being for fear of losing everything. I stood up in the bath and soaped myself from head to foot. Then, I lay down in the by now tepid water and rinsed myself, then got out of the bath and dried off, and chose my clothes for the day.

Inside the greasy spoon, I huddled in a corner and ate ham, sausage, eggs, fried bread, and drank bad coffee. Ate slowly, quietly, feeling the weight, the unnameable weight, lift, lift, turn into something small and round and blue and beautiful and float off like some alien probe and I made notes on things. It was a relief, a sense of renewal. Something had changed. I had stories about people in buildings. I had read the paper and eaten my breakfast slowly and made notes of things in the greasy spoon.

After breakfast, I walked home to the white room. Three thousand, two hundred and fifty-eight paces, each pace approximating half a metre in the morning light. I took the long way home and the long route involved traversing the city centre. I was, I suppose, out for a stroll.

The rain that had started during breakfast, stopped. Between the clouds, the sun had risen, between the trees and the questionable horizon. On the white floor, beneath the indivisible speeding sunlight, I marked its progression across the room, noting the date and time. By three-thirty in the afternoon, despite the increasing gathering of the clouds, I had timed the progression of the light and shadow across the room. I noted it carefully in my notebook. Then, satisfied with my work, I lay on my bed and played another game of chess in my head. I was getting better at that. Before, I had been able to hold only so many permutations of moves in my mind. Now, I could progress half way before the pieces would fly off into the oblivion of my exhausted imagination. I lay and dozed for a while and decided once again against masturbation as a futile act, as the question of their being a self to stimulate in the first place would cause more grief than joy after the event. Deciding that I had, somehow, once again, successfully checkmated myself, despite the use of the Alekhine defence, on the twenty-eighth move, I turned over and napped once more for a while.

Waking up, I looked at the wall and noticed that the sun had approached the gradation of the evening apogee and hunger was gripping my thinning frame, I decided against food until a few questions remain questioned, but inevitably unanswered. I walked over to my desk and looked at the manuscript. Only a few pages, but it is a beginning. I thought of the other possible careers I might have pursued:

Some useful things to do (possibly without the rest of my life)
One: Play chess.
There is nothing like a bit of strategy to keep the mind from thinking.
At night: Review the notes.
Two: Measure varying gradations of light and shade that creeps through the white room during the day.
At night: Review the notes.
Three: Note changes in Sycamore tree as the year progresses.
Describe using non-specialist nomenclature in three hundred words or less... 50 marks.
At night: Review the notes.
Four: Become a lawyer doctor mechanic gardener storm trooper detective proctologist dentist clerk used car salesperson. Every young person needs a career.
At night: Review the notes.
Five: Get social. Go to parties. Meet People. Be witty and interesting. Drink beer, wine, spirits, smoke dope, talk too much cover up the dark. Eat bread and cheese, vol au vents, tasty snacks that make you sick. Visit the relatives on a Saturday and admire how smart and pretty

their children are becoming. Look forward to a better start. Tell them all you've done. Tell them about the promise of a bright future, just beyond the horizon. Be amusing and self deprecating. Use your knowledge as a defence mechanism. Remember Christmas and picnics and holidays in the sun. Don't ever review, reflect, remember. Don't ever review notes.

At night: Review the notes.

In the distance, there came the drop, the falling of an envelope, the sound of a letter being pushed through the letterbox and then the grip of gravity. I had put a cardboard box in front of the letterbox to stop the annoying letters getting all over the floor. I walked over to the letterbox. More mail was falling into the cardboard box. I picked up the first letter and opened it.

It was from a billing agency. 'Congratulations Mr. Kruger you have been pre-approved for a credit card.' Thieves, I said to myself. Thieves in business suits. I tore it up.

I picked up another. It was a gas bill.

Another. A letter from the local residents association, giving a yearly statement of income and expenditure.

Another letter gave an offer from a roofing contractor. Another was a wrong address.

I sat down in the middle of the hall and began to go through all the letters, out of a compulsive curiosity. I separated those letters from people or institutions that were looking for money, in other words, bills, from those who were not. I disposed of those letters looking for money. In the midst of those that were not looking for money, I came across that letter I mentioned earlier from the publishing house in the UK, wondering if I was the same Arthur Kruger who penned the Ten Short Novels and if I had any other finished manuscripts, not to hesitate to send them to this little publishing house, as they were always interested in any work by the author of such a book. I read the letter again, in case my senses had deceived me. I stood up and put the letter on my bed. It was dated six months ago. I took out a sheet of paper and wrote a letter.

> Dear Sir or Madam,
> Thank you for your letter of interest in my work. Yes, I am the same author of the work you mentioned, the Ten Short Novels by Arthur Kruger. I do not know how you got my address, but I am glad to hear from you. I have been not myself for a while. But I am better now. I have begun a new book, which I am calling Stories About People in Buildings. I am in the process of writing it, and I am not sure just when it will be finished. If you have any interest in seeing the manuscript, I would be happy to send it to you. Please reply, as I have only now received your letter after six months.
> Yours sincerely,
> Arthur Kruger.

I sat back and read the letter I had written to the little publishing house in the UK. Good.

I leaned back on the bed and smiled up at the Sycamore. It was outside the white room. I thought of all the time I spent staring at those white sane white walls, those white tablets with nothing written upon them, after day after day of waiting, day after day of stopping and, there, in the reflection, the soft words linger like ghosts, words like ghosts, spoken in insubstantial whispers, words from the tongue reach, reaching proboscis like for the object of their love, lingering like heroin in the dead veins of the insubstantial Ophelia Aron. I felt the love again, the beginning again, the. In the beginning, there was just this moment, and the memory of others.

7

NOVEL V

I Believe In What You Do

I am in my dead son's room.
My dead son. Arthur. Arthur tossed himself in front of a train.

This old house still hasn't been sold. Perhaps they will never find a buyer for it. I can always rent it out, though. A few hundred from the funds should be enough to do the renovations necessary. One could turn it into four or five flats. They won't notice the ghosts and the visions that frighten me. They aren't for them and they aren't born to see such things. After all, you could say that I have been made sensitive to them. They cling to the walls and whisper from the ceiling. That is how it seems. I am afraid. I am always afraid, but it doesn't matter. Maybe the only way to escape it is through burning the place. I feel like doing it. Some days. It is insured, so there will be no loss to me anyhow.

Some days I feel this. This grip. The grip these things, this room, has over me. Sometimes, I cannot think clearly. I remember my mind as once different. Sharp. Sharp as steel. Kitchen knife-like. Now I have moments of clarity, only moments though.

I fixed this room up. Arthur's room. I changed everything, the decor, and the furniture. I even widened the windows in this room to give it more light. I kept his desk. The room looks better now. It was so dull and smoky when he was here. All those cigarettes and pipe tobacco. Sometimes it doesn't look so good. I remember, you see. Sometimes seeing is enough. Sometimes, seeing the door is enough.

I come here now every so often. I come here to remember. Not so much to be maudlin or wallow in the pain. I come here because I have to. Some days, I can pass that door back there. Some days, I cannot.

Some days, I see the door and the attraction is too much. It is like that for so many mothers and fathers and sisters and brothers in my place. They all do it. It is not a museum to Arthur, my son.

I fixed this room up. Arthur, my son, had not lived here for years and he took everything, save a few boxes of redundant papers, that turned out important only to the detectives that called after he was dead.

It would be like this. I would see the door. I walk up to it and here I am. I fix the room up every so often. I repaint and replace the bed and refurbish. It looks nice. He does not haunt this room. I do. He didn't care much about his stuff. His books or papers. Once or twice we caught him putting everything in boxes to sell.

It bothered him to have things. He wanted to get rid of everything: Money. Books. Words. Stuff.

Words bothered him. As a consequence of being bothered by words, he was addicted to writing it all out and saying little. He couldn't see the point of words. He was out to get those words and make them talk.

He said that to me once, when I was talking to him about respectability. He asked me why I needed all those words and weren't they a bother to me. These respectable sentences. Having all those words. Wouldn't it be better to just let them go? I hit him hard across the face for that. There was no other answer. He was being disrespectful to me.

I stopped talking to him much after that. I left it to his father. His father didn't say much.
His father kept asking questions.
Well... hum... well...
How are you then?

What are you doing with yourself?

Do you have a job?

No answer for a while, an awkward silence and then the words would mutter themselves out, like reluctant conscripts forced out of the trenches to certain death.

Yes, he said, I have a career. As a member of the unemployable classes. His father tried, you see. Then I tried. Then we tried again. Nothing. Believe me, please...

I mean, it wasn't us. I mean, I know we shouldn't. I mean. What I mean is. When we heard what had happened, that we had, he had... I mean... That he had thrown himself like that, in front of the train, you see... I never thought that he was capable... I never thought he was so serious about it all... I think we pretended it was not like that, that he was confused and that his father and I got unlucky. Some people are born confused. We wouldn't dare say that. It would be – hurtful...

We naturally felt. We thought about it and we felt a lot about it, you see, and, and, the police came to us. They wanted to see everything Arthur had put down on paper and we let them go through his stuff. But then I said, Arthur took everything. The detectives smiled and didn't listen. One of the young detectives took the stuff to Aron and she read it to the young detective. Then, the young detective came back and he seemed different. He asked me if I had read any of my dead son's work. I said no. He didn't like that. I knew he didn't like that.

The young detective sat in Arthur's room for hours. He was a nice young man. He sat in Arthur's room so professionally and read through page after page. I didn't realise there was so much material. Arthur didn't like visitors and didn't go in for quiet chats about what he was doing and where he was doing it. I think he had a lot of friends that his father and I didn't know about. I don't know, but I think that.

Information is sketchy, I said to the detective. He was a secretive boy. But I think he had friends. He came and went at all hours. All hours, I told the detective. All the hours. After all, I told the detective and the young detective reading at the time, Arthur used go out for such long periods. But the detective wasn't listening. The young detective was sitting at Arthur's desk, just sitting there, looking out the window at the back garden. He had put down what he was reading. His hands were draped along the two arms of the armchair and he was gazing, just gazing. I felt unwelcome in my dead son's room. I think I might have said something that might have upset him. But he wouldn't tell me. He took some boxes of stuff away and then I didn't see anyone. A week later, there was the funeral. It was a beautiful day in June. Aron was there, and she alone, and there was no other friend there. Just his father and I and Aron. It was a quiet ceremony. We insisted on a religious funeral, despite Aron's loud objections. It was such a bleak thing, the Mass, the near dead flowers draped over the coffin lid, the slow movement of everything, the horror of separation, the dry mechanical solemnity, voice of the priest, the clear sunny day, the clear clearblue sky, and the sound of the birds. The crunch of new shoes on the pavement. The goodbye. I think he was glad to be dead, glad to be out of the terrible business of living. Maybe that's what the young detective found out. I think young Arthur Kruger didn't have the will to go on. His father and I had the will. I think we failed him in that regard. We failed in giving him the will to go on.

Then the detectives came back and asked a thousand questions.
How would you describe your son?
He was a good boy. He had his own ideas about things.
And did he have any friends that called for him regularly?
No.
Did you have any disagreements with him?
No. Hardly ever.

How would you describe yourselves?

What?

When was the last time you saw or spoke to Arthur?

Six months ago.

Did he call home often?

What?

Well, thank you for that and we are sorry for your trouble.

And they were returning a probable conclusion to their investigations of death by suicide.

Then his book came out. About six months. Aron had found a publisher. She got the advance fee, and the royalties for the moderate sales over the following years. It was hardly ever out of print. That was the strange thing. I read it. Awful.

We couldn't stop it. Such an awful, awful thing. I read a little of it. Then I put it down and a few weeks later read it through. Awful. It hurt his father terribly.

He had married Aron. Aron was a lovely girl, I must say. So quiet and sensitive. I think she understood him. I envied the understanding she had of him. A good girl, I must say. And we still are friends. I get the odd card from her, the odd phone call. Not too often, mind you. At least she accepted him. We tried to get to know her, to try to reach out, you see. In a real sense, she was all we had of Arthur. But she didn't want that, though she kept up contact.

Aron came for dinner, you see. And I cooked my best and Arthur's father helped and we tried to have a good time, but we knew, even then, it was a doomed thing. The silence and the tension. It was a doomed thing. Each of us sitting across from the other, wearing our

best evening faces. With our polished knives and spoons glinting in the candles. We sat across and tried to smile. And Arthur's father asked questions.
Well.
And how are you keeping?
And.
When did you and young Arthur get married?
And.
Then.
And what is it that you do?

Well.

We didn't know that. We didn't know till much later that she and Arthur had married. We just thought they were living together. It came as a shock. He had excluded us from so much. We felt even more shocked. These whole lives he had conspired to live without us. I was so hurt and angry. So hurt. Aron didn't tell us till much later. She said that she understood that he had nothing to live for, except what he wrote. No one could change that she said. It was the way of it. She said she understood that soon after she met him. She said she didn't know why.

She had the right to do with his estate, well, whatever she wanted. His estate fell to her. His estate was the one manuscript and the boxes of stuff, mostly notes, left behind. Pens and typewriter and the odd bits of clothing Aron had kept him in. Our lawyers told us so. So the book came out. Awful.

Arthur was born into love. But love was not enough.

He was a bright boy. Perhaps that was it. Something shone from within him. He was a beautiful child. I thought it was such a miracle when I held him in my arms. Such a beautiful child. Though, every mother will tell you that.

Some children are not quite right. Born, you see. Not grown, like now. Now, you can pick the sex and the intelligence, if you have the money. I read the papers. Born into the love that is never quite enough. Born into the love that can never be forgiven.

They learn to mistrust love and blame it for their misery. They become the gene police. They never forgive the love.

The love a mother feels is different. It never dies. It is an affirmation of life and that they too have life inside them. I knew that feeling when Arthur was born.

I held him in my arms and I knew I was someone. I had taken a step forward. I had taken the step.

Some mothers feel that cold dutiful love. Some feel not even the cold duty that they deem to be love. But not I. Arthur was conceived in love. Arthur was wanted. When he was born, I had a clear sense of liberation, not a sense of imprisonment. No. I was ecstatic. It was a difficult birth, a terrifying thing. A horror and an ecstasy of death, those things from which comes new life. Death and birth and the two sides of the one coin. Only a mother could know. To know birth is to see the other side of death. But that's something entirely else. I remember the hospital. I couldn't deliver. They reached down into me and drew him out. Forceps. I don't know if they do that anymore. I don't know if it was what he wanted. I sensed he was disappointed with his birth.

It was not quite right.

But where was his father? Well. He was on his way. His father insisted on a room to myself in the hospital. We could afford it, but I was not so sure about it. I thought it might have been better to talk to other mothers, something I am not so good at. But his father, didn't want that. He didn't want his wife in a public ward. I guess I didn't want that either. I didn't want to be a bother. But the snobbery of it left me alone. They had to induce birth and I was terrified alone.

The pain was unspeakable. It was only a child, I said to myself, not a tumour. Really. But young Arthur would not be born. They said there were complications. So they made it happen. They reached down into me and drew him out. He didn't want to come out and when he came out, the pain ended. I knew nothing until he was born. And I held him and kissed him and was in love and then we slept. The relatives and the friends and the acquaintances and the professional associates and the neighbours all came. They came and they told us what we already knew. They said that the baby was beautiful and we should be happy. We were happy.
I was happy.

And then he started to get sick, and young Arthur back home only three weeks. His faeces was green and he could hold down no solid food. Crying day and night so much laying there, his ears filled with tears. And then the child went silent. And that was scary. Still baby. All of a sudden, you see. It was heartbreaking to see him like that, could do nothing, and the little one once upon a time screaming and screaming and the pain, the pain. Then still. Not a gig. Rushed to hospital. Called the ambulance. The doctor could do nothing and the hospital. Isolation ward. That was the beginning. Complete isolation for the child for weeks and weeks. We could do nothing, except look in through a glass wall at our little Arthur.

He came home on diets and isolation and surgical conditions. It cost us a fortune on medication alone.

So he lived only to die. He survived a bad beginning, only to die. At thirty-one, he throws himself in front of a train.

There was something not quite right.

Of course, a child never understands what a father and mother go through. How he came to live like that. The circumstances of his existence beyond all our controls. His parents' history. Their parents' parents' history. History was another thing he did not see. All the fights that went on. All the things that keep us going. All the arguments with my parents. Truths and misunderstandings. These things, little things, that pass us by, only to take a little from us, as they pass us by.

He went into his own world. Not one for friends. Of course he had friends. School friends. People, so unlike him, who came to the door and asked if he was in. Yes, yes. Arthur is in. Arthur, some of your friends are here. And they would play football with him. For a while. He did so well. For so long. At his lessons. He became the good little boy. He tried to please, but trying to please was all too much for such a fragile psyche.

Loved to play. Happy little boy. So it seemed. I was too hard on him. I knew it. I said sorry son. Sorry, Arthur. I had guilt. Guilt too late. I ruined it. I don't know how. I know he doesn't blame me. How could he blame me? I did nothing, nothing...

After he left school, he couldn't keep a job. The effort to succeed had warped him. His father found him work, gave him money. But he would stay for a while in whatever job it was and then go quietly into the night. He would go out at eleven or twelve o'clock and walk the city for hours and come back when we were all in bed and drink tea. We kept to our own routine. Then he would go to his room and read or make notes.

This was his life.
He would sit in his room alone. And no one would see him. For hours. Fewer and fewer called for him. I suspected homosexuality, pederasty, witchcraft, serial killing, masochism, death threats, robbery, murder, drug addiction, mental illness.
It was worse than that. He was writing something.

He would not come to the phone as a rule. If he were alone in the house, he would never answer the phone. We had to answer the phone and then get him. If we managed to get him to come to the phone, he would mumble monosyllables into the speaker. Words and half words. Yes. Good. Right. I guess. Right. I see. Great. I see. Okay. Well, thanks for calling. Right. Goodbye. He would smile. And I would ask who that was. And he would smile and go back to his room and my eyes would follow him up the stairs and I would wonder who that was, or if it was anyone.

And I would ask him why he never called anyone.
I would ask him if he had girlfriends.
I would ask him who that was at the door, on the phone, or who he was out with, answer my question please, I'm your mother, your parent, please talk to me, will you talk to me?
Please?
Would ask him was happening to his life.
What was going on?

Arthur?

What were you doing in that damn damned room?

Alone?

Why he spent so much time alone.

What was wrong?

What were these notes?

Notes everywhere.

Are you depressed, lonely, feeling your life is going nowhere?

You know we love you, your father and I love you.

Anything, anything at all, yes, we mean that, we do.

It didn't seem right.

He said, I don't know. I don't understand this either. Didn't call anyone? Never had anyone over for drinks or talk? Never got introduced to a friend. His father and I often mentioned it. Jack said not to worry. It was just another case of history repeating itself. I said there was more than just history repeating itself. It was his history coming to an end. And, one day, he said he wanted to leave home. Of course, we said. Of course, we would love to help.

Then there were the jobs. Working in hospitals, bars, fast food places, strip joints, brothels, coming home at five in the morning, exhausted and drunk or stoned, sleeping till five in the day, coming down the stairs dreamy and distracted, leaving money on the side of the fridge and then dressing, and then gone again, until he would, for no reason, leave only to sit alone again, for days, until he left everything. Working for the.

I don't know. I really don't. Sorry, sorry.

I sought family therapy. He argued with the therapist, saying that the notion of the family as the fundamental social structure was a capitalist bourgeois construct. His father and I looked at each other in astonishment. Arthur said that human relationships were the fundamental structure of our social charter, not just or necessarily the family. The therapist didn't bat an eyelid at young Arthur. She said, so what? So fucking what, she said? This infuriated young Arthur. He said, stop playing games with me. She said, this is not a game, this is not a family review. This is your life. No it is not, said Arthur. No. This is the end. And then he walked out. I had never seen him so angry. Though, he would never admit to being angry.

He disappeared. We called the police and then one day he rang. It had been a month. A month without so much as a word. The police couldn't find him. He said he was living with a girl, that he had been living in some old hospital, that he had met a girl and that he would call up. So we had dinner. His father questioned him as to what had happened, why he had left therapy, why he was so angry. He said he was fine, that he had money, that he had a job and that there was this girl. Her name was Aron and they were living together. But the truth was he had nothing. The truth was he had no job. She was looking after him. Perhaps they loved each other. I didn't know that they were married. It was only after that the book, that awful book, came out.

In the end, I honestly felt it was as though we did not exist for him. I did not know that he was a writer and that he saw himself in that light. It seemed so arbitrary and delusional, so outrageous, considering everything he had seen and done. Writing was the last thing we expected of him.

But it was worse than that. Neither his father nor I ever knew what we had done to be shut out of his life. Perhaps it was that we did not understand. He had gone cold. I looked into his eyes in the way a mother would understand and I was uncertain as to what I wanted to see. A memory of something that we had. Then I stopped looking.

It wasn't all silences and division. There were long periods of us getting along. Love and other loving things. There are the compromises one works at. We tried then for some time. While he was alive. We weren't good at this, I said to myself. We weren't good at playing the role of the bad parents that he has cast us in. We didn't do the disapproving distant parent act well. And one of us would call Arthur, or Arthur would all of sudden call us. I guess he thought he should. We didn't know why.

Then we would talk. He would detail the graphic nature of his feelings of being misunderstood and alone, his feelings of being unloved. I think it was something he learned in therapy, because, though we tried to listen to him, we didn't have a clue what he was taking about. We never failed to love him. He just was different. He was born that way. We were not the enemy.

Then would come offers of reconciliation. A decision to dialogue that reverted to discussion. Yes, we understand your need to follow your own destiny. Yes, I accept that life is imperfect, that sometimes misunderstandings occur. We will put it all behind us.

To try to be better parents. To say sorry and hug. To send gifts and friendly cheques that support the arts in the post. To hope for a publication. To remember Christmases and birthdays. To carry on regardless.

I took courses and reskilled myself, lest I become depressed. I got a good job and worked hard.

I too attended a therapist, as was considered necessary and fashionable for my status as the mother of a troubled child. As I said, I reskilled myself. Allegedly, I got a life. For a while, I wondered what we were doing all those years. Arthur's father distanced himself from the drama of mother and son trying to understand each other. He adopted the stance of the distant father. I shouldn't say this. Shouldn't obsess. Shouldn't be in here if the truth be known. That's why we're renting. Part of the process of letting go. Getting out, in a way.

He lived an isolated, self-contained, self-reliant life and assured himself of sufficient security and income to guarantee his self-reliance. In a sense, he was just like his son, only with more money. But he continued to talk to his son. And, for the time being, it was enough. So we thought.

A mother can see when her child is going away from her. It brings on a panic and confusion all of its own. He was made bitter by living with people who were bitter themselves. We blamed him for our bitterness and our own sense of failure. Perhaps if we had had other children, someone might have been born who understood and bridged the gap. But he was somehow long gone, long before we understood.

I think I passed all that on, a dissatisfaction at something neither his father nor I understood. There is more to ordinary unhappiness than the ordinary. He took on a type of passive resistance to what we held to be true, to our ordinary unhappiness. He rebelled. He rebelled against nothing. He took up writing as an exercise in futility and we couldn't understand. We couldn't understand because we wouldn't understand.

I figured that out after he was gone and he had killed himself. We made him so unforgiving in so many ways.

His father was more inflexible in other ways. Would never give up a point, never surrender a principle. I think that's what made his son equally so. There were two of them in it, too. He was never a respectful boy.

But his bitterness was lost on me. I was desperate and relentless. And my desperation, my relentlessness, reached out to him long after he was gone.

You know, I can see him at times. I walk down high street, or walk in the park and I can see him reading on park benches, or sitting in the windows of bars with a note book. They say that is part of the mourning process. I would feel the old anger at the waste of it all.

That was the nub of it. I was addicted to him. I couldn't let him die. So he did it anyway. After all, they are a part of you. Their life grows inside and, after they are gone, one is the lesser for it. I can feel it. Feel. One of my turns.

Dear Arthur, or should I call you son. Should I call you. Dear.

Dear Arthur. Jesus wept. I cannot touch you, except with my mind. Dear Unperson, or should I call you Hero… As a rule, all my life I have ignored you. I worked at it and ignorance was a roaring success at its job. Unfortunately, one cannot always legislate for the completely unexpected. Crisis struck like the bubonics and brought me retrograding to my sense of humour. It was my sense of humour that brought me back to basics. Now, I am full of jokes. Perhaps that is what I am. I have become a story with a comic ending. I am full of anxious banter. Perhaps I am dodging the main event. I am full of dreams and other mental games. Perhaps the tedium of this place is too much. I look constantly for alternatives. I drink too much. I have casual sex. My husband doesn't know me. There are always possibilities, I am told. I am full of integrity and scheming sinful deceit.

I am Mother. There is no reason for fear. This is my dead son's dead body. Move along please. Nothing to see. Nothing to see. This is the day. This is the light from beyond this room. This is the time. This is it.

Like ants, we seem to be scrabbling over sandcastles through forests and cities, until the wind and the rain files it all down into the dust, into the reports filed away by another office full of secretaries.

Shouldn't be her. Aron.
Shouldn't be here.
But here I am.

Switches on the bedside light and pages through the stastical manuellas of the psychiatrical angels of desolation. I see the lords of the underworld heave mightily downwards as the tectonic plates of the last words before lightnight splinter and crackle like an old hags mother last laugh on a brighter note. There is no better life to be sought. I thought they thought, nothing to be understood seen, prophesied over, but that's another question for another day and whom but the mothers of desperation take comfort in oracles?

What we see, do, and have done changes little from one age to the next, she thinks and smiles, turning the covers and fixing the mantelpiece and goes towards the door...

The hatchets are batoned to death. And the wood walls rot eternally and the storm rages unto its last breath, and the new borns scream hollow in the gales of laughter, and the squalls of the young melt like ice into the storm walls of rage.

That wash the universe of light, you hear me can you see me can you can you can you hear me love I believe in everything you do I do, believe me.
Mmhhh? What's that sound?

Turns, turning round. Frowning from closed lids. Closing, closing the door...

Days darkling before unblinking sleepless eyes peeled rimless eyes watching, watching, as the curtains in the bedroom quiver and scratch against the heathcliff glass. God knows I'm good and it's a darling day outside, the clear light of dawn choking the dark in a fit of hate. Moving other than the wind pulse, making everything naked, sweeping under the door between chair legs, under the blanket covers, shivering with age. Just don't tell me. I don't want to know. Don't want to see. Don't. However did it come to this? You, you again. Always you, my love.

NOVEL VIII

Genuinely Interesting People

Though I have little talent for friendship, I once was a friend of Joseph Pinkers. Successful and brilliant and irrevocably alone, Pinkers made a religion of intimacy in the way only the lonely could. Pinkers, the perfect academic machine, utterly dedicated to self-advancement, rose through the academic ranks of the English Department like a force of nature few could resist. Established early in his career with a series of groundbreaking articles on Samuel Beckett, he followed them with a singularly beautiful collection of "Stories about People in Buildings," some of which had been published in the New Yorker just before he got tenure. Then came professorship. He knew he had arrived.

Talented, charming, articulate, moneyed, successful, I was bitterly jealous of him. By comparison, I was a non-entity. I luxuriated in my unhappiness. I was talentless, abrupt, nervously tongue-tied, an unsnappy dresser, girlfriendless, a common or garden failure. Suffused in the neurotic knowledge of my own non-entity, Joe rarely neglected to pay me the complement of his company. I basked in the iridescent glow of his magnificent, impenetrable, urbane, knowledgeable, sociability. My fear and self-dislike worshipped at the altar of his posturing at intimacy. I remained in awe at his talent for making alliances and social contacts feel like lifelong friends, lifelong friends that loved one another. I am sure they still call regularly to see him when he is at home.

Rachel looked stunning the night she introduced us. I lingered over her body as she came out of the crowds in this magnificent night-spot, the latest trendy bar she typically arranged for us to meet in. Tonight she was going to introduce her new man. She cut through the knot of people already gathered about her and her man, put out her hands to take mine, and kissed me on the lips. Her kiss felt like being touched by God. Why does she not love me like I love her? I thought. Then, with flawless grace, she took Joe Pinkers' hands, and introduced us.

"Arthur, this is Joe. Joe, this is my good friend, Arthur Kruger. Arthur, this is Joe Pinkers."

"Hi," Joe said.

"Hi," I said. "Rachel, can I talk to you for a second?"

"Sure." She stopped smiling. We stepped away from the group.

"You didn't tell me I was getting into this."

"Into what, sweetie?"

"All these people. These... attractive people."

She looked coldly at me. My eyes luxuriated in her cold, gorgeous disapproval.

"Hateful, isn't it?" she said.

"What?" I said.

"I mean having to deal with nice people who want to talk to you, and even to one another, I mean, God forbid we communicate."

"Don't do that."

"Do what?" She said, getting increasingly irritated with me.

"That's not what I meant."

"I know what you meant, you anti-social jerk."

"There was supposed to be three of us, that's all," I said.

"Control freak."

"Am not," I said.

"Joe had to invite his friends along. They turned up at his house."

"Unannounced?"

"What can I say? People like Joe." She shrugged her shoulders.

"Now that really is hateful." She kissed me on the cheek and smiled. "Still love me?"

"Don't do that."

"What?"

"Kiss me. Like that."

She looked me in the eyes, and pretended to ignore what she saw.

"You know, Arthur Kruger," she said.

"What?"

"Nothing," she said.

"What?" I said.

"You and I are going to have to have a talk sometime."

"Except for the last few weeks, we talked most days," I said. "Then you found Professor Big Brain with his 'friends', and I don't hear from you."

"Don't worry, Arthur, yours is bigger than his,"

"I'm greatly comforted by your measurements," I said.

"That's not what I mean," she said, getting increasingly awkward at our sudden bout of unwarranted honesty.

"I know. We need that talk."

"Maybe. Maybe not. Now let's get you away from ink and paper and known to a few interesting people, okay?"

"Ink and paper is honest."

"Ink and paper is safe," she said. Then she took me with a long soft hand and led me to the group. I ached for her.

"I think I'm going to have a breakdown," I said.

"Wait until after, okay?"

"Whatever," I said, dreading the following hours of chit chat, probably of the very clever rather than the merely clever kind.

Pinkers watched us with a cold analytical eye behind a convivial smile. I saw him watching us in the midst of his friends, making flawless conversation as he amassed new data, eliminated what was useless to his advancement and therefore uninteresting, and promoted that which brought him more power. As I watched this fascinating sociopath, this predator, I tried to imagine what he was really thinking, rather than what my mistrusting paranoia told me he was thinking. I couldn't. He had a poker player's unreadability about his features. Pinkers was an attractive man. He looked in his early forties, clean shaven, well proportioned, athletic without seeming self consciously physical, the type of person who did not need high maintenance to appear fit and well to the casual onlooker, and, though his clothes did not particularly suit him, they were expensive, probably designer labels, and carefully and inappropriately chosen.

Eventually, despite my best intentions, I was formally introduced. My previous meeting was conveniently forgotten. I looked into his cold eyes and watched him download my soul piece by tiny piece. Rachel stood between us and smiled excitedly.

"Hello there," he said. "We seemed to have missed each other."

"Delighted," I said. I loosed my right hand from Rachel's and put out my hand. He smiled. I saw he had most of his chestnut brown hair with a little grey visible here and there, the accomplished look of the intelligent forty-something emerging, despite his overall youthfulness. Good genes, I thought. One could see from his clear blue eyes and good skin that he ate well and enjoyed decent health. His face was handsome, but not too handsome. It was the type of face that was a little thin to be striking in a crowd.

"Kruger. Arthur Kruger? Now that's a fascinating name. South Africa, I believe. Do you have relatives there?"

"I don't think so. I never went to the trouble of researching my name. I think my grandfather moved here in the fifties, when my father was in his teens. Hard to believe I am the son of an immigrant. I don't know the circumstances. It's a family fable, if you like."

His voice was soft with a self-conscious timbre, born from careful though by now unconscious elocution, a voice that amused rather than engaged. His face had clear thin lines from rim of nostril to mouth. His hairline was slightly receding, though self-consciously combed not to be so, with woven crows' feet pattern about the eyes that defined a person given to smile easily to cover up intense feelings.

"I see. Would you like a drink, Arthur? Rachel says you love pina coladas."

"Thanks. I do. I believe you teach college."

Pinkers nodded to the barperson. The barperson came over. He handed a large bill to him. The barperson smiled.

"English Department. Modern lit."

"You work there long?"

"I've done it for about twelve years or so. I like it. I enjoy teaching, and I write myself. So what do you do Arthur?"

He smiled at me in the way he had smiled to the barperson.

"You know the answer to that question"

"Do I? Eh?" he asked.

"Same as you know you could attract that pretty barperson's attention. You already tipped her hugely last time. To get her at your beck and call. You know I work casually. You know I had a good job I left. Rachel told you."

He patted my shoulder, smiling and gazing with reptilian precision into my eyes, trying to find the core of me, and, for that moment, find what he most needed to take from me.

"That's not true, but I appreciate your insights."

I felt there was no need for me to speak, reveal myself even. Pinkers had decided on my truths. He seemed dedicated to verbally mapping the labyrinths of his universe only, and to inculcate others into its endless wonders.

"Right now I'm unemployed," I said.

"I don't think so, Arthur."

"For the last few years," I said.

"You have never been unemployed, I think, a day in your life," Pinkers said, with a knowing smile.

"I get work here and there."

"Nonsense. That gives you time to do real work. Rachel says you're a writer."

"No, no, Rachel's wrong."

"Rachel is very insightful," Pinkers said.

"I'm trying, that's all. I don't know what I am."

"I'd love to see your work."

"I know she showed you some of my stuff. You wanted me here. You asked for me, summoned me for an audience. Right?"

"You don't like me, do you Arthur?"

I loathed him, but I didn't tell him that.

"Don't patronise me. What did she show you? They were for her eyes only."

"She showed me a little, a few poems here and there, a few pieces of prose. I'd like to see your novels. Ten of them, is that right? That's a bit unusual."

"It's unimportant."

"Perhaps, if you're interested, I might show them to a few publishers of my acquaintance."

"No."

"They are always interested in publishing something other than the usual stuff, so long as it's good."

"I don't think so. I don't want to show them. Not at the moment."

Joe raised his eyebrows a little. He looked perturbed at my refusal. Then he handed me a pina colada.

"I mean, I could imagine what you'd think of it and all," I said by way of possible self rescue from his disapproval.

"No, I don't think you could," he said and smiled.

"I mean, you've published a book," I said, beginning to feel desperate.

"Two, actually," Pinkers said, "And fifteen articles. Besides doing the odd bit of writing, I teach creative writing courses. And I'm lucky to have friends and colleagues who encourage me. You should drop by and meet some of my friends. They might be able to help, maybe."

Rachel's eyes widened with glee and delight for me. Her chestnut hair folded itself just off her forehead, framing her oval features, her clear, intelligent forehead, her pale skin, her soft pool blue eyes, her ivory teeth. I took in her obviously new party dress that hugged her perfect figure. I ached as I looked, recorded every detail to feed my doomed obsessive agonised hunger for her. Then, realising I was exposing an open sore, I returned to my role as playful, depressive, amusing, slightly eccentric, yet interesting, companion. Rachel nodded at me vigorously, indicating I must assent to what Pinkers was suggesting. I wouldn't. I was, once again, throwing away golden opportunities, ruining a perfectly good chance to be one of the in-crowd. She frowned when I didn't react. I saw more people arriving. Pinkers greeted them, one after another. Rachel nudged me to accept the non-casual casual invitation, to come visit within the Pinkers continuum, and meet new people. Clearly Pinkers was bent on impressing his new love.
Rachel smiled. "Of course Arthur wants to come visit. He is a bit of an idiot. He keeps to himself too much. I think I'm his only fiend, I mean friend."
"Thanks," I said. "I like the Freudian slither."

Pinkers smiled and nodded, took another sip of mineral water and looked around the lavishly refurbished pub. Rachel sipped her mojito and talked too casually to a few acquaintances, acquaintances I was then non-casually, casually introduced to. I then moved away. Rachel's excessive shyness led her to babble, to repeat oft remembered stories about her life, her experiences, to espouse hackneyed opinions. I was introduced, in rapid succession, to Margaret and Louise, who wrote a horror fiction novel together every year and a half, had a baby, and had recently moved in together. Then there was Philip, who played for a chamber orchestra and studied music, and Luke who worked as a cameraman at the United Nations, before it was disbanded. There were others, many others I was introduced to, but I couldn't remember their names amidst the noise and the banter and the smiles and laughs. I felt they'd arrived as I had arrived, for casual drinks, in the way one pretends such invitations to casual drinks are infinitely less precious than they really are. I felt happy. I didn't feel alone. Then I ended up talking to Joe again. He seemed determined not to leave me in peace. I saw him stroll up to me out of the corner of my eye, and, leaning against the bar beside me, began talking.

"You know Rachel and I met in a bar just like this?"

I didn't answer.

"Arthur? Are you listening?

"No."

"I said Rachel and I met in a bar just like this. I was in the middle of a discussion, well, rather, I should say I was in the middle of listening to a graduate student, can't remember her name for the life of me, expound some difficult aspect of higher math. You know these types."

"No, Joe. I don't really."

"They have this overblown notion of their own significance."

"I don't know anyone skilled in higher math."

Rachel smiled, stroked Joe's face and said, "Joe does. Joe's a genius." Joe ignored this remark with a professional detachment, though clearly pleased with the vote of appreciation.

"Of course, you don't know such people. They tend to be rather unskilled socially. Well, let me see. I imagine her behaviour had something to do with the social status attached to doing a Ph.D. I remember being that insecure myself when I did my first. But she was a very nice person, I imagine, and, from all reports, a competent student. I think they were thinking of offering her a job at the college once. Now, mathematics is not my thing usually, but it was something I was thinking of using in one of my papers. I sat and listened to this student and tried to keep up, what with all the technical language and the factors and the vectors, and there, in the midst of it all, I saw this vision, whom I now know to be Rachel, out of the corner of my eye. I waited for this student to finish her extremely long, not terribly interesting, complex point of contention, looked at her, smiled faintly, and excused myself."

"How?"

"How, what?"

"How did you excuse yourself?"

Joe didn't seem to really hear the question.

"You know this used be a Greek Orthodox Church?"

"No, I didn't."

"Sure, Arthur. There wasn't enough of the community to maintain it. They built it in 1754, held services until 1976, and then sold it five years ago when they finally ran out of money."

"What about the penal laws? They were persecuting Catholics then," I said.

"Now, we don't talk about that," Pinkers said.

"I don't want to talk about it, either," I said, and finished my drink.

"The altar is a control room for a multimedia centre, you know? Another?"

"Great, thanks," I said.

Rachel slightly frozen smile broadened a little, and deepened in its icy aspect. She took Joe's hand and gently stroked his palm, trying to get his attention, trying to warm things. He smiled lovingly at her and continued talking.

"They can tell by looking at a screen if they are running low on towels or soda water. They have three bars in here and run a hotel on the next floor," he said.

"Nice," I said.

"Joe, Joe," she said.

"What?"

"Arthur was asking how you ended the conversation, with the student?"

"Quite right," he said.

"Doesn't matter," I said. I just wanted to leave this place, and go home.

"I'm not really sure, Arthur. I don't exactly remember."

"That's okay," I said. "As I said, it doesn't matter."

Then, for a moment, Pinkers looked extremely irritated. The small group that had gathered since our discussion had begun seemed to palpably hold its breath. Then Pinkers, looking around, suddenly smiled and continued. For a moment, he had revealed himself. With his smile, the temporarily suspended buzz of conversation resumed.

"I imagine, at the time, I said I had a friend I had to speak to, and, if this research student wouldn't mind, that we could continue this discussion on another occasion, that I must go now and speak to this old friend. And that's how we met."

"Right. That's nice, really sensitive of you," I said.

Rachel and Joe kissed. Then she smiled herself into the surrounding circle of sophisticates. My head spun with the peculiar blood pressure of meeting people. I continued to be introduced to lecturers and editors and translators and poets and musicians and academics and others at the centre of things. These were interesting people. I also met those on the fringes who made dark, brooding, brilliant, sexually, charged, anti-authoritarian conversation. As I listened to them, Rachel came over to me.

"So are you having fun?" she asked.

"Wonderful, mixing here with the frauds."

"You need to lighten up, Arthur. Joe knows so many talented people. He thinks you are quite brilliant, you know."

"Yes indeed," I said. "There are a lot of clever people here in this very hip hostelry."

"Aren't there?"

"They who have plundered the minds of originals thinkers exist on all ends of the spectrum, and they are here, with you, and Joe. And Joe gains their confidence to plunder them."

"God, Arthur, sometimes you really disappoint me," she said, and walked back to Joe.

I didn't speak to her again until very late that evening. I hung, for the most part, with they who dwelled on the periphery of Joe's group. They were looking for promotion, a break into the centre. This would come from acceptance by the right people. For acceptance brings peace, and peace brings an end to struggle, the vegetative calm of self-belief, from the powerful mapping out of your place in the world, a meeting with faculty members, a job offer, or a meeting with editors or publishers, or an offer of work, company, a circle of interesting fun people. Or the lonely meeting a lover, for a time.

So as I said, later on Rachel appeared again.

"Hi," I said.

"Hi," she said.

"You sure about this guy? I never seen you like this."

"Like this? What's this? What are you saying?"

"I mean, do you know him?"

"I'm in love."

"I know. That's chemistry. We're all susceptible to that chemistry. But we have a problem. You know him?" I asked, pressing my forehead to hers. Someone nodded to Joe. Joe saw, but did nothing.

"You're jealous," she said.

"Of course I'm jealous. I'm human. You're so taken so quickly."

"You know I still love you, Arthur."

"I love you too, Rachel. You are my best friend and—"

"I know you only want what's best, Arthur, you're such a sweetie. It's just all so sudden."

"My point exactly," I said.

"When I met him, he didn't seem married."

"Is he married?"

"Divorced."

"He doesn't seem like a one woman person."

"I'm not a one woman person either. You don't like him?" she asked, pleadingly.

"I like him, sort of —" I said.

"No, you don't."

"No, I guess not," I said. "I think he's a vampire."

"I think he is the one, Arthur."

"Naturally, you would. You would think that. Tell me, grasshopper, is there a one?"

"What?"

"I was wondering is there such a thing as 'the one' in the 'Neo, you are the one,' sense of the word," I asked.

"There has to be a name for what's wrong with you, Arthur Kruger. Sure, sure there is, a 'one', chemistry aside." Rachel paused for a second, looked down embarrassedly as she saw me looking at her breasts, and she said, "You know, he's asked me to move in with him, twice."

"Dear God," I said.

"Don't do that! Arthur!"

"Dear God," I repeated, this time more as a prayer than an act of despair.

"Do what?" Pinkers asked, appearing on the scene, as a cat burglar steals into the study where he instinctually knows all the good stuff lies hidden.

"Arthur is just too sceptical for me. It's partly why I love him," Rachel said brightly to Joe.

"I know you do. Do you love Rachel, Arthur?"

"Absolutely. I'll always love Rachel."

"I can see that. You like girls, Arthur?"

"Would it matter if I liked girls or boys? Would it matter to you?"

"No. Not at all. I don't care about things like that. I'm curious that's all. Rachel has interesting friends. You're a genuinely interesting person."

"Now that sounds ominous. Portentous even."

"Really? Why?"

"I love Rachel. That's what matters. Right now, Joe."

"I think you have talent, Arthur."

"Thank you. I'm not sure I agree. Look after my friend."

He didn't answer, but went on about his favourite theatres and movies and music and his students. And, as I listened to Joe Pinkers' carefully elocuted voice, his fabricated rolling intonations, his manufactured, folksy condescension, that gave no clue to his class, or race, or personal history, the shell game sleight of hand that was his invented self, I saw Rachel withdraw into herself. I saw she saw things weren't happening right. She saw I did not adhere to the one true faith, that was her beloved adored Joseph Pinkers, her own personal Jesus just for now. This was an irreparable breach in the solid world she needed to get by.

"You're jealous," she said. Her eyes filled with bitter tears. I reached over and kissed her on the lips.

"It's more than that. You know I'm not a petty man."

"Just a jealous man. Maybe if we slept together, it might fix things."

"I'm open to that experiment," I said. She smiled and went to talk to Joe.

Rachel remembered the night she met Joe Pinkers. She had checked his slim soft hands as she took one that night and wondered what those hands had felt. She remembered giving him a little shy glance when he smiled for the first time at her. Then she feared appearing too vulnerable, too nervous, or too eager, or too much of a party girl. But the hands say so much. We protect our faces or our legs, but our hands tell our story. They have the marks of our charted world. She looked for either the recent signs of a wedding ring or its real presence, but his long hands were more or less the same colour as his face, sallow almost tanned, with thin reaching fingers that deftly closed the paper he had been carrying while talking to that other woman. She wondered what he did for a living, wondered if he liked his work, wondered if he was driven by money or power or love.

"So... what do you do?" She moved a little closer to him.

He began, "I work in a college. I teach. What do you do?"

"I work a help desk. I'm one of those people always looking for promotion," she said.

"What does that mean?"

"I'm ambitious."

"Why?"

"You ask a lot of questions. I'm not one of your pupils."

"Sorry."

A silence descended. Each of them fondled their drinks. Pinkers asked her to tell him what she did, if she wanted to.

"People call in when their systems, you know, computer systems, break down, and I help them get it together. Or, you know, if things are really bad, scheduled service staff to go out to fix things up. The company I work for fix any kind of system. Some of them, the other companies we compete with, they will only fix their own systems, won't touch the other types..."

She remembered she was too nervous, lost in the details of her life. Pinkers reached over and touched her hand and caressed the back of it with his soft slim fingers, enough to signify his desire to calm her mounting nerves. She withdrew her hand a little, looked at him suddenly, afraid of feeling too drunk, and then looked down at her empty drink glass.

"You must like what you do…" she said to him…" Do you..?"

"It's important to me…" Pinkers began. "People are important to me too…"

He so wanted her to believe that, but, because she had heard him say it like that, she couldn't be sure of it.

"Are you married?" she asked him.

"Not any more."

"Why?"

"I had an affair…"

"Was that the woman?"

"Student. She was a student, a maths student. Very boring. The woman, the other one you asked about, is remarried. Gone. Long gone. Big, stupid mistake. I make them regularly."

"Children?" She asked, looking about the bar, unconsciously fixing the creases in her dress.

Pinkers shook his head. "No children…"

"I see…"

"What do you see? Tell me, what you see?"

Rachel remembered that question he asked her that night as she looked at the group gathered around, as she looked at Joe, now her lover, who had repeatedly asked her to move in with him free gratis, and saw Arthur listening sceptically to the people talking.

"I have my own place, my own life, my own friends," she said. Then she had told him about Arthur. Pinkers wanted to know whether she and Arthur had ever slept together.

"No," she told him.

It had begun with Pinkers meeting Rachel in his car after she'd finished work, taking her out to dinner, buying her clothing and spontaneous gifts of the useless, but adorningly beautiful, type, romantic weekends in quiet tasteful locations, and because of his job and lecture tours and books and broadcasts, Joe was never short of money.

"Why are you doing this?"

"What? The gifts. I like to buy gifts. I buy gifts for lots of people."

"It's just," Rachel paused. She felt bought. How do you tell an overgenerous lover he was trying to buy his lover's affections?

"I'd be honoured if you would consider moving in with me. It's a big place, after all. You could rent out your place and pay the mortgage, and it wouldn't be like you'd lose your independence. I never like to invade people's space."

"You don't need to. You just learn everything about them. You've got them in your head."

Joe looked angrily down. They were racing through traffic.

"Slow down!"

"You're being unfair!"

"Slow down! Joe!"

Joe stopped the car. Rachel got out.

"Next time, I'll take the bus. Lunatic!" And she stormed off.

Pinkers, however, didn't surrender to Rachel's declaration of independence. Tearful reconciliations followed a long silence that settled between them. I thought, to my secret glee, that it was all over between Rachel and Joe. I imagined scenarios whereby my own declaration of undying love might find an open ear. But then Joe invited her out for coffee, followed by dinner. Then, the following day, six months after she stormed out of his car, she rung me to tell me she had moved in with him.

"This will end in tears," I said.

"I stormed away before because I was deliberately pushing him away, deliberately trying to sabotage our relationship, because it was the way all my other relationships had gone."

"Those sentences have a suspiciously professorial tone, Rachel."

"I'm happy, Arthur. So fuck off."

"Sorry. I'll call you later."

I remember seeing them seemingly so happy together, those smiles that said 'I am in love, can you see how much I am in love?' I kept imagining them together and hating it. Despite how I felt, I strove to be the friend. I tried to be entertaining, to be emotionally honest, polite and deferential, a raconteur and joker, vulnerable but kind, witty and simple. To an extent, it seemed to work.

I remember parties that lasted all night. I remember vast quantities of alcohol and drugs consumed, brilliant conversation that sparkled with Saki-esque wit, speculations in philosophy and religion and a search for life outside the box of birth or death or marriage or career. It was a competition for immortality, designed to kill the life inside.

"So, Arthur, you having fun?" asked Pinkers.

"Why does everyone keep asking me am I having fun? I'm not wearing my 'Suicide is for quitters' T-shirt this party season. In fact I haven't taken it out this year, not once."

"You work too hard at being clever, Arthur."

I ignored Pinkers' attempt to probe my psyche.

"Sure, Joe. Great party. Lovely people."

Pinkers grinned.

"What's so funny?"

"Nothing."

"Rachel told me."

"Told you what?"

"You hate this. You only come out of loyalty to the friendship. You find it all fake and it makes you angry and this is why you are so kind and friendly and funny."

"I think that's unfair. I am very unfriendly, honest."

"You are that, Arthur."

"And I think there are some nice people here. I just don't do so many drugs now, you know?"

"These people are old friends," Pinkers said.

"Do you have friends? I mean, I think you have subjects and people who feed your creative needs. But friends, in the sense of people who are your equals who you are emotionally honest with, and trust, I wonder about that," I said. "I mean, Joe, I have a certain fascination with the shiftings and orbits and movements of this new universe I find myself inhabiting."

"Really, that must bring you relief from having to face up to your own bitter disappointment, your distrust of people, and your negativity."

"I'm long past disappointment, Pinkers."

"What are you saying? Arthur? Are you trying to hurt me, compete for Rachel, is that it?"

"No, Joe, but you are not fooled by your own performance at living. You go on like this life is working for you. You cultivate the self-obsessed misery of the privileged; pursue therapy, because it satisfies your own self-deceiving need to be seen to be seeking personal well-being in all its forms."

"Who told you I was in therapy?"

"You just did, but you never take responsibility for how another person might feel because of how you treat them."

"And how do I treat them?"

"You pretend you're a giver. But you're a taker. You pretend you're an artist, but you're just a very smart hack. You come up with nothing new, and that's why the market likes you. You're safe."

"Really?"

"Yet you never really take any effective step to better anyone else's lot save your own, while at the same time giving every signal of being genuinely caring."

"You really want me to hate you, don't you? Just because I have this and you never will?"

His hand holding a glass of mineral water swept around the room, mirroring yet another fabulous soiree filled with the brilliant and the best.

"I won't do that, Arthur. Never," He smiled and waited for me to continue.

"I'm onto you, that's all. These people are just filling your void," I said. "If you want to feel fulfilled, resign your job, sell this place, and go somewhere no one knows you, and start again."

"You're wrong."

"You like me, Joe Pinkers, because I'm not a winner," I said. "You like these people, because they have talent, but little or no self-belief, despite all they have achieved."

"You keep telling yourself that."

"I don't need to," I said. "I heard myself the first time."

Joe didn't approach me after that, ever really. Rachel questioned me about Joe.

"What happened?"

"We had a disagreement."

"We have disagreements. What happened? How did you insult him? How did you ruin this particular relationship?"

"Excuse me?"

"I know you, Arthur Kruger. You can't help yourself."

"Words were exchanged. I don't believe in this social whirl. I can't help it. We got talking about ourselves, and one thing let to another and—"

Rachel began to cry.

"Couldn't you keep your mouth shut? For once?"

"I'm sorry, Rachel. I don't trust him"

"You don't trust anyone. It's a sickness with you."

I was always invited to soirees and get-togethers as Rachel's closest friend, but, deep down, I didn't care how frosty people were to me, as I regarded friendship as the centre of a universe of fear and uncertainty and self-destruction. In order to be one with these people, these beautiful, selfless, kind-hearted people, these warm loving souls,

I would have to become a believer, a believer in this world of success. I would have to be like the apostle Peter and deny my own personal salvation in my darkest moment.

I was not alone in this darkness. I stayed in my flat and did what I thought was work. People came to my door. I went for drinks with them. Mail was delivered. I received packages with things I had ordered inside them. Then, I got other jobs and began to make a little money, travelled, and new horizons began to open for me. But I could not escape the Pinkers continuum. Occasionally, I would receive gifts of money or tickets to the theatre from him. Apparently, I had been forgiven. He wanted to meet me. He wanted me to come to his parties and get-togethers. I declined. I began to suspect things were going wrong for Rachel. She called me especially to ask me to come to a little Christmas get-together.

"Joe's mother is sick. He won't be there. I need the company."
"Okay then."
We were sitting together that Christmas, by Pinkers' big fireside. The usual warm hum of conviviality vibrated around the hive epicentre of the great gas fire that imitated a log fire. It was eleven o'clock. A few people came and went. Rachel was playing host. I looked at the fire for a long time and saw how Rachel drank and shook the ice left in her drink after she made small talk with the visitors. She had a new dress on.
"Have you rented your apartment?" I asked.
"They haven't got back to me yet."
"Who?" I asked.
"Hold on," Rachel said.
"Okay."
She went to talk to someone. Then, a few minutes later, she sat back down.

"I like your dress."

"Thanks."

I looked at her lips as they touched the lip of the glass, and the ice melting against her tongue. It irritated me. I couldn't understand why I was so angry with her. Perhaps it was a sense she had put herself in an impossible situation that gave me no control over her. I didn't know why I wanted to control her, to own her, capture her, protect my love of her by having her in my possession. I will never do that, I thought. Never. As though sensing my obsessions, she began talking to me again as the room started thinning as it got too late.

"People are going home, to their wives and husbands."

"It happens," she said.

"Right," I said.

"Listen, Arthur, listen, I wanted to ask you something..." she said "...and I want you to tell me the honest truth..."

"Well," I said. "You don't ask much."

"What do you mean?" Rachel said.

"Be that honest... there's a challenge. Most friendships never survive honesty..."

And she leaned close to me and I met her dilated pupils with a scared sexually inadequate look. I lingered on her soft tanned skin and citrus smile and moist soft lips and I imagined sex with her once again for the thousandth time and she said:

"Why haven't we slept together? Why not, eh?"

I looked around the room in this heart attack moment. I looked around, in case anyone overheard us. There were still lots of people left and I smiled and Rachel looked at me with those sea green eyes and, like all the other times she had asked me these searching questions, the kind of stuff so hateful to answer, and she sat back, drunk, and watched me swim round in the fishbowl of my own fear and embarrassment.

She didn't mind having sex with me, if I wanted it, she said. Sex was nothing, like a hug, a mere passing thing. If I had suggested it, we would have had sex.

"I don't know why," I said.

"Sure you do, Arthur. I know why. I see you... looking at me."

"Look, Rachel. You ...you are drunk. Leave me alone."

"Answer me..."

"Shyness, I guess. I suppose, it isn't because I haven't thought about it..."

"Me neither. We would always be friends..."

"Right..."

"It wouldn't matter if we did it or not."

"Sure..."

"Always. You know I had a twin?"

"I would remember if you mentioned it."

"I had a twin. A twin sister."

"I see."

"Her name was Aron. She died. When we were little babies."

"I'm sorry about that. Aron, what an interesting name."

"They were hoping for a boy, I guess," she said.

Rachel was beginning to weep a little, remembering her little baby sister who didn't make it past infancy.

"You know, Arthur, I sometimes feel her around, looking out for me. All my life I have felt her there, and it makes me lonely. I miss her. I feel something's missing without my baby sister."

Rachel cried in my arms for a long time. I thought about the years we had been friends, how we had survived all those crises and failed relationships maybe because we never had crossed the sexual line, though we had come close to it. Precise details escaped me in that hormonal moment, as the years bled into each other. I held her, feeling helpless, patted her shoulder, and rubbed her back, and tried to kiss it all better.

"Look, I have to ask. Why are you bringing this up? What's going on between you and Joe? Trouble?"

Joe was in the process of taking my only friend away from me. Rachel was looking for tangible ties between us, something tangible like a sexual history, something more tangible than time. Maybe she didn't know.

"Rachel, just what do you know about Joe?"

"Lots of stuff. Why?"

"Pinkers is crippled by his addiction to his own cleverness."

"What the hell are you talking about?"

"He has hidden within his own thinking skills all his life."

"You just want to believe that."

"Rachel, he is not capable of really giving, only taking."

"He's taking care of his sick mother right now. I call that giving."

"I wondered what he told you about himself."

"Lots."

"What?"

"I can't tell you. He made me promise."

"Have you met his mother?"

"Sure, sure I have, a couple of times."

"Right."

"What?"

"Nothing. I, I think he had it tough as a kid. He became the machine he needed to become to excel. Now, he's looking for love and finding the machine has no heart. Things are crumbling."

And she got up and fixed us both more drinks. It was Christmas. The guests were leaving. I decided to stay and slow down my drinking. Then the hours passed.

"Do you think he is seeing someone?" I said.

"I don't know. I'll try his phone. His mother is sick."

Rachel left her fifth message. Joe still hadn't come home. We called it a night after finishing those last drinks. I got a taxi home. It was four o'clock in the morning.

I lay in bed in my little flat and read myself to sleep and cried as I finally drifted off. I knew I was losing Rachel. Expressing such confidences were a last act of desperation to cement over the cracks of our love.

I kept away from Pinkers for a month to two. Rachel didn't contact me. Then, as usual, I got a letter from Joe.

Dear Arthur,

I miss you. I tried telephoning over the last weeks on odd occasions, but sadly the phone seemed to ring out. I can only conclude you are angry with me over something. I would be happy to talk over the matter with you, if you like. If you don't want to, please do not feel the compulsion to talk over anything. Rachel misses you too, so she says, and she finds this unaccountable tension that seems to exist between us very trying. She says you and she had coffee just last week. This Friday, we are having a little get together, just a few friends and it would be a rare delight for me if you would attend. It is to celebrate my publishing a small book I have been working on over the last year or so. I enclose an advance copy dedicated to you. Looking forward to seeing you then.

Love

Joe.

I rang Joe.

"Hello?"

"Joe. It's Arthur."

"Arthur! I have a student with me right now. Can I call you back?"

"Whatever."

"Thanks. Talk to you."

Ten minutes later, I got a call back.

"Hi Arthur, where are you?"

"I'm in town, Joe. I got your letter."

"How are you? Are you okay? Do you need anything?"

"I'm fine."

"How's the writing going? Rachel says you're still rewriting ten short n–"

"I'd like to meet."

"Great. How about lunch at Chapter One? My treat."

"Fine."

Pinkers was sitting reading when I arrived. He smiled and waved me over. A waiter immediately came and asked me what I wanted.

"A salad please, and a glass of chardonnay."

"Fine, sir, sure, and what will Professor Pinkers have today?"

"The usual, Tom. How's the play coming on?"

"We're going for a first reading this Friday, Professor."

"Please, call me Joe. I told you before."

"I know. I'll get that to you right away."

The waiter disappeared, beaming into the kitchen to expedite the dinner orders. The high status restaurant began to fill with the great and the good. I recognised theatre people, some of them nodding to Joe, then others studiously ignoring others. Our food arrived with lighting speed.

"There we are. Enjoy your meal."

"Thank you, Tom."

"Yes, Prof – Joe."

Pinkers smiled.

"So, is there something you wanted to say to me Arthur?"

"Yes."

"So?"

"I think we should end our friendship."

"You do, do you? Why?"

"Because we don't fit. Because we're opposites, and opposites detract. Because you feed on the souls of your so called friends. Because you are a fraud. Because your career is built on ego rather that the pursuit of knowledge. Because you are capable of anything. Because you are the kindest, most giving person I know. Because you are a genuinely interesting person. Because I hate myself."

Pinkers closed his book and looked quickly around the by now full, noisy lunchtime restaurant. He saw Tom serving nearby. He beckoned to him. "Tom, Tom?"

"Everything all right?" Tom came over and smiled. He looked extremely worried.

"Tom, I hate to put you on the spot. My friend here thinks I am a vampire."

"I never used the V word," I said.

"Okay, then. He thinks I feed on the souls of those around me. That from what I can gather, I attract people of potential, and stifle their lives. Don't answer if you don't want to. But if you do, what do you think of that?"

Tom smiled broadly. He didn't hesitate for a second. It was like asking one's boyfriend if one's backside looked big in one's newly purchased ball gown.

"I think it's not true. You are one of the few gentlemen who come in here. All the staff like you. Okay, Joe?"

"Thanks. Sorry about that." Tom looked bitterly my way. Then Tom went back to work.

"So?" Pinkers ate his meal. I drank my wine and nibbled my salad.

"I once rescued a cat and kept indoors after I had it spayed. I stopped it from repeated impregnation, various diseases and an early death. I gave it food and warmth. Unfortunately the cat didn't see it that way. It wanted to harm me every time I brought it food and cleaned its cage. Eventually it bit me badly, escaped and I got a nasty infection."

"That's a sad story, Arthur. What's your point? That the cat would rather die than lose its freedom? A cat is not a good example, what with their suicidal curiosity and all."

"Maybe." I finished my wine and ate the last of my salad. "I have to go."

"Don't go, Arthur."

"Why?"

"I have, over time, managed to get more than a dozen writers with a fifth of your talent published. Your work is too experimental to get anywhere without all the right levers and switches in position. I can do that for you. I am in a position to help. Let me help you. Don't ruin your life."

"I can't believe you are actually jealous of me."

"I think it's the other way around, don't you think, Arthur?"

"I have a lot to be jealous of, but not the kind of person you are."

I looked into his eyes for a long time.

"I don't trust you. And neither should Rachel."

He didn't answer.

"Have you asked her to marry you, yet?"

"Mind your own business, Kruger."

I walked away and didn't go to the party that Friday night. Months passed. By now Rachel and Joe were rarely apart. I waited for the inevitable announcement of a whirlwind engagement, a tornado marriage in some exotic location. But there was no such announcement. I was too angry with Rachel to meet her socially. My money ran out. I took an office job.

"Kruger?"

"What?"

"Call for you."

"I see we're on a second name basis, Brad."

"Sounds serious."

"It does?"

Brad, the company secretary, made a crying face. I nodded. So, someone was crying.

"Thanks."

I took the phone.

"Hello?"

I heard crying. Then I heard someone calling me.

"Arthur, Arthur!"

Someone was shouting for me in the office. I indicated I was taking a call. I saw who it was. It was Mary. Mary was my boss.

"We need you in here, Arthur. This is no time for personal calls. That is a personal call, isn't it?"

"Yes Mary, this is indeed a personal call. I am indeed speaking to a person."

It was Rachel who was ringing me. Rachel was crying freely.

"Arthur. I'm in my apartment," she sobbed.

"Rachel! I thought you had rented it out."

Mary did not move from where she was standing. She looked coldly at me. I was challenging her sovereign authority. My attitude problem had been alluded to more than once. I had been given a good talking to. I apparently had a listening difficulty I should look at.

"Right now, Arthur."

"Rachel? Rachel, don't go away, okay? I'll be back."

I covered the receiver. Then I turned to Mary.

"Mary, can we agree that I am poor, being in my thirties and working as an office temp and that I really can't afford to lose this job, so maybe you might conclude from that I need to take this call right now, seeing as I have a very old friend in a distressed state. So go away, okay?"

I put the receiver back to my face. Rachel was becoming hysterical.

"No, no, no. Oh, God. No. Please come over. Please."

"I'll come as soon as I can. We're in the midst of a crisis here."

"Please. Please. We broke up."

"Okay. Leave it with me," I said.

I went to my boss.

"Sorry about that."

"Forget it," Mary said. "You are an ass, by the way. I need the following orders processed stat, A109, B457…"

"So, here's the thing," I said.

"No way, Kruger," Mary began.

"Why does everyone call me Kruger? Everyone else is on a first name basis."

"You are not leaving here because some friend broke up. We need you here. Fact is I'm thinking of offering you an extension on your contract!" Mary slapped the desk and pointed to my desk.

"Listen boss," I said. "I have a real crisis. A crisis of family proportions, epic proportions. Heartbreak, tragedy, loss, agony unto death. I need time out. I need to just disappear from the office for a few hours. A dear friend, a lifelong friend is in trouble. I don't know how much trouble, but I need to go to her right now. I don't know if she will be okay if I don't. I'm sure you understand."

And Mary said "No."

"I have to."

"I separated from my husband last month," Mary said.

"I wonder why," I said.

"Go and you're fired," she said, her chin wrinkling with suppressed tears.

"Okay," I said.

So I went to Rachel's apartment. They had broken up, in a way. Joe had accused her of terrible things, sleeping with other men and women, of sleeping with me, stealing money and saying malicious things about him.

"What things?" I asked.

"That he was a failed artist."

"So? He's also a monumental jerk."

"That all his money and success and connections covered up for his deep rooted sense of failure," she said.

"I didn't say that."

"You did to me," Rachel said.

"Okay, but you didn't repeat it to anyone. Did you?"

She shook her head and began weeping again. I wasn't sure I believed her.

"He was like a madman," she said.

"Unsurprising," I said.

It all had erupted after she had gone through his clothing during a post coital romantic whim. Rachel came across photographs of Joe with other women. These photographs were of other girlfriends.

"I wanted to know why he didn't tell me about these other women."

"So what did he say?" I asked.

"He had said they were of old girlfriends, that he had introduced them to me here and there, that there was nothing between these people and him now."

"But you didn't believe him."

"You don't keep pictures of former lovers in your jacket pocket if they mean nothing to you."

"I guess," I said.

"There was something in his voice, something about the way he looked at me. I knew he was seeing them. And matters built up and the screaming and fighting started." She stood up and paced the room. She didn't speak, just paced and paced.

"Don't pace. You know I hate it when you pace."

"Sorry," and she sat down and lit a cigarette. I hated it even more when she smoked.

"I see what you mean," I said.

She said it got so bad, so violent, that she ran out of his house and taken a taxi to her own apartment. I looked at her and I was horrified.

"You don't look so good. Why don't you stay over with me for a few days? He's only going to find you here. Right now, that's not good."

Rachel didn't seem to hear such an eminently plausible suggestion. She looked destroyed. Nothing visible on the outside, the same perfect body and lovely face, but the eyes were dead and there were tiny red smears about the eyes and cheeks. She was stoned.

"What are you on?"

She said nothing and lit another cigarette.

"What have you taken?"

"Uppers or downers or both. Smoked a little pot, you know? Oh God." She was weepy and wearing a white towelling robe and slippers, her face red and a little puffed from crying. It was the eyes though, that was most upsetting, the eyes of someone hurt beyond expression, the old look in Rachel's eyes that had been gone for a little time when she was going out with Joe first, but was now back.

"He hit you?"

"No. I hit him. And he restrained me."

"And that's why there were bruises on your wrists?"

"That's where he held me," she said, showing me her wrists.

"Did he hit you? Really?"

"No."

"Tell me."

"No!"

"No, he didn't hit you?"

"He didn't. He's not a hitter."

I held her hands for a while and stroked them. She leaned into me and reached out to me and kissed me at first gently and then harder. Suddenly my desire for her, the desire I had held at bay for so long, turned to revulsion, and I pushed her away.

"Sorry," I said.

"Okay," she said.

"Bad timing."

"It's okay," she said, and took to pacing again. Maybe, I thought, this kind of rejection defined her. I walked over to look out her balcony at the passing cars and the passing people and the darkening buildings and the lights coming on one by one and the other people arriving home to dinner and television and calls from friends and family. She was still quiet. I wondered how many drugs she had taken, if maybe I should call an ambulance. It was looking out from that balcony, taking in the panorama I knew she was not the person I thought she was. I knew I had been in love with an idea of her, not the person, the needy heartbroken social climber indoors.

The heating was turned off in her apartment. I quietly switched it back on as the place seemed weirdly cold, as though haunted.
"Have you seen any ghosts?"
She looked at me strangely, and then discarded my question.
"Doesn't matter."
She repeated the story of what had happened with obsessive detail, as though her rage at Joe magnified her ability to amass damning evidence against him, twist the facts sufficiently to make it seem it was his cruel selfish mind that had ruined their happiness together, that his singular vindictive needs to control the relationship caused things to spiral out of control. I listened, and looking around her spotless, sanitised, impersonal, bright Van Gough sunflower coloured apartment, with its obligatory framed prints that investors and landlords and landladies put on apartments walls painted over industrial plaster, so as to engender a superficial welcoming air of depth and meaning and experience, and I felt desolate. A drying out, dusty pot pourri bowl perched itself at the epicentre of a low-legged steel and glass rectangular coffee table.
"You hungry?"
"I couldn't eat now, I feel sick, I feel as though I have been kicked in the stomach... I..."

"I'll make tea, and I'll order take out…Chinese or Indian take out… and 'll get a bottle of wine, or something…maybe you will get hungry."
She watched me eat in silence, picking here and there like a robin with a bleeding heart. I left the house at eleven o'clock at night in a taxi, having said little for the entire night, feeling guilt and complicity in my silence, wanting to ask what possible joy could there be in torturing each other, what possible satisfaction in twisting the truth of events and past lovers, but being afraid of hurting her more and pressuring her at a bad time.

had lost my job. I was running out of money. I went down to the employment exchange, looking for work. I got a job as a hospital porter at the local ultramodern heartbreak hospital. And, as I worked moving patients, Joe and Rachel made up.

Joe told Rachel she had become the single object of absolute obsession in his mind, the measure of his heartbeats, the oxygen that filled his lungs. Joe had, so he said, fallen absolutely passionately totally for Rachel, and such devotion is rarely easily forgiven or desired or understood. Rachel too had seen her longings fulfilled in Pinkers, but she felt devoured by him. Deep down I knew Rachel only wanted the little things, a nice man, someone weak and sincere and sensitive, and nothing too big that would change her comfortable unhappy life. And, because of these desires, she chose Joe, who had none of these qualities. Worse still, Joe had been ambushed by his longings. The fabric of his universe had been rent; her perfect body adorned his soul with a new vision.

One tried to see what Joe saw: that Rachel was attractive and desirable, but even Rachel knew she in no way lived up to his image of her. She became afraid of the pain and the desire she had inadvertently provoked, for she did not love him as he did her, nor had she ever loved anyone as Joe loved her. Furthermore, Joe never believed himself capable of the madness he was going through. He was hardly in work before he was out of his office or drinking somewhere, his lectures were poor, his work output dropped, he seemed exhausted, distracted. He rarely turned up for lunch on campus, preferring to buy a sandwich and eat alone in his office. He was frequently drunk, writing reams of low quality literary criticism, trying to read students' essays and falling asleep on the job, or hating what he read so much that he got offensive in his comments. Students complained but nothing was done. Occasionally, his next-door neighbour would pass his door to hear Joe laughing to himself, talking out loud, or crying a little. He would not answer the door when someone knocked at it. Joe made sure it was locked for the time he was drinking. Aside from colleagues, his publisher called a few times looking for him, and once called in person. His book deadline was approaching fast, but he wasn't returning calls or mails. Things could not get any worse. His colleagues saw all these changes with a much gossiped-about grim satisfaction. At last, he got what he deserved. Some were worried as well as satisfied, but no one would risk breaching the high maintenance defences of Joe Pinkers.

Rachel called me often, telling me about how things were with Joe, that Joe was crazy, raving and weeping and begging and fighting. Rachel said he was begging her to marry him, to, at least live with him again, so that he could begin to live again. But Rachel wouldn't. She stayed over with him every so often as a type of concession to the pressure he put her under. Love was the killer, and this insane passion in Pinkers made me loathe him a little less and forgive him just a little. One imagined telling him how it was, that this disaster that was love was not a moral failing or the product of some trauma, but Rachel was not the person he needed her to be, that he should just let go, that there was a terrain where the mind cannot go, a region of desire, that was ost there. But one didn't want to get involved. This felt too much like he end. Perhaps, like his colleagues one felt gratified at his suffering, o my endless guilt.

Even more insanely, after rejecting Pinkers as a friend, encouraging Rachel, his lover, to leave him, insulting him, I was once again a visitor o the Pinkers continuum. I could not break away. The soirees and the drinks and the evenings out became the polite social torture one imagined hem to be, and I endured them because I had nowhere else to go. Rachel too had as many problems breaking away from Pinkers as I had.

"Arthur!"

"Hey sweetie, how are you doing?"

"I got promoted."

"That's fantastic."

"In London."

"Oh."

"It's a kind of little village in itself. The company have so many facilities or socialising there, dining areas, two gyms, free weekends away for op employees, pubs, coffee houses, every other week it seemed the company was growing…"

"I attended the staff briefings too," I said.

"I know you lasted six weeks as far as I remember when I got you a ob in my office."

"What was it? Trying to strengthen inter-office relationships, trying to complete the incomplete world of the job. Employees should see the ob as a way of life, a 'complete life cycle' as they put it in their mission statements. The new corporate village built in the financial quarter in London. It's a huge promotion. You should take it. Does Joe know?"

She shook her head.

"Gotta go mingle."

"Ah, the duties of hosting. You can't beat a quiet one to one drink in a spit-on-the-floor pub. No pressure."

"You keep telling yourself that, Arthur."

"See you later."

"You too," and she glided back into a group.

The last time I was with Joe and Rachel, as a couple of sorts, was that informal summer party. I remember the glow of candlelight and the smiles and laughs and the ease and the fun we had, as though we knew that things had changed, a great pressure lifted. Rachel wore a gorgeous cyan silk dress that she said she had bought that day, and Joe, who rarely wore a suit, wore a black suit despite the soaring temperatures outside.

After dinner, which was a strange mixture of fish delicacies and odd salads I hardly touched for fear of indigestion, we sat out in the garden amidst a plethora of candles that shone like tiny sentinels and lit the glowing shadowy, laughing faces of the party people. We drank white wine or beer and listened to the practiced conversationalists practice their art. Joe was moving around the group, smiling more than laughing, listening intently in a condescending deferential way, commenting occasionally, and after the allotted time had passed, moving on to others to say hello. He sat beside me and put his arm around my shoulder. I smiled at him and commented on his suit.

"You must be boiling hot in that, eh?"

"Yes, I am," and he took off the jacket. A light dusting of sweat was just visible in the candlelight along his sallow, smooth neck and clear shaven, shining cheek and chin.

"Have you talked to the professor? We have an expert on William Blake here this evening, you know?"

"I didn't feel qualified," I said.

Joe grinned and tapped me on the back in disagreement.

"I couldn't keep up with him myself," he said.

I had begun to shiver. I wanted to huddle up to the candles for their tiny warmth.

"I think I have something coming on, hot then cold. I spoke to some others. Nice people…"

I went to go indoors. Joe stopped me. I sat down, surprised.

"I have something I… wanted…"

Joe folded his black, newly bought summer suit jacket carefully and hung it on his arm. He had lost weight, and, in that millisecond of seeing, seemed older and sadder. I sipped a little white wine and said nothing.

"I know she doesn't want to stay, to be with me…"

"You'll find someone else. Someone to interest you, to act as a focus for your energies, if you haven't already. I'm sure you have someone lined up already."

"Why do you come?"

"What do you mean?"

"Why come here, to these gatherings. You obviously hate it, and me…"

"I don't hate you, or anyone. I disliked you a lot, for a while. Rachel is my friend. That's why I come. In another life, we might have been friends. In another life, I might have been you. I feel sorry for you. You have traded a lot for what might be called respect."

He rubbed his eyes and face and said nothing for a minute or two, as though his mind had failed him as it had so often during his time with Rachel. He looked across at her and caught her eye. She looked at him and smiled, then Rachel looked at me for information, and I knew she knew. She knew our friendship was over. Then, Joe looked at me and said:

"You knew that she didn't want to stay, didn't you?"

"As I say, I am a friend."

He put his hand on my arm. I looked at the long dexterous spider like fingers. They seemed to have intelligence independent of their owner. His hand and fingers were warm and a little moist. His grip had a controlled feverish intensity to it. And then he looked at me with an unspeakable sorrow, got up and walked away. I sat there for a half hour till I started to shiver again. A few people asked me excruciating questions about what I wrote. Eventually, I said my goodbyes and left, feeling another psychological flu approaching.

She was gone in a week. She sold her apartment and moved to London. Two years later an accountant from the company's financial department, Charles Greene, asked her to marry him. I met Charlie. We went for drinks and dinner and drives in the country. There were these warm conversational evenings of sharing and friendship. She wanted us to be friends. Charlie was smart and moneyed and kind and warm and sensitive, but not too much of anything to be scary. I did not go to her wedding, pretended to be ill. She never forgave me for it. She sent me photographs. It seemed to be everything she dreamed of. But I was happy for her. It was a good arrangement. I met her first child, named after his father, only last month.

So, this is how it is. The phone stills rings at my house now every so often, and I know it's Joe. I would be reading or making notes. It would be five o'clock on a balmy Friday summer's evening and the phone would start ringing. 'Just making contact,' as he would say. And, sometimes, I would be enlightened enough to understand. And we would meet, and just make contact. It was, if nothing else, genuinely interesting.

NOVEL IX

DR. KAFKA DECLINES THE NOBEL PRIZE

Aron Tully was born in Dublin's Rotunda Hospital, probably by now a long long time ago, to be unspecifically specific. No one is quite sure, as the records have been strangely lost. But Mother Tully remembers that Little Tully successfully completed birth and emerged Dadaesque, with the umbilical cord wrapped tightly about her neck, without a hint of irony. The umbilical knot tightened and the baby began to die and her mother named her Aron, for no other reason than Mrs Tully, stoned on all the painkillers the hospital had given her, forgot she was not a boy. But Aron lived on, despite that initial act of theatre strangulation. How did I manage to get that cord around my neck, and so young too, she often mused afterwards. Following the usual short rest, due to lack of hospital beds, she was released to her family's questionable care, came home and Aron started to grow and live through the unforgettable horror of childhood and girlhood and youth and to survive so-called education and become the poet she was born to be. She survived the domestic gulag, was helped to leave home so as to evade the relentless love and pederasty of the Tully household. And how she tried to forget, deny, rationalise, slice open the past and let in bleed out. But forgetting didn't work, as memory and feeling were killers she couldn't evade. My special little girl. Our special little secret. She tried to evade memory in death. Suicide and all its seduction.

Unfortunately, she was unsuccessful. After accepting her lack of talent in the area of self-termination, and an accidental discovery of her destiny as a human being, she turned away from the void and got good at, if not living, then surviving. She did not die, or become an addict, or wind up in some respectably toxic marriage, or become a well-toned, well-known executive. It all went right because she found friends, good friends. This put off death for a later date, possibly old age, with accompanying senescence. These friends she found offered her lodging. They took her into their executive suites, deciding one good deed was not as good as another, and that a good deed was something not at odds with their self-image of Jesus-Zen-loving, meditation-addicted, computer-literate, left-wing, well-paid, corporate-friendly bohemians. But Tully was happy. She, too, was in the happy habit of looking on the bright side of things. Indeed, it was worse than that. She was in the habit of idealizing people. This habit was a reaction to being constantly disappointed by people, of finding others apathetic, cold, heartless, merciless, brutal, avaricious, evil and for so long without the possibility of change. Now, any act of basic human decency was an extraordinary revelation to Aron. It was a happy thing, she noted in her notebook. A happy thing to find friends who would take her in. My lucky, lucky star, she thought, as she looked up through the attic skylight the night she moved into the cool clean apartment. I'm not dead and only a little raped and pillaged and scarred for life. Lucky me.

The apartment would be warm and dry. It would be peaceful and happy. At least until she found a job. At least a little precious time. A little time is everything between friends. A little wine and a few olives and a few friends. A party of one. There was a kind of idealism about these friends who smiled and prayed and loved the love of God and wanted her to come to meetings and seemed so knowing and so understanding. These friends who took her in knew the score in Aron Tully's life, all she had gone through in her parents' home and they had intervened, had put Aron wise to her own predicament. They had the compassion of the converted on the postulant. They had performed the required intervention, the gathering of the arms about her and the inspired psychobabble that saved her life. They intervened in the mode of seeing the truth and acting upon it and said that her life, such as it was, could not go on, that she was dying in her home, that, if she did not go, something terrible would happen. As if it hadn't already, Aron said. Worse might happen, they said. We have seen it. Aron acquiesced. Things had all changed for her so suddenly.

She had met these people by accident. She had gone to a prayer meeting, of all places, through drinking too much and wandering into a church and sitting at the back. The entire chapel was aglow with the soft skin coloured light of candles, the candlelights dappling off the walls and columns and flying buttresses, as the meditating people sang old hymns and read from the gospels and the psalms. Tully sat there, her drunkenness opening her to a connectedness she had never felt for anyone or anything. She sat there and tried to pray, tried to reach out into the infinite nothing left. Dear God, she prayed, dear God, help me, and please please, she prayed, and then she closed her eyes and began to dream of God. And she was woken by one of her new friends, who shook her gently awake and told her did she know she had been crying in her sleep. Tully looked up at these kindly folk and told them that she had not been sleeping, but had been praying. And they smiled and that night they filled Aron Tully with coffee to sober her up and Tully told them everything and they offered to take her in, so that Tully could get away from home.

They had an apartment on the south side that they showed her. It was by South Great George's Street and from downstairs came the constant buzz of vehicles during the day, the homicidal gridlock of human traffic, the cappuccino-grabbing, multi-tasking multitudes, filled with objectives and clear margins of thought and awful loss and a keen awareness of the tiny differences they make. Aron was terrified of this possible change, terrified of herself, afraid of her mind and the tortures it might wreak upon her if she disobeyed its obsessive compulsions. She feared breaking the cycle of dependency and servitude. She feared what might happen if she left home. She feared what might happen if she stayed at home. She agonised. Then, after the appropriate period of agonising, she saw that her friends were right. She took the step and it all turned out okay.

Her departure from the well-regulated, carefully controlled Tully home was an eerily simple matter. She was having breakfast and, in the midst of the cheery gossip and chitchat about what it says in the news and who said what at the office and what the neighbours are doing, she stammered that she was leaving. Leaving? Was the response? Where are you going? Leaving, she said. Going. Not coming home again. Ever, she said. Not coming home. Ever. She had thought of saying other things, crafted a speech in her head, so crafted it sounded crafted. So she said nothing else, saying to herself that silence is my weapon. I will use it to good advantage. She thought too much about everything. More to the point, she was too afraid. So she went upstairs. Walking up the carefully crafted, woodcut stairs, with the excessive tacky religious iconography, passing the bedrooms and the study and the box room, into her own room, which she had defiantly self-furnished, she made a phone call to her friends to come get her. And she packed her clothes, books, records, notes, drafts for unfinished novels, poems, notebooks, intimate letters to boyfriends girlfriends friend friends and acquaintances into two suitcases, and she sat there in her room with her life in two suitcases, and waited. The friends should be here, she over-thought and over-worried and then feigned external calm, in case some family member was monitoring her, or would come into her room as she tried to look idly out the ill-lit window in the evening gloom, listening for the sound of her friends' urban assault vehicle to crunch up her parents' tiny driveway. But there was no legate from the bosom of the family; no one tried to reason with her. Eventually, at around seven o'clock, her friends came. Still no one came to say goodbye. No one spoke to her as the doorbell rang. No one answered the doorbell. She answered the door with her suitcases in hand, smiled, and got into the vehicle, and then she was gone. Forever.

From the parental perspective, they were prepared, with the omniscience of the parent who had borne and raised the child. They had read the volumes, had sought professional advice as regards the matter of their daughter. They had explained to the professionals that you do your best to inculcate a certain set of values into a child, but there comes a point when they become responsible for their own actions. Only Aron would have fully appreciated the extraterrestrial irony in such a value system. But it didn't matter. The professionals with whom Aron's parents had spoken told the Tullys to let her go. This was why there was no scene of heartbreak, no tearful goodbyes, no attempt to reason or unreason with their daughter, their beautiful, intelligent, resourceful daughter, who had achieved nothing in her life, who had been such a disappointment. Well that's life you see, they said to themselves, in the inevitable self-justifying post-mortems that follow a family tragedy. You never know how they turn out, they reason. Tearful reflections. You do your best to bring them up, as damaged as you are. You do your best, you see, and then this is how they repay you. They leave. In the end, they all leave. And, so, she left.

At first, Aron slept a lot and read the newspapers strategically left on the dinner table for her when she woke up. They were trying to help her find work. With the undisturbed rest and the regular life, she began to feel better. She had her best suit cleaned, and began to march out by day to find work.

After several months of predictable failure, she found employment in the offices of Kafka insurance. This was not a difficult task, for Dr. Kafka was still in his offices at the time of her summons to be interviewed. She arrived at the busy offices of Kafka Insurance at ten o'clock, as summoned. The thin Dr. Kafka spoke softly and smiled at Aron. Kafka sat behind his desk, with his carefully calibrated notes before him, fingered them a little, then asked Tully to explain to him why he should hire her. At this stage, Kafka had decided to hire her. He knew her. Tully looked into the eyes of Dr. Kafka and, in that moment, she had a revelation. His eyes were the eyes of stars, the eyes filled with a terrible light of knowing, the eyes of fire, the explosive origins of time and pain and horror and creation and destruction, and she saw in them the possibility of future employment and substantial, but unrecognised, art. And it was then she knew she had to have this job. She knew then why one is obliged to lie at interviews. One is obliged to lie at such times because Tully, like so many others, had nothing to offer, except their unrealised potential. It was Kafka's task to see such potential. The past is dead at a job interview. They want what they want, and what they want is what they think you can give. And, what you can give is not yet given. And so Tully talked and talked and she gave him her babble and Dr. Kafka took a long calm smiling careful look at Aron, as was his wont, and knew she was lying. His thin tapered fingers, his slim nose, his clear shining forehead, his glowing eyes, his spotless dark brown suit, his spotless shoes, his soft voice — it was so beautiful, so delicate. He raised his hand, and smiled. "That will be all Ms Tully. I'll let you know. Thank you."

He terminated the interview, having decided to give her the job. He instructed his subordinates to draw up the necessary paperwork to have Aron Tully employed by the company. He liked her. She had lied well and with undeniable style. Tully was overjoyed. She was free. The wages of sin were a monthly cheque. She, thus, won the necessary personal freedom to live in derelict estates and bombed out, condemned buildings, away from those awful, hypocritical luxury apartments where her loving friends resided. She could lurk with the undead, the waged and the corporate executives. She was financially independent. It had been such a strain living with the friends, despite all their kindness and spiritual seduction of her needy, desperate soul. All that love can suffocate. It was so unlike the real world.

As soon as the wages came through, she moved out of her friends' apartment and began sleeping in vacated business premises and hospitals. The nuclear glow of such buildings kept her safe and warm. She acquired a gun for protection and only occasionally had to use it. The other vagrants who lived there left her mostly alone. They feared being shot if they tried to molest her and Tully made no bones about using her gun.

But living in bombed out buildings lacked something. She found that the ghosts that haunt such dwellings were unfriendly. They had mostly died violent and bloody deaths, generally at the hands of drug-hungry surgeons and corporate takeover hit-people, fulfilling lucrative contracts and mob hits and political assassinations and murder rape killers, and other sundry undetectable dyings, handed down from the anonymous above. The targets were, for the most part, people who knew too much. She reflected that these horrors should attract her, that she should feel a certain affinity for such things, all these nice dead people and all they want in death is to suffer an eternity of gut-wrenching, lonely torment in peace. Who could argue with that? Died alone and friendless, for their friends had betrayed them, and they were bitter and harsh spiritual companions. Though Tully could see them, they had no desire to keep her company. She would call to them to come back and at least chat, but they would leave to annoy someone else. And the evenings became emptier and emptier, and there were only so many books one could read in a night, so many words written and so few of them useful.

She moved around a lot during the first months of working in Kafka Insurance, because she felt restless and unsure wherever she tried to settle. Things were good in work. She liked her colleagues and the business was doing well. Dr. Kafka expressed discomfort at the increasing bureaucratisation of his, by now successful, business venture, and warned everyone to read his work on the dangers of making procedure quality assurance, and other sundry bits of paperwork, their God. Kafka

Insurance had become successful because it was about people, not just the money, so he said. Kafka liked the work, though it was affecting his writing. He had sought professional therapeutic help since his recovery from tuberculosis, had cut down on his excessive writing obsession, resolved his issues with his father, and focused on his life-long dream of running a successful business. He had already, it was rumoured, turned down several major literary prizes in his lifetime, including the Nobel Prize for his unfinished classic, The Castle. He kept notes for possible endings at home in a locked closet, fearing becoming unwell once more if he ever succumbed to the urge to write again. It was such a dangerous occupation. He also feared if he produced another book it would attract unwelcome media attention, disturb his deep need for solitude, and ultimately destroy the purity of his art, which was now his life. Dr. Kafka had worked hard to save himself, had a good business going, and money and fame would not bring him closer to that truth he had for so long sought. Kafka was happy at last and things were going well down in central command.

As the months wore by, Tully was required to do more and more overtime and Dr. Kafka expressed his gratitude for her industriousness and meticulous attention to detail. She bought a business suit, a briefcase, and moved again to other accommodation. She decided on the shell of the old Children's Hospital, Harcourt Street, as her permanent temporary residence. She paid rent to the local drugs lord who came around demanding monies with menaces, that is until she became friends with Tully. Then the rent went down and the local drugs lord used call for tea and a chat. Tully liked the local drugs lord and they usually went for a drink after their tea and their chat. Together, they drank in the local cocktail bars where the lawyers met to discuss their respective cases. Tully's friendship with the local, smashed out, drug lord became something of an inspiration to her. Tully felt something akin to companionship with that stoned out queen of chemical distraction.

She would call and talk about everything. They liked the same books and went to see the same movies and plays. Aron grew to love her. They became fast friends and exchanged favourite books every so often, and hung out in their favourite shooting gallery. Despite the warm joy of a newfound friendship, Aron knew this was an unsuitable life for a writer. Having known and grown to love and respect the remote person of Dr. Kafka, who had given up writing to save his life and sell insurance, she knew herself to be a writer. She knew no other writers, and did not know what was fashionable or marketable, and, aside from the bombed out junk queen, she didn't see many people outside her job. She wanted to work, not have a job. She wanted to find a space where she could work. She decided there was only the now. Living in the moment only occasionally seemed to give one hope. But she took the now for what it was worth. Aron began her novel. It was a short book on the reality of bears and other significant creatures, such as badgers and cats and dogs. Sleeping in the old hospital, with its weird midnight noises, the sound of old souls whispering, the scratch and the strain of the structure underfoot, all these things conspired to make her write when she came home from Doctor Kafka's firm of brokers. She kept her conspiring to create the reality of bears a secret. She sat up in her hospital bed, with its spotlessly clean sheets and small bedside camp light and the sounds of earth world playing on her bedside transistor radio and she wrote into her notebook, Chapter Three, On Being a Bear. Night after night after night, she sat there, sketching structure and parameters of the book down, fighting sleep, keeping going...

And, then, Arthur Kruger found her. He came to hide his manuscript, which he claimed was a bomb. She told him it wasn't a bomb, but he wasn't hearing her. He arrived months later, when the dark of winter came down. Until the night when Arthur Kruger came to call, everything was calm and well and she had almost forgotten her loneliness. Then came Kruger, and suddenly it was all different. She heard him coming, heard his footsteps and she knew that Some One Different This Way Comes. She had grown hypersensitive to every sound in the old hospital building. She could hear the creak of the old drunk junkies' bones. She heard the clink of late night oblivion drinking. She heard the rattle of the old steel beds. Then the hush and howl and screams of the infant ghosts. The crossing of landings by long dead doctors and their patients. The dead come, still looking for love and morphine in the night. She heard them all. But this was a different sound. A human footfall, both old and young. Not a ghost. Kruger carried the heavy weight that was himself. She took her gun and laid it across her breast. Disposing of dead bodies isn't easy, she thought. I hate this. Even in a hospital, disposing of dead bodies isn't easy. Then, the sound approached and with it there came Arthur Kruger. Something was carefully slid under the bed. Perhaps another body. She took the gun and pointed it at Arthur Kruger's head.

"Hello," said Kruger.

"What are you doing?" Aron Tully asked the young old Arthur Kruger

"Putting this bomb under your bed, actually."

"Bomb?" she asked.

"Bomb," he said. "You know – boom. I am putting the device under your bed because it seems to be the right thing to do. I thought, somewhere inside, you would understand. It only does damage if it goes off, you see."

"I can see you've thought this out, carefully."

"No, it's safe. I mean, it's safe now," Kruger said.

"And I see you were a science major, a very long time ago."

"You have no idea," Arthur Kruger said.

"You need help, seriously. You also might have asked if I understand, and maybe even if I accept," Tully said.

"Agreed," said Kruger. "Sorry about the not asking you thing. Is it okay, by the way..?"

"Well, this might be totally unimportant," said Tully, still pointing the fully loaded gun at Kruger, "But what if the device decides to detonate and I am here asleep, or reading, or writing, would that not constitute an act of premeditated homicide?"

"Very likely," answered Arthur Kruger. "Sorry again about that. By the way, I am Arthur Kruger. I apologize for trying to kill you."

"I gather you weren't trying to do that, in fact the opposite."

"How, um, rational. Would you perhaps like to go somewhere for a drink and put away the gun? I am sure there are bars open at this time. Please put the gun down. Put it in the suitcase. You are completely safe."

"Completely?" said Tully. "I think not. And I must respectfully decline this drink offer. I am... rather tired."

"Please come. I feel bad about all this," said Arthur Kruger.

"No, I need to sleep," said Tully. "I have work tomorrow."

"You work?" asked Kruger "And live here?"

"Yes, I work at an Insurance Brokers."

"Which insurance brokers? I am thinking of getting some insurance... for the bomb, you know."

Kruger was, of course, lying. He thought Tully was very attractive.

"That's great," Tully said, deciding on this person's, Arthur Kruger's, complete insanity. "Call in anytime. We are always in need of business. Doctor Kafka would always understand."

"Dr. Kafka? Kafka insurance... that fool turned down the..."

"The same," Said Tully. "Turned down the Nobel Prize – and for an unfinished book to boot. Such a crazy guy. He could have greatly expanded his business with the prize money and the increased sales of his books. It always gives a writer a boost if they win prizes. It's the equivalent of the Palm D'Or or and Oscar, you see..."

"I might just do that," said Kruger, "I might just see about the insurance thing, I mean. To go back to what you were saying before. Insurance, now there's the thing. Look after my bomb. Would you mind? I have problems with it at the moment. I might call in over the next two days. You are safe now. I would have it in my apartment, except there could be trouble if the landlady found out about it."

"That's fine," said Tully. "I understand your predicament," she said, moving and feeling the suitcase was a tad light.

Kruger stalked off. Tully dragged the suitcase from under the bed and forced it open. She found the suitcase empty, but for a few bundles of carefully written upon manuscript paper, wrapped in plastic and sealed using waxed twine. 'Ten Short Novels,' She read. Mmm. The waxed twine she also liked. It was, she noted, the type obtainable in any common or garden hardware store. She went back to sleep, dreaming of Kruger and his Ten Short Novels. It's a bomb script, you see, so she dreamed.

Arthur Kruger came back the following evening about seven o'clock as Tully tucked into a vegetable teriyaki and peanut stir fry with fried rice, purchased from the local Chinese take away. She shared the food with him, and the drunks and the junkies stayed away, because they knew of her gun and her propensity to use it and her mad friends. Kruger didn't eat much. The dope queen came by to exchange stories with Aron, but left after a while, feeling rejected by Aron's new choice of intimate companions.

"So what's with all the paper?" she asked Kruger. Kruger looked at her, puzzled by the question.

"Paper," he said?

"The 'bomb'," she said. "The paper bomb," she said. "In the suitcase."

"There is no 'paper bomb'," Kruger said. "You would want to be careful with…"

"Right," said Tully.

"I am a writer, you see," Arthur Kruger said.

"Goody for you. So am I," Tully said. "And quite the diplomat too. Inviting a girl out after giving her a bomb."

"That's great. So what about that drink?" Kruger said

"I assume you have no money," Tully said.

"Correct," said Kruger.

Having no money was excruciatingly embarrassing for Kruger. But he did not want to be alone. Not this time. The hospital was getting so cold and hollow, now that night had fallen. He did not want to go onto the streets and home to his place by himself. He heard noises. She said that there were parties downstairs.

"Some of the local poets," she said.

"Sure," he said. "Let's go with them. They know the best places."

"Great," Aron said.

"I see you didn't call on Dr. Kafka," she said, putting away her things into her bag and checking her revolver. "I mentioned to him of your interest in insurance. He was delighted at the prospect of a little business. Is it your life you are interested in insuring?"

"Insuring my life might be problematic," Kruger said. "I've been dead more than once."

"I see," she said.

And they took the stairs. The lift had long stopped working.

They went on down to the bar with the matter unresolved and they sat together in mostly silence, watching people come and go, listening to the poets recite their work and applauding, occasionally commenting on the clothes, or the attitude accompanying the clothes, about who was speaking to whom and why they felt they had to talk like that.

"I don't envy those who talk a lot," Kruger said. "It's such hard work."

Tully was familiar with the local gangster element in the bar crowd. She knew who was talking to whom, whether it was with regard to a deal or a truce or a bribe or a payoff. She knew who had just got out of the jail and what they were doing in a bar like this. Kruger was astonished at the depth of her knowledge and asked her how she knew so much.

"How do you know all this?" he asked.

"No reason," she said. "No big secret, I naturally absorb that kind of information."

"Right," he said.

"And that's important," she said.

Kruger looked at her with a mixture of fear and desire. She looked back at him, impassively meeting his longing silence with calm, distant, watchful, smiling silence.

"What's wrong?" she said.

"Nothing," he said.

Endogenous compression of the thought faculties, he thought. God knows I spent too long on your trail, he thought.

"Then why are you so quiet?" Tully asked.

"No reason," he said. "I am not much of a talker, lucky for you," Kruger said.

It gives me peace at last, Kruger thought, to find you, like religion, in the end. We all sell out then, you see. This thing, this being with another thing, this feeling with another feeling, for another thing... it's... confusing

"You are lonely?" Tully said, beginning to mistrust the silence between them.

"Yes," Kruger said. "I have spent a lifetime to meet this moment."

"Whom do you write? What you do write, I mean. I mean is there anything you write about?"

"No idea. No apartheid in my texts. But this is the thing: since I decided to leave home, I have been unable to write anything. The days tend to be long. I keep notes," Kruger said. "Notes about notes. Notes about ... stuff... things seen and heard... and felt..."

"Why don't you kiss me?" Tully said.

"I know," Kruger said. "I want to. Kiss and be kissed. The meeting of all opposites in a kiss."

But, then Arthur Kruger stopped dreaming. He drifted out of subconscious into conscious, like a diver surfacing. He could see that she saw the distance in him, that he had gone somewhere, and was now back.

"Well," he said. "That was a very nice drink."

"Yes," Tully said. "A very nice drink. I like this place. We are a suitable part of the clientele."

"That's not... important to me," he said.

"So, what's important?" Tully asked.

"I think it's important to have enough money to live on. The rest is speculation, I guess. Outside of that, I do what I can, is that okay? I ..."

"So what do you do," Tully asked. "What exactly is it that you do?"

"What I can," Kruger said, "and I'm not jesting. Come home with me, come home, don't leave... it... like this..."

"What? Who do you think I am?" Tully said.

"The type of person who does what they can."

And, she stopped and looked down and a faint recognition seemed to cross her expression and, she smiled at him and she looked at his already smiling, shy face, and reached across and she kissed him gently, feeling at last this was not wrong. They put their arms about each other and stood there outside the bar. This was right. They felt it, holding each other, sensing the sea change in the ether. They did not know how. Sensing a primordial knowing, that together they would be in less pain than before, that there was a chance of freedom that they wanted to take, she went home to the privacy of his bed sit, carefully avoiding the landlady, who would disapprove, they made love as awkwardly as they ever would, with fear and trembling, chuckling at their endless naiveté for people who had seen too much of life too soon. She called in sick the following day and they spent it together. They ate in cheap but nice places and Kruger got his clothes cleaned and pressed so they would get into some of the better bars and eateries in town and not the filthy places he grew accustomed to before. She was amazed how he stayed a stranger wherever he went, how he didn't say much to anyone, how no-one greeted Arthur Kruger, and, if they did, he would hardly acknowledge them, how he didn't look you much in the eye. When she asked him about that he said it had always been like that for him and he had grown used to it over the years. He did not expect, or notice, attention. He expected not to expect, so things were fine. Tully said that would be something she could never get used to. Kruger smiled and said he had to get back home. He had work to do and Tully said yes. She had to get ready for work in the morning. That too.

Kruger felt good to be with this person, clinging to life as he did, okay to be alone and not alone all at once. She seemed to instinctually let him be. And he left her to be herself, knowing full well that love is never enough, that love paves the road to hell faster than good intentions. Something always happens. Better off being sure.

"Your family will come looking for you and perform black masses in your presence. Or a stranger calls. It happens in the best biographies and sometimes in life."

"A stranger?" she said.

"A stranger. Believe it."

"You are crazy," she said. "Crazy."

"Look," he said.

"Yes?"

"Look... Everyone is a stranger in a hospital. If we live between two places we will just be living apart. I know I have no money. I am sorry. I'll get a job if you like. If we allow money to determine things. We can't end up living by accountancy."

Tully was more than sceptical. She was afraid of being with him. Afraid of the invasion she would feel, but felt too that this was right. That deep down it felt right. That it was okay to feel this afraid. Survival of the fearful. She said:

"And what will you do all day?"

"Try to write."

"You expect me to pay the bills? What about my writing?"

"No... No... I'll get a job..." he said.

"No you won't. You'll never work. Never."

"No. So what will we be doing?"

"Me?" she said. "I'll muddle through."

Kruger looked half sneering, feeling more than a little jealous of the certainties she had in her life.

He said, "You have a plan and an income. I can see it makes you happy."

"Happy is a strong adjective," she said.

"You have your drug fiend friends and your job with Dr. Kafka," he said. "I suppose he has something in the works too."

"I don't know what Dr. Kafka plans," she said. "He is something of a mystery to us all. But I like his spirituality and his great talent."

"Oh please, he likes feeling special, that's all. I thought you got along with him. I thought you and he had coffee together, in the Jonathan Swift definition of the term."

"I do. But he never talks about himself. He likes the theatre and politics and theology. He likes movies too. He goes twice a week to watch movies."

"A fun guy. I like that. Party animal."

"No, Arthur. I've thought about it. Moving in together is not a good idea," she said. "I won't do it. It's not right. It's crazy."

"Very likely," Arthur Kruger said. "Totally crazy. Right? I'll go home now," he said, getting out of bed at four o'clock in the morning. He smiled at Tully's smiling face and said: "We'll talk." And kissed her. "I have to go now."

"Call me," she said. "Call me in work. You're sure you are not hungry? I have some bagels in the fridge over there."

"No thanks. I am not hungry. How come the fridge works?"

"A few plugs work on this floor. Most don't. I even have a little light and heat," she said.

"Right. I'll call you," he said.
"Bye."

But they moved in together anyway, despite the madness of it. They moved into a house off Prospect Avenue, deeming it cheap enough and giving suitable accommodation. Tully's confidence had taken a quantum leap. Her work rate got better. She slept even better at night. She became a productive member of the burgeoning Kafka Insurance business. She was sick less frequently. Her success rate in selling insurance and consolidating deals with small and medium sized businesses increased. Others in the office looked upon her with a mixture of fear, anger, jealousy and admiration. Tully was too strange to do well, to secretive to be liked, too good to be true, so they decided. Some, whom she had thought of as friends, no longer associated with her. She felt lonely and hurt. But she buried herself in work and it had its own rewards. Dr. Kafka, who believed in rewarding excellence, took her aside and suggested she take further exams in Zen and the art of insurance and achieve a higher qualification. The implication was that if she had such a higher qualification, then Dr. Kafka could promote Tully in the bigger firm of Kafka Insurance. There was no commitment from Dr. Kafka in this regard. But Tully understood and was elated at such a compliment.

She rushed home to tell Kruger. Kruger simulated gushing admiration, but found it hard to feel anything. This was a good thing, he thought. But it also meant he would see less of her now. She stopped writing. She was too tired to do anything in the evenings, except watch television and drink wine and fall into bed before eleven at night. But she feared for Kruger. She tried to get him to take a job. At anything, get him out of the house and meeting people, making friends. He refused to sell insurance and became deeply depressed at the prospect of office work He got a job for a few weeks in a small bookshop. But Kruger struck the owner after he accused him of stealing some morning coffee from him and books too. Kruger was taking the books home and reading them and bringing them back. The owner of the bookstore did not sue him. But Kruger lost another job. So, he was at home becoming increasingly anxious and guilty over being supported by Tully. And she would hound him about his writing.

"How many words did you write today?" she asked him, in Andy Warhol mode.

"Life is short. Time finite," he said.

"How many words?" She would ask. "You can't expect me to support us if you do no work. How many words?"

"None today. I have nothing to say."

"If you have nothing to say," she said, "Then steal. There are so many lives out there. You have ten novels in you."

"Ten Short Novels," Arthur Kruger said. "Yes," she said. "Ten Short Novels by you know whom. Steal," she said. "You have a suitcase filled with notes."

Yes. Why not steal? So he began revisiting the unfinished bomb script and stole wholesale from the lives all about him. Ten short novels. He stole from her soul, as his own had been long hollowed out. He stole from the souls of her friends, relentlessly plundered their fictional lives and tried to get it all-real. He stole Brad and Mary and Joe from her soul, and then gave it all back, for he felt himself misdirected. He met them all, with their friendly voices and their interesting well-reflected-upon, educated conversation, their well-attuned gossipy, perception of others' lives. He went for drinks with them. He had them over for dinner. Then there were the others, the dozens of others, who had no other lives, save for the lives his imagination gave them. They all lived and he gave them life and histories and forgot the line between the real and the fictional and the fear that he would one day wake up and have lost control of it all. And Kruger liked these people, some carbon-based life forms, some not. But he could not steal for long.

Then he wrote down the title of the book. The rest he had written was merely a library of notes to focus the mind on the atoms of his world. The title was the start. He would write ten short novels, each one of them a perspective on the labyrinth of being alive. About the Bomb. About the dark. It would be the freedom, from himself. The end was nearer than he thought, and further than he could ever imagine, past the interstellar void. Beyond the comfort of career, beyond family and attendant finance. He sensed that no good could come of this for himself. But he had nothing else to do. There was a sense of inevitability about it.

It became his one true obsession. Although he lived with Aron, she knew quickly she had lost him to the very book she had suggested he write. It distressed her greatly. But she let him go. He would have died sooner otherwise.

His day started at about eleven in the morning. This tardiness in rising came from Kruger's insomnia, fed partly by his nervousness, partly by nightmares. Nothing matched the desolation following a vivid nightmare. Thus, he developed a schedule to escape these dreams and restless waiting, though vivid dreams and restlessness fed his writing. The book became the reflection upon which he saw his fragmentary and elusive self.

He used the night time as best he could. If he was not too tired, he would work till two or three in the morning, sitting up in bed with the manuscript balanced on his lap, until sleep, or exhaustion, came. He could sense whether or not it would be a good night by the types of dreams and feelings that would visit him the moment he finally closed his eyes.

He would vaguely hear Tully rise at about seven or so. She would come into the bedroom to kiss him goodbye for the day and then he would go back to sleep for another few hours. Then breakfast and to work again, sitting in front of his screen typing out the book. He called on no one during this time, heard from no one, save her, and drank heavily at night to bring himself down to earth. He slept badly generally, and Tully complained endlessly about his habit of struggling out of bed in the small hours and the freezing cold to go downstairs, insomniac, to write. His mind was the storm the words made and left him running running until. Until the word running left.

The book progressed quickly. The chapters cohered into their own weird non-predetermined order and progression. Kruger found himself as the one following orders as the words marched from the nowhere at the depths of it, placing them down as they said so, marshalling the sentences and the paragraphs as the dark so directed.

These words, these saddening suppositions, he thought. Where did they come from? Were they who he was? He watched them come into existence. Perhaps it is the feeling of stillness that the words evoke. Words, like sentries in their solitary station keeping, eschewing any safety in numbers. They stand alone. They drift through the mind's eyes, running on emptily, meeting in forms of one, melting into the completeness of the unknowable one word at the end. Perhaps one is equality in unity, wholeness in isolation, and the loss of the other together, alone with the other stranger that I am to every other like myself, he thought.

I stare at them in space, somewhere along the continuum between thought and action, along the stratosphere of eternity, or in self-sufficiency, across pages to see their effect on one another. Perhaps I am built from these particles that form the bomb, those I know and the many others I have not met. It is quite remarkable how they interact, the legion of solitary angels that hold me together. And I never hear them speak.

He would sit at night, after a day's work and read over the text he had written to see if any of it needed reworking. More often than not, it needed changes. And he wrote and rewrote until it came together. He would make them there and then, and try to sleep. Occasionally, Aron asked to see finished sections, the short novels as she liked to call them. Kruger would print it up and she would curl up on the sofa in the front room with the television on and read through the text. She liked what he was doing. It was going to be alright, she beamed. Their lives were taking shape, she thought, and, yet, at the same time, it was running out, for she saw too much of him in these words.

But he seemed happy, such as happiness was a recognizable entity. He seemed productive, finally getting to sleep at night, seemed fitter, seemed getting there. It was like having a strange alien creature as a companion, someone who had no home but chose her as a companion, out of love, or its nearest substitute. She let him live and tried to live herself. But never saw the end coming when it finally happened.

He had been working for nearly a year, hardly going out and day and night at the desk, saying it was nearly all over, that an end was in sight. He seemed so happy, then finally, one day, he rang her at the office saying it was over, all over, that he had finished and there was nothing left for him and that she should forgive him.
"Forgive you for what?" she said.
"Everything."
"But you have done nothing wrong…"
"I suppose," he said, and then he had to go.

And all day long, the brief exchange she had with him lingered, disturbing her concentration at her work to such an extent that Dr. Kafka took her aside and asked her was there anything amiss. And she told him what Arthur had said to her that morning and how it had worried her, that it all sounded not right and Dr. Kafka nodded non-committally and said it did not sound good and that she should go home and see to Kruger, see what was wrong, that things would be okay today, just this once. Dr. Kafka decided, at that moment, to promote Tully, to give her the position of junior partner in the firm of Kafka Insurance. He saw then, in a flash of intuition, that she had the potential to go anywhere she wanted.

Tully drove home. She had bought a car the previous autumn from a long overdue bonus cheque. Kafka had appended a written apology to the cheque for the delay in getting it to her, but Tully was not the complaining type. She banked the cheque and bought a car with it within a month.

When she got home, Kruger was not in, and she had no idea where he was. In his room, the finished manuscript sat on his desk with a dedication 'To Aron Tully' on the first page just below the title and author. She felt terrified and began to weep uncontrollably. Something had happened.

Arthur did not come home. At about ten o'clock that same night, a policeman arrived to deliver the news that Arthur had thrown himself in front of a train. She rang Dr. Kafka at home and told him the news in quiet tones. Kafka sympathised and told her to take a few days leave, to try to come to terms with it all, and, if she wished, he was there to listen, if she wanted to talk. There was an inquest within a week that returned a verdict of death by suicide. Several witnesses saw him throw himself in front of the train and a few tried to stop him. It was all so very public, making it so much the worse. There was video footage of the event. At the funeral, Arthur's parents approached her and invited her over sometime for a meal and to talk things over. Arthur had made a will, leaving all his manuscripts, not to his parents, but to her. But Tully said she would keep the most recent work, dedicated to her, but they could have the rest. This seemed to be an acceptable arrangement and she had dinner with the Kruger's twice, usually a sad affair, but they talked and cried together and she felt the better for having gone. They were, she decided, truly lovely people.

The doctor prescribed antidepressants and sleeping tablets for the time being and she began to attend bereavement counselling and Dr. Kafka, in an extraordinary act of faith in Aron Tully, made her a junior partner after only two years superhuman effort on her part and her lover dead a month by now.

Two nights after her promotion, Tully came home late and slept in the following morning. She woke about eleven o'clock in the day, ran a bath and took a razor blade and slashed her wrists and remembered nothing until she woke in hospital with Arthur's parents and Dr. Kafka and doctors attending. Inexplicably, she had survived. A kindly spirit, perhaps, had come to her aid.

"She had tried to kill herself," a hospital psychiatrist said. How did I do that? she thought. Where did all the pain come from to make me do such a thing? Just how depressed have I been all this time?

She cried a little and asked how she was still alive and they told her someone had put through an anonymous emergency call at the right place at the right time. Someone was looking out for you, they said. You have no idea how lucky you are. No idea. Dr. Kafka smiled his quiet brilliant smile, his gentle face and dark eyes looking into his new junior partner, intimidatingly understanding more of what was happening than he would ever say. He told her to take as much time she liked, that er job would be there for her. He sat by her bedside for much of the following days, reading Proust and making phone calls to the office to ensure business was being taken care of. Kruger's parents had stopped in for a half an hour and had long gone. Tully's parents came mostly in the mornings, wept, talked to the psychiatrists and doctors a lot, and then left. On the fourth day Tully and Kafka began to talk. Kafka asked about Kruger.

"He was mad," Tully said, "but fun. He had a lot on his mind. He was fun, a funny guy."

Kafka smiled. For a moment, the glow of tuberculosis seemed to return to his omnivorous eyes. They didn't call it consumption for nothing, Tully thought. His mobile phone rang. He answered it, nodded, then hung up.

"I have to go back to the office. Meetings. A crisis. I'll call back this evening."

"Tell me, Dr. Kafka," Tully asked, "Why did you decline the Nobel Prize?"

Dr. Kafka shook his head and did not answer. And Dr. Kafka smiled and said, "That was a private matter. I will call in this evening or tomorrow to see how you are doing."

And Aron smiled and turned to go back to sleep. The hospital psychiatrist would be calling in to see her. She needed to get a rest in for that particular meeting.

NOVEL X

I AM ANOTHER

I wake up. Where am I? Then I remember. This has happened before. I get this mostly in the mornings. It's just for a minute or two. I don't know why it happens. I have this panic. That there's something wrong with the world. And then I calm down. Yes, it's okay again. Wish I knew what it was.

I can hear the sounds. My breathing. Then the radio sound. I hear the electric click of the radio switched on too loud. That's what woke me. The trigger click. Then it's turned quickly, crackly down. Then the sounds of movement downstairs. Then the sound of discreet female feet. Someone downstairs. Someone aware that I might be asleep. Then the self-obsessed clumsy, childish bang. And the little boy laugh. Aron and Joseph are having breakfast. These people are family. I am here. This is my life.

I turn over in my bed, remember the time, and decide to wash and find some clothes. The house is warm and, as I go into the bathroom, I feel it a relief not to have to shiver at this time of year anymore. I have time only for a shower. I walk back into the warm bedroom with its heavy deep red wall hangings and paintings and mirrors and heavy pull blinds and music playing off in the distance. I select a good suit and comb my graying beard and hair and put on clean fresh crisp clothing over my fresh clean-smelling body. Being this clean and presentable makes me feel good. I call a cab, and, as I wait, I have this sense of having travelled here from a great distance elsewhere, from the bathroom down the hall to here. I have a sense of a calm arrival that seems to have arrested my frightened moment of awakening. I check my suit and crisp shirt in the mirror. I am almost good to go.

I can hear Joe downstairs, talking to the dog and throwing things. I hear the odd crash, probably a toy chucked about the kitchen, as breakfast is reluctantly eaten by the little boy, who wants his friends forever to be the toy soldiers he loves and the football games with other little boys.

I try to picture Joe, right now, as I check my face for lines and blemishes, my hair for baldness and more grey hairs, my shirt for unwarranted creases. I look at myself, and, for a second, see myself, catch the happiness and the sorrow in the expression, the unusual youthfulness in my eyes and skin despite my years, that smug sense of having overcome the odds and kept it together, my sense of self-identity imposed on my reflection, my self-expression in my mirror. I picture the clear eyes of my son in my own reflection and, then, suddenly, I can hardly see myself. Instead, I see decaying skeletal remains, bits of flesh being eaten away from whitening bone. I am shocked. I look again and see myself and then I see the old Arthur, my clean crisp confident air, the lingering sense of self-possession that I give, is in place. I am Arthur Kruger, I say to myself.

I pause at the top of the stairs and listen to Aron and Joe talk to each other.
"Be a good little pussy cat and eat your breakfast."
"Don't be a silly mommy, I'm not a pussy cat! I'm a little boy!"
I walk into the kitchen and on the breakfast table beside Aron's coffee I see a copy of *The Castle*.
"Kafka for breakfast, how uplifting," I say and kiss her good morning. Joe wants a hug as well as a kiss. Aron continues with the Kafka witticism.
"I was thinking of reading a little to our boy, just to kill off any illusions he might have about how things really are."
"Great," I say. "And we'll charge the therapist fees to your credit card."
"Get them while they're young, that's what I say. Isn't that right sweetie?"

"Pussy cat," Joe says by way of response, and picks up his favourite toy train. "Daddy, Daddy, Daddy, we missed you…"

I kiss them both once more and sit quietly down to breakfast, trying not to let my anxiety show. I have about eleven minutes. I can see I have dilly-dallied too long upstairs, lingering in a kind of vanity. I see Aron looks lovely today, a beautiful dress, black shoes, and her slim muscular body clearly imaginable underneath the beckoning clothes. No time for sex. Ten minutes. If I eat too quickly and just leave now, I'll get indigestion, I think. If I eat too slowly, I'll get in too late. I eat slowly, deciding that things will work themselves out anyway.

"You look gorgeous in that dress, by the way," I say.

"You charmer you," she says. "I thought we might have a little dinner this evening."

"What about himself?" I see Joe is conducting a crash test between his favourite toy train and a toy soldier. "That's an expensive toy train," I say.

"Stop, darling…" Aron says.

"Bang! Crrashhhh! Bassssshhh!" Joe says.

Joe bangs the toy soldier harder with the train. Then he runs him over and over. I feel panicky. I take the train from him. I haven't got time for this, I say to myself.

"Noooo, no no no no. Please Daddy, noooohhhh…"

He shouts at me, then whimpers, then shouts, then sulks, and tries to grab the train from me. Then I raise my index finger at him in warning.

"Now, now, young man," I say. "You will get your toy train when you promise to finish your breakfast and not be so noisy when Mummy and Daddy are having a chat. Okay?"

The boy does not easily submit to my negotiation skills. I give in to him too easily, I know that. Aron is aware I will be out the door in minutes, whether or not I have eaten.

"What about Joe?" she asks.

"Yes! What about meeee?" Joe says.

"You might go see someone." Aron frowns at Joe. I put more food into my mouth. Joe stamps his foot.

"No stamping!" I say. My tone is severe. The boy pipes down. I am irritable myself. I didn't notice that. Aron seems calm, though. She has plans for us this evening, and I feel there is nothing for it but to comply. Her focus on this matter seems complete, her planning insurmountable. I have six minutes. If I start saying I have so little time she will get upset. Time is irrelevant. I don't know what I want. I want the easiest out-clause obtainable. I want to get to work.

"He might pay a visit to his granny this afternoon, about five maybe. I'll leave him into Montessori, and you could collect him, and bring him over to Rose. I'll call her and maybe bring over a basket of fruit as a thank you…"

"And a bottle of Sicilian White. She likes Sicilian white. Be nice…"

Aron raises her eyebrows at me, as Joe is on the verge of bursting into tears for my theft of his brand new train that Granddad gave his favourite grandson. I hand Joe back his train and he takes it from me, hurt that I would defy him so. Two minutes to critical mass. One minute fifty seconds to departure…

"I have to go. Two minutes…"

"I see…"

"I really have to go…"

"Why take a taxi?"

"Drinks last night. Left my car parked in the company garage," I said.

"I forgot. I'll call you. What time did you get in?"

"About twelve."

"I didn't hear. I mean, I didn't hear you."

"I'm silent when drunk. Gotta go. Bye…"

"Bye," she looks a little lost, playing mother as her boy plays trains, her mind elsewhere.

"Call me after eleven o'clock in the day," I say to her as I close the hall door. I forget to ask her what she had to do today. All I can think about are the meetings I will attend.

I taxi quickly to work, traffic good, no bother. The taxi man veers right, down the last road; turn right, past the motorcycle policeman, and I'm at Watani. I recognise a few of the cars in the parking lot. Everyone who is anyone will be hovering around today. I can tell from the quality of the vehicles. I see Shelvin's car, feeling my anxiety mount over this meeting today. Shelvin has his office door open. His office is down the corridor from mine. His office door is left open when he is monitoring who is around and who is walking with whom. Shelvin calls me as I pass by.
"Arthur, do you have a minute?"
I had to pass by Shelvin's office to get to my office. I was his obvious victim, his crime of opportunity.
"What is it?"
"I see you're in a particularly good mood, today"
Shelvin had the health and sense of well being of the insensitive person, the good digestion of one who does not stomach the pain of others, who does not think about the consequences of his words, who sleeps well because he has, by some alchemy, forgotten how to care, has made his love conditional and his hate a moral obligation given by his own personal cruel and unforgiving God.
"Max, please state your business. I'm tired and I have a headache."
"Come in for a minute."
Shelvin's still well muscled body and clear, slightly tanned skin and formidable smile filled the room as I came in. He looked as though he had been waiting for me, or if not me, then someone of my grade to pass by.
"Okay, what is it?"
"The system, your system, is simply inadequate for our needs at present."

"We've been through this before."

"It is too slow, breaks down too often."

"You won't learn how to use it properly, that's why it breaks down."

"I mean, I have five people inside trying to get a lot of stock out, five people with so much depending on them…"

I looked at him. He had started talking and I just couldn't hear him. A great gulf seemed to separate us and word salad came from his lips. I thought of all the rumours about him. I hoped all of them were true.

"Shelvin. Stop speaking."

Shelvin was in full flight, babbling about the deficiencies of the system that I maintained that operated his stock control, how unhelpful my staff were, how many more reports were needed from that system, that as I was the systems man, how could I fail to see that all the important work he was doing needed my support?

"Shelvin, I have a meeting."

"You are in a meeting right now."

"Shelvin, I have to go. I'll get Brad on it."

"Brad's useless. He's a snake. A diplomat."

In front of him on the desk were milk and biscuits. He still hadn't stopped speaking.

"Max, you need to shut up. Right now. Shut the hell up. Every day you complain!"

"Who the hell do you think you are?"

"Shelvin, in another life, you and I would have had a serious confrontation, something unforgettable, perhaps terminal. Now back off, and I don't mean just now. If you compile a report on what you deem to be the shortcomings of the system, then mail it to me, I'll get Brad to fix your latest round of pointless complaints."

"I could have you jailed for this. Are you threatening me?"

"No, Max. I'm telling you I'd like you to liaise with Brad."

Shelvin looked shaken. It was as though someone else had spoken, not me. Then he seemed, for a time, to recover his equilibrium.

"I think you should take the helm on this one," he said, weakly.

"I know you do. It's not possible. Call Brad."

"Okay. If that's the way you want to play it, it's fine by me."

"Look Max, I don't care what you do. I don't care how many reports you compile or fusses you create. You're just making things worse for yourself. I keep records of everything, I mean everything."

"I see. So do I."

"Every keystroke. I'm the systems man, as you say. Don't fuck with me, and I have a really expensive lawyer. I'll sue you for defamation."

I left the office, worried that my loathing for the man was colouring my ability to deal with him.

I arrive at my desk. A message awaits. The meeting scheduled for this morning had been cancelled and rescheduled for next week same time. I wondered what failure of tactics, or lobbying, or stage-managed-speechmaking lay behind the paper thin excuses I read on that note that caused the meeting to be cancelled. Who is blackmailing whom, I ask myself.

I tossed the note on my desk and saw that the office was busy with usual busyness, with phone calls, people coming and going, clutching files and planners and folding their arms as they make sincere, open, on the spot discussions of critical company matters. A few came up to me with system problems, and I dealt with them and sat down to answer my mail. Brad was sitting opposite in his usual silence. Mary had called in sick earlier. Mary was a far better programmer than the silent, sneaky, non-committal, watchful Brad, who liked weight-lifting and line dancing. Brad makes no personal calls in the office and if he takes a personal call, knows how to speak in whispering tones as he leans into the telephone receiver. Brad, unlike Mary, does only what's necessary, volunteers for nothing and, like all those destined for promotion, will never tell you what he is thinking.

"Morning, Brad. You might get a call from Shelvin."

"Okay."

"Make sure he sends you a memo on what he wants."

I spend the day coding up some reports that I decide, for the sake of having something to do, are long overdue. What is necessary is decided mostly on the basis of an arbitrary judgment of what top management considers necessary and expedient. I say little to Brad. He sits away from me. I leave quietly at four o'clock in the day, relieved to have had nothing further to do with Shelvin. It will take a day or two before he finishes his typing.

As I go down to my car, I worry about what might happen if Shelvin confronts Brad before I have the opportunity to explain things to Brad. But then I figure I am getting hyper-anxious, as I know that Shelvin usually waits for lesser mortals to come to him rather than lower himself to go anyone lower than my grade. I drive to Joe's day care. I lack professionalism and objectivity. I am late as usual. I am late for most appointments. Aron didn't ring me for the day. How strange is that? Stranger than strange.

I try to think, but nothing appears, except the vague anxious glow of Joe's finger paintings as he presents them to me at the end of class. They are vibrant and awash with colours and he screams with delight as I heap praise on them. The child gets so high, literally shakes with excitement. Other parents are gathering their children to them and giving the appropriate affirmative noises, as they hold their children's paint flecked hands, sending them in for a second and a third wash so as not to destroy the car seats and their hair and clothing.

"We'll go over to Mamo," I say.
"Hurray! We go over to Mamo."

Joe loves Mamo, my mother. Mamo was the name given by Joe to his grandmother. This naming was unaided by either of us. Joe and I hug and we get into the car and he helps me fasten his seat belt and we drive over to Mamo, with Joe telling about how he played ball with Lily, who can run much faster than he can and faster than Terry and about Terry who paints faster and threw a sweet at Miriam and how Miriam cried as the sweet stuck to her hair and she had to go to the bathroom and the running they did and the trip to the pool and what teacher said about looking at things and how it was important to listen and not to speak when other people were speaking and I pick up my mobile phone and ring Brad.

"Brad, this is Arthur. Look, if Shelvin is looking for me, or starts asking questions, tell him he needs to put everything on paper before you start doing anything. He needs to clearly define the problem he has with the system before you start wasting time you could be spending on real problem solving. We'll talk tomorrow. I am not available this evening."

This has to stop, I think, has to stop. Now. It all ends here.
"Daddy!"
"What, sweetheart?" I hang up.
"I was telling you something!" He elocuted his complaint very clearly, almost coldly, like someone making an announcement about the weather.
"Sorry, sorry... I need to finish this..."
I ring back and finish the message to Brad, because I cannot leave an unclear message for a subordinate. It would look bad. Once I finish the message, I don't think about the job again for the evening. Then my mobile phone rings once more.
"Hi Arthur!"
"Jane!"

"Remember me? Your sister?"

"What's your point? Are you ringing to pick a fight? You are on speaker, and Joe is here, by the way."

"Hi Auntie Janie."

"Hi Joe!" Auntie Janie calls out. "When are you going to call over to see me? Your Daddy doesn't bring you so often now."

"Daddy has been very busy. We will bring Joe over sometime next week," I say.

"Is that a promise? I forget what you look like it's been so long."

"Promise. We are going to Mamo's right now. Heavy traffic. Bye Janie."

"Byee Auntie Janie. Love you," Joe chimes in, as we disconnect from one another.

We drive on to my mother's and I hide my guilt in chitchat and embarrassed questions and nervous cheerfulness. Joe rattles on about glue and food and Tessa his teacher and running in the park and big crow with big black eyes he saw perched on a railing today. I saw the movie, I thought.

We arrive. Mother is waiting, smiling and waiting. Yes, my mother is waiting, armed with a meal.

"Here we are!"

"I have something ready..." she says, leaning her right cheek near for me to kiss in matriarchal mode.

"Mother..."

More food. Food not just for Joe, but for both of us.

"You so love to provide unwanted meals for all guests," I say.

Joe folds himself into her arms.

"I can't stay..." I say.

Mother purses her lips and looks away. She walks hand in hand with her grandson, dispensing attention to him in disapproving silence of my initial sentence. As we pass through the hallway of their house, I catch sight of a huge basket of fruit and a bottle of white wine.

"Who brought the fruit..?"

"Your sister."

"She just rang me."

"That's nice, dear," she says.

The fruit basket sits on her sideboard, to typify her dowager like appreciation for such tributes and pacifying gifts. It would stand thus until she felt it appropriate to move it from its place of exhibit. We turn to go downstairs and Mother is talking to the child in her arms, walking and hugging.

"Well now, isn't this so wonderful. And how is my handsome cabin boy?"

"Have you any idea what a handsome cabin boy is?" I say.

"Yes, yes I do. But he doesn't, so that's that," she says.

Mother gazes longingly and smilingly at her grandson and, once again, I feel strange about leaving Joe with someone who so desperately loves and loves, but always needs a full refund. Mamo looks deep into Joe's calm, unafraid eyes, and tells him one more time how handsome he is, how wonderful his painting of the trees and the sky and the birds and his mother and his father were, how well he looked in his new outfit we got him recently, and that she had food ready for him to eat.

Three minutes.

I can do pleasantries. Three minutes. I start inquiring about the house, about my father's endless supply of work.

"How's Dad's job?"

"Good."

Then, I start to think of movies, and I talk of those I had seen that I figure Mother might be interested in. I have talked for five minutes. Eight minutes have passed since we arrived. Joe seems so happy. We are downstairs in Mother's newly installed kitchen, with new oven and dishwasher and air extraction system and mahogany presses with brass knobs and the walls with angled lighting and that sense of money. I talk on. Twelve minutes. Every modern convenience was here. Fifteen minutes. The chairs were hard backed. The floor was stone, a cold earthenware brown colour, not unlike the walls. The kitchen was below street level, so the natural lighting that came through the window was poor. The newly fitted artificial lighting was too bright and disconcerting. Twenty minutes. I am given a salad.

"Eat up," mother said.

Joe said he wasn't hungry. He had opened his books and started drawing from them. I took my snack plate and sat down on one of the overpriced high backed wooden chairs and smile my most congenial smile. Mother looked at me with those clear bright blue eyes.

I thought: Less than two minutes, maybe. I can take another two minutes of this and then my exit strategy comes into play. More than two minutes and I will start screaming.

Around that time, Mother searches my face for signals from my inner self, inquiring without words where I was at. I tried to give only a little away, enough to keep her satisfied.

"Something small," she said, indicating the plate of salad.

"Yes, very nice…" I said.

"Your father was called away less than half an hour ago. He was just about to sit down to his dinner when his phone rang. You might say I was less than pleased to see him go at this hour in the day…"

"I could imagine…" I said.

I sometimes slipped into an adolescent sarcasm, listening to my Mother's naïve disapproval of a man whose ways she had all her life defended. My sarcasm was in my voice, and she never heard it.

"…and the evenings closing in like this. It can't be easy driving for him. Still, he likes to keep busy…"

Work had always come before life for my father. Work is always easier than life. Therefore, work. Simple.

"...indeed... very..." I say.

"He says to say hello. He will, of course, want to know how you are..."

Father might call, I thought. Such a busy man might call.

"Well, how have you been, darling? Your little boy looks as lovely as ever."

My son responds for me. He holds up another drawing to her.

"Look, Mamo. Do you like?"

"It's lovely dear..." she says, looking at me with a questioning eye.

"Has Aron called?" I ask.

"Why, yes. I just got off the phone from her. She was saying you and she are going out somewhere tonight. She didn't say where. I think she might be afraid I might let it slip..."

Heading for time. I avoid the pitfall of responding. Heading for one minute.

"Did she call from home?"

"I think so... So..." She said gently, watchfully, without letting on.

"So... how are you. Are you tense..?"

Joe climbed up on her lap. She put her arm around him and stroked his blond hair.

"So, I have something I'd like to bring up with you while I have a few minutes of your time, and I hope you don't think it pushy of me..."

"Not at all..."

I sat and looked at Mother, already feeling a sense of dark uncertainty. I looked at my Mother's calm, smiling expression, as she returned the warmth she received from Joe. Mamo did not have a beautiful face, but the kind well-formed, handsome features and figure of a woman who thinks others should see her own value and importance. Her hand was on my son's shoulder and she was aglow. I watched her aura at that moment, with the eyes of the interested initiate. It was the glow of the cult member in love with the idea of being in the arms of a loving family.

Mother had her fantasy family. Then I arrived every so often and she communicated from within her longings for a warm well-fused family. She didn't keep it as real as she thought she did.

"Your father and I are worried about Joe's spiritual well-being."

"Joe, will you go and play in the other room, for a minute..?" I said.

Joe smiles and begins to leave. This is too easy, I thought. He is going to break something next door...

Mamo is not happy with this arrangement.

"There's no need for Joe to leave," she suggests. "For clearly we are not speaking about him."

"Okay," I say, "he stays."

"Good!" Joe says.

"Okay, what's the problem with the spiritual development of certain unnamed parties?"

"You put things so cleverly, son. I can never compete with how cleverly you put things. I often wondered if it was not you who is the writer, after all."

Mother looks awkwardly at the fire and settles herself for saying something unpleasant, and squirms a little in her seat.

"What I mean, and I am sure your father will agree with me on this, is that your, I mean that children, generally, should be baptised."

"What's baptized?" Joe tugs at me and climbs into my arms. Mother smiles and nods at me, as if to emphasise her point.

"Look," I say, "I know what you are going to say and you know what I am going to say and there is no point..."

No point in making a scene. All the old stuff, like acid, like fire, burning away...

"Absolutely, absolutely. I never argue about religion or politics."

Good. Late already.

"...Okay, I..."

"But we have to consider what is best for the child. Don't you think that the child comes first in all of this, don't you, Son..?"

I smile at Mother and look at her and smiled again and she smiled back at me and I stroke Joe on the top of his head.

"You didn't secretly... Did you..?"

"Did I what... baptise... I can't believe... I can't believe you..."

I know she did. I can't believe this. Can't imagine it. What time is it?

"I was asking you if you did it..."

I envisaged her baptising him in a dark quarter of the house while no one was looking, just in case. Mother was very hurt. Her eyes filled with tears.

"I know... I know you are... and that's what shocks me so..."

Time for me to go. Thirtysomething time. Late.

"Let's just leave it at that, shall we..?"

"...believe in something when I don't."

She purses her lips in anger, and clutches the hand towels that were folded over the back of a nearby chair.

"I have to go. Mother, I'm late. Don't exorcise the child while I'm out, or ordain him a bishop or anything."

"What's a bis-shop?" Joe asks.

Mother smiled ruefully.

"How did Aron sound to you?" I ask.

"Wonderful, son, great. Really excited. She has a nice night planned for you two, I think..."

"It's just that, well... I... haven't heard from her all day"

"Did you check your messages? I left a message..." She looks at me, a little hurt at the possibility I had ignored her messages.

"I got it. I just didn't have a chance to..."

"I see...well...if you don't get back till late, we'll tuck our little friend up in one of the beds, not to worry..."

"If that happens, we'll call..." I say and turn to go, blowing a kiss at the busy boy.

"Bye Daddy..." Joe seems content to stay with Mamo. Content and safe. He resumes running around the kitchen

"Bye Son, you be a good boy..."

"Bye-bye Daddy…"

I left the kitchen, trying to contact Aron. Her phone was switched off. She could be out of touch for days, away somewhere if working on something, without telling me she was working on something, leaving me to handle things. During those times, I would come home to a house in chaos with her in the back room writing, the floor strewn with empty bottles of wine, the child asleep in its cot, and some awful music playing in the background. This was why we employed a cleaner and the occasional nanny, too. I also bought her a mobile phone, but, since she saw little use for such intrusive accessories, she rarely bothered to switch it on. I tried her number in the car. It rang, and she answered.

"Hi, where are you?" I asked.

"I had an idea today."

"Where are you?"

"In a pub…"

"How much have you had to drink?"

"I went away to the library. Then I went home. I tried to ring you but you weren't answering. I didn't leave a message or anything. I was confused, a little, a little dizzy, you get me?"

"Sure you're okay?"

"Sure, sure. Come on down and we'll have a few. I got the restaurant all fixed up. I made a few calls and there's this really wonderful place in…"

"Just tell me where you are, and we'll meet up…"

So we met up in the Thomas Reads bar and we sat there. She gave me a long lingering kiss, the type she gives when she has had too much to drink and is drunk or stoned, worked too hard. She was full of enthusiasm and delight and happiness to see me and was all questions about Joe and what he had to eat and how he seemed and what he had on since this morning and how his day was at school and she wanted to ring him again, just in case, but I say no, he is fine and he will be fine and not to worry and we sat down to a gin and tonic each.

"So where are we eating tonight?"

"The Zettel"

"…That's a great place. And no unexpected arrivals, no guests, no one else?"

"Nobody… you and me…"

"You have this awful habit of inviting, you know, people, editors or publishers or publicity people, and all I want was just you and me."

"I promise, no one but you and me."

"Okay, then."

The energy from her was different then, shy and subdued, possibly a little stoned. Detox mansion beckons once more, I muse.

"So…" she smiled lazily and looked around the pub and saw no one she knew but me. She lit another cigarette and waited for me to initiate conversation. I said nothing and smiled. There was something going on.

"So what did you do? All day, I mean?" she began.

"Wrote programs mostly."

"Wow. Fun," she grinned sarcastically through half glazed eyes.

"Don't do that. Don't disrespect my work. I supported you for long enough."

"You're right. I'm being a bitch. I took a few pills to chill. Sorry."

I went on. "And I caught up with jobs I had been putting on the long finger… I avoided taking calls, so we may have missed each other… I hear you and Mother have just been talking…"

"I've been thinking about you," she said.

"Yes… I have too… thinking about you… I miss you. When you go missing into your books, I miss you."

Her face was a strange mixture of beauty and suffering, her eyes were warm with love and despair, hidden behind the smallest spectacles. She was full of a desire I felt I could never satisfy. She smiled and leaned over to me and whispered.

"I want to write about you, I want to write something that will tell your, and our, life story. Almost like a biographical novel but not quite one."

"My God... are you asking my permission?"

"Maybe a series of short novels... mind?"

"I don't know... How long have you been..?" I wondered, "I mean everyone would know who I am. That's the thing..."

She lit another cigarette and inhaled deeply. She takes a long time to answer.

"Is that so bad?" she asked.

"No," I said. "Not so bad... what about little Joe?"

"He wouldn't be in it," she said.

"Right. Like you are going to not have our son in a book like that. I'll agree if you stop smoking permanently," I said.

She looked at me too carefully, ironically, through the cigarette smoke wafting like incense at a temple. I was being examined. Hers were the eyes of God. She was the scientist of love. I was inside the lepidopterists jar of her mind.

"We can't do this. Think about what it might do to us..."I said.

"No, no!" she said and she looked down at her empty place. She looked upset. I felt I had hurt her terribly.

"What I was saying is," she began. "What I was saying is I have an idea for another book, but I need your okay before I go any further."

"Because it's about me, right?" I said.

"Because it's about our life."

"Everything, well most things you write about are about us. I mean, I see us in it."

"Well, they have us as a starting point, I guess. But is doesn't end up that way, you know"?

I would be written up, suffer possible distortion and reinterpretation, would die and arise as someone else. I would become another, possessed by those who would read her. I would possibly never recover from it. Then, I realised how I would no longer be myself, that I would be another. I was happy. The fear fell away. I was ready to die. Die and be reborn.

"I kept thinking about where you were all day, you know?" I began. "Then, just now, I remembered something my mother said to me, just before I moved out."

"You moved out. I thought they kind of, you know, kicked you out."

"She told me it was a matter of time before the hammer fell on you, and you have to get a job," I said.

"Your mother and I enjoyed a long and warm relationship before the hammer fell on her and she joined the realm of the afterlife," Aron said.

"My mother is alive, Aron. Don't say that!"

"It was hate at first sight. She detested my marrying you. She wanted someone else, someone respectable."

"I always thought we would make up as she got very old," I said. "I hate how we don't get on. It's not good, and I know you and she don't get along either," I said.

"I know. And near the end is too near the end to make a difference. Deathbed reconciliations are the ambit of those who have lived their lives in guilt. Omygod, Arthur, I'm sorry, my love. I don't mean to disrespect your mother. I'm sorry. I'm stoned, I guess. I can't believe I just said all that."

"It's okay. She is my mother. And she never really gave you a chance. I wish she had."

I breathed deeply and felt an excess of longing rise up inside me.

"Okay?" I said sharply.

"Okay," she said. "Okay," and kissed me again.

We finished our drinks and went to dinner. As the waiter explained in broken English the combination of herbs and vegetables and fruits and nuts that made up the cornucopia of starters that they lay before us, I saw that we had been spotted. They looked carefully at Aron as they left, expecting at some stage, an ostentatious tip. Later, I saw them discreetly comment to each other just who Aron was. She leaned discreetly over to me.

"Look at them," she said. "Look at them, it's as though I were made of money."

"Do you want to go somewhere else?"

"No, do you?"

"No, no. I like it. Is this a problem?" I asked.

"Sure. I want a quiet dinner with you."

"Nice to hear it," I said. "Look, if you want to do this novel thing, fine. But it's better not to mention Joseph."

"I hadn't intended to," she said.

"How long have you been thinking about this?"

"A few months…"

"So what's it about, I mean really about?"

"I think it might get taken the wrong way. It's about… redemption…"

"Right… that's really good. What does that mean?"

"It means you, darling,"

"I have no idea what that means. Redemption."

"It means death is not the end."

"How comforting. Is this something to do with…"

"With what?"

"Reincarnation?"

"I'm not sure. You, well not you, your incarnation in the novel, he is very disaffected with the world. Eventually he, you, kills himself."

"Oh, joy. But I don't feel that way about life…"

"I know you don't…"

"Right… that's scary… People will think…"

"But this is a fiction. You know that. The myth is always more important than the truth. For him the world is beautiful and horrible..."

"So what happens?"

"Doesn't die. He moves from job to job, from life to life, moves through history learning, all the while accumulating experiences... Let's not talk about it. I'm hungry. I haven't fully decided as yet."

"That's more than a thumbnail sketch, though, isn't it? I mean you have a plan, a roadmap."

"Just talking about it helps, I guess. Great food."

"Lovely," I said. "It might work out after all."

"What?"

"The thing," I said.

"Probably. I might be less of a failure than usual. Where do you want to go after this?" she beamed.

"I want to go home. I want us to take a few days off and celebrate..."

"Sounds like fun..."

I called Mother. Asked her to keep Joe over. She said she would be delighted. I remember us driving home that night. We talked about friends and the car and Joe and the food at the restaurant. We talked about the book she was going to write and about how I felt about it.

We made love in the front room, too excited for caution, too nervous and fragile to take our time. I felt happy, holding her, lying on the front room floor, talking about the little things that add up in the end, knowing that I, like her, was not myself. That I was another.

"You know," she said.

"What?"

"I thought of something today."

"What?"

"I only started writing after I met you."

"So? You had other things going on for you before we got together."

"It's like I write for you."

"No. Not possible. You do it because you can."

"No, it's like you give me something, you release it."

"Is that why you didn't call today?" I wondered.

"Its like it came from you." She sounded dreamy, as though drifting away.

"So the novel is like a kind of revenge on me?"

"No, an acknowledgement, a gift," she said.

"That's impossible. It can't be from me," I said.

"How do you know anything is impossible?" she mumbled.

"I don't, I suppose. Not provable, I suppose."

"Mmm, this is good," she said, as her eyes began to close. I looked around the room, my eyes growing heavy too. Yes, I thought. This is good, and I picked Aron up, carried her to bed. And we slept.